# THE CACTUS LEAGUE

## EMILY NEMENS

Farrar, Straus and Giroux ⊘ New York

Farrar, Straus and Giroux
120 Broadway, New York 10271

Copyright © 2020 by Emily Nemens
All rights reserved
Printed in the United States of America
First edition, 2020

Portions of this book previously appeared, in slightly different form, in *n+1* and *The Iowa Review*.

Library of Congress Cataloging-in-Publication Data
Names: Nemens, Emily, author.
Title: The cactus league : a novel / Emily Nemens.
Description: First edition. | New York : Farrar, Straus and Giroux, 2020.
Identifiers: LCCN 2019037899 | ISBN 9780374117948 (hardcover)
Subjects: LCSH: Baseball—Training—Arizona—Fiction.
Classification: LCC PS3614.E45244 C33 2020 | DDC 813/.6—dc23
LC record available at https://lccn.loc.gov/2019037899

Designed by Abby Kagan

Our books may be purchased in bulk for promotional, educational, or business use. Please contact your local bookseller or the Macmillan Corporate and Premium Sales Department at 1-800-221-7945, extension 5442, or by e-mail at MacmillanSpecialMarkets@macmillan.com.

www.fsgbooks.com
www.twitter.com/fsgbooks • www.facebook.com/fsgbooks

10  9  8  7  6  5  4  3  2  1

*For Dad*

# CONTENTS

# FIRST

Welcome to Salt River Fields, the newest spring training facility in Scottsdale, Arizona. Turn east off of Pima, drive down the fresh boulevard, Lions Way. You're flanked by parking lots so new they still smell like tar, their white hatching wet: ample parking for the anticipated crowds, already sold out for opening day. Note the median's plantings: environmentally sustainable xeriscape. Of course, this *is* 2011, and the club cares about our natural resources, is mindful of the perpetual drought in Phoenix metro. A few Christmas cacti bloom, despite it being February.

And here, at the terminus of the boulevard, the centerpiece of the multi-field complex: the twelve-thousand-seat stadium that will be the new springtime home of your Los Angeles Lions. Take it all in—the crisp-chalked diamond, the ruddy arc of infield, the bright checkerboard of the outfield. It's not easy to grow grass like that in the desert—I offer a hat tip to the grounds crew. And see out past the warning track and fence? There's the shock-green tilt of a well-watered general-admission lawn. Farther still, on the horizon: a ridge of mountains, jutting into the blue like the teeth of some mile-high rusted saw.

Take note of the architecture, too: the exposed steel beams and brick, a slate-gray cantilevered canopy over a sunken seating bowl, the polished concrete rotunda and concourse. A classic-looking stadium. Timeless in design, some might say, even if it's anything but. Nothing is static, not the bluegrass-ryegrass blend growing out there, not the architecture, not the angle of the sun hitting the seats. And not a man's career, especially not a ballplayer the first weeks of spring. His batting average, his ambition, his hopes: all is in flux. I'm looking toward Lions left fielder Jason Goodyear as I write this, coming off a Gold Glove and a close second place in American League MVP voting, coming off a possible divorce and a lonely drive across the desert in his busted old Jeep. (Doesn't Cadillac *give* you a car if you do that many ads?) But that feeling of uncertainty isn't reserved for All-Stars and the freshly dumped; it could apply to any player on the squad, any coach on the bench, any man in the executive suite, any fan in the stands. I'm looking at his entourage: his agent, Herb Allison, his maybe-wife, Liana, his favorite minor league batting coach, and the devotees who would give an eye tooth just to be near him. It's all up in the air.

Here's the thing about baseball, and all else: everything changes. Whether it's the slow creep of glaciers dripping toward the sea, or the steady piling up of cut stones, rock upon rock until the wall reaches chest high, nothing is still. Sometimes change comes as quick and catastrophic as a line drive—hear the crack of wood displacing a sphere of leather, yarn, rubber, and cork; watch how it pushes the ball flat and then, just as quickly, forward. The action springs the left fielder from his squat, and the man's metal spikes tear into the turf, kicking up tiny wedges of grass, sending them toward the sky.

Sure, I followed I-10 across the desert to write the story of one remarkable man, but baseball's not that kind of game. It's too long and complicated to say, *He did this, he said that, then this happened.* That sufficed when I was first working the beat, still wet behind the ears and liable to get lost on my way to the press room. Back then, it was *Get the score, get the quote, add a little color, and file*—162 times a year. (More if you were lucky and your team took any sort of postseason run. September, October, that was the only time the rest of the newsroom took us serious. And no editor was ponying up for spring ball—that's what the wires were for.) I was such a kid, spooked by his own damn shadow, downright fearful of asking any kind of tough question, something that might be construed as disagreeable. Now, I'm no muckraker, and not setting out to take down a great man, but in this life things *are* complex, some questions *are* hard, and that's why I drove to Arizona in the first place.

It's not that those early reports of mine were totally off the mark. Ask any fan, and she'll tell you there's something satisfyingly linear about baseball: three strikes, three outs. Four bases, nine innings. A *line*up, for chrissake—you don't need to be an etymologist to see the meaning in that. But at the same time as that steady progression of three up, three down, then the next, then the next, it's going around and around, cycling through the order, running around the bases. Things get parabolic. There's the arc of up and down through the organization, from Single-A Carolina to the big time in Culver City, the tight arc of an infield-fly out and the majestic one of a game-winning homer. Charting the line gets mighty complicated: there are so many men playing together, so many more behind the scenes, coaching and cajoling and sometimes sabotaging the game's progress, pulling the line until it goes bonkers, more like a dance chart than any sort of arrow.

None of that nuance goes onto the score sheet, none of it gets printed in the next morning's recap. The paper's box scores, like my early reports, don't hardly scratch the surface of what happened: there are so many stories behind that neat summary. Triumphs, failures, vindications, yes. But just as many stories end not with "out three" but "out maybe"—fly balls that never do fall, men who never stop running 'round the bags.

So to tell Jason Goodyear's story will take a while, require not just Jason but a whole web of people who are touched by him, and a few who long to touch him, too. I know it sounds crazy, but when it gets down to telling the story of the league's best outfielder, as much will happen in parking lots as on the field, as much in backyards as in deep left. So no, it's not as easy as, *He did this, he said that, then this happened*. It's more, *He did this, he said that, and then the whole world unfurled*.

It's how things go in baseball; after decades on this beat I should know. And so, I'd encourage you to find your seat, settle in, and get ready for a long game.

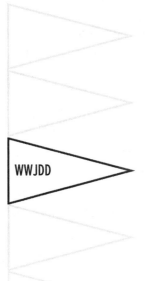

**WWJDD**

Audrey and Michael Taylor have been traveling all day, since before the sun rose on their daughter's snowed-over Milwaukee suburb. Now, late afternoon, Michael directs the cabbie from Sky Harbor and Phoenix's loop freeway into Scottsdale, toward their development—a square mile of adobe-clad ranchers—and finally, down their street.

Theirs is halfway down the block on the left. "It's that one," he says, his wrinkled finger jutting into the front of the cab, indicating a house that's so orange it's nearly pink. "The salmon."

He tips the driver well—Michael always tips well; it is part of what he considers his character—and the young man happily unloads the Taylors' coffin-size suitcases onto the curb. Forty-nine pounds each: the Taylors have been doing their off-season circuit for so long Audrey knows exactly which sundresses and sweaters to include, every wool blazer and light jacket and pair of slacks Mikey will need for Thanksgiving in Chicago, Christmas in Virginia, the month of January with Katie, their youngest, and her four kids in Wisconsin. And now, February and March in Arizona, where the desert can swing from the thirties at night to the nineties at noon.

The lawn looks dried out—the timer on the sprinkler must've malfunctioned, Michael thinks. He's bothered by this; he prides himself on his perfect little patch of bluegrass-ryegrass. The neighbors appreciate it, too—Mr. Baseball knows his grass.

"How's that for peculiar?" Michael says to himself as he jiggles the doorknob. He tries the key again, no luck. He checks the others on the ring—stadium entrance, supply room, and office (all to the old stadium—was he supposed to turn those in? he forgot to, in any case); Scottsdale safe deposit; spare set to Betty and Dave's (those he definitely should return); the Camry; and the new, beloved Cadillac. He cannot help letting his thumb linger on that smooth black pebble, its silver shield a pleasing ridge under his thumb. He tries the house key twice more before stalking past the picture window to the side gate. There is a hide-a-key under the back mat; he'll get in that way.

"What's going on, honey?" Audrey missed his defeat at the front; she had her nose in her phone, texting one kid or another. "Did you forget your keys?"

"No, Aud—my God!" Michael bellows. The gate, now open, reveals a backyard in disarray—trash is skewered on the spines of their saguaro, and it looks like someone played whack-a-mole with their potted plants. A tower of crushed beer cans is piled on the patio table, and pizza boxes, stacked like so many beach towels, sit next to the Taylors' small in-ground pool. The pool's water is murky, with strange, bright blooms skimming the surface.

The cardboard panel in the back door's French window leers at him like a smile's missing tooth. Michael punches the cardboard out, reaches down, and opens the latch from the inside.

The alarm system should trigger, but it doesn't. Instead, he hears the sound of feet on gravel and Audrey's gasp. He barks, "Now just hang on, Audrey." His wife, fretting her hands by the patio furniture, nods like a bobblehead. "I'll take care of this."

◇

When Michael bought their Arizona house, brand-new in 1971, guys on the team thought he was crazy. But Michael thought they were crazy *not* to buy. Why spend their meal money on six weeks of hotels every spring when they could be putting their stipend toward a mortgage? Scottsdale wasn't quite tumbleweed-down-Main-Street back then, but it was a lot different. Small, for one. It stopped around Indian Bend, mostly just cacti and the old army airport past that, the ghost of Frank Lloyd Wright hanging out on some distant hill. Other players rented convertibles and bought clothes that impressed only whoever else was eating late-night at the Pink Pony; Michael paid down his banknote. A career in baseball, or at least one going the way he had imagined, was a looming unknown, but some things you *could* count on. By thirty, he and Audrey already had their retirement home. When it was clear his shot at the majors was done, that thrift felt more important than ever.

And while their official residence is Salt Lake City, home of the Stallions, the Lions' Triple-A affiliate, the Arizona house is their favorite stop on the yearlong, countrywide circuit. These days, now that all the kids are out and mostly on their own, Michael and Audrey spend eight weeks in Scottsdale every spring and fall. It is well lived in, and well loved, but not any sort of run-down—Michael makes sure of that, always sprucing up the yard and keeping the paint fresh. There is something very cathartic about everything being in its right place, especially after so many months on the road.

◇

The first thing to hit him is the stench of decay, a garbage smell, but he also detects the acrid aroma of something not meant to burn having been burned. It is cool—downright cold—the thermostat doing its best to keep the house at sixty against an eighty-five-degree sun. Michael shivers.

"Anybody home?" he calls. It sounds ridiculous, he thinks, yelling out as if he were some overcurious neighbor. Like this isn't *his own home*. But Michael can't think what else to say, what else to do. So he calls out again, and then he listens.

No answer.

He surveys the kitchen. Wadded-up Pop-Tart wrappers spill across the counter, dishes jam the sink, and then his eyes go to a dark, sticky-looking stain on the floor. Blood, Michael thinks, and his breath pulls up short. Only when he kneels down and sees the overturned bottle of Hershey's syrup wedged underneath the fridge is he able to exhale. A trail of tiny ants march from the spill to some unknown world behind the cabinets.

The security system, once mounted next to the thermostat, is now smashed plastic and a knot of clipped wires. The dead bolts in the front and back have been replaced with some cheapo set, the locks sitting loose in their casings. One mystery solved.

Michael pops out the back door. Audrey is gingerly gathering takeout containers and depositing them into the trash. "Leave it be, Audrey. Those are filthy."

She looks up. "How is it in there?"

"Not good," he says with a grimace.

He does a quick survey of the dining room. At some point, a

meal had been set for four, premade lasagna by the looks of the caked tinfoil casserole. The Taylors' nice china, stained orange with grease, is spread across the table, crusted and crumbed. He inspects the sideboard, the small liquor cabinet and wine rack atop it. Their visitors drank every ounce in the cabinet and every bottle in the rack, including a 1999 Mouton Rothschild Bordeaux Michael was saving for their fiftieth. "Those shits," he mutters.

In the girls' room—now fitted with two sets of bunk beds, for when the grandkids visit—all four beds have been slept in, none of them made. Something squirreled in the corner catches his eye. An assortment of Michael's sports memorabilia has been gathered from different parts of the house and deposited, improbably, here. The ball from his first home run. His collection of cards, all the way back to his squinty rookie year. He'd been handsome in 1965, even if the TOPPS photographer had surprised him, asked him to turn around and smile right into the sun. Michael didn't know he could ask for a redo, not until the team set came in and the whole clubhouse laughed at his squished-up mug. He slips the card into his shirt pocket. Also in the pile: a framed clipping from 1974, that lucky moment when they made it all the way to the World Series, and *he* was the Lions' backup left fielder. No ring, though—they'd lost in five to Saint Louis. His retired gloves, their leather gone soft and then stiff again. Ball caps from every level of the organization: Carolina, Kansas, Salt Lake. The medallion the Lions organization gave him for forty years with the club—for those, *major* or *minor* don't matter, nor do *player* or *coach*. It is about being loyal—which he is, faithful as a border collie. If only the feeling were mutual. The last time he encountered Stephen Smith, the head of the ownership group, the man couldn't be bothered to hide his sneer, making a face like Michael were a stain he'd have to scrub out.

In the master bedroom, the bed is unmade, the sheets strewn like something violent happened. He stands in the threshold, listening to the ticking of a quiet house, wanting and not wanting to hear something more. As he waits, he can feel his blood pressure going up. He has meds for it, and he takes them dutifully every morning. But a tiny pill can do only so much when someone's been living in, and messing up, your home.

Those little white pills—he charges into the master bath and throws open the cabinet. He shakes one bottle after another, hoping for a rattle. They ate everything but the stool softener. "No respect," he says to himself.

Closing the cabinet, Michael catches his reflection in the bathroom mirror. Blue eyes rimmed pink, jowly, a carbuncly nose that keeps getting bigger, his hair bright white—he sees very little of that young man from the TOPPS card staring back at him. He'd been handsome, he'd been strong. He looks down at his wrist, the threaded bracelet embroidered with the letters W-W-J-D-D. What would Joe DiMaggio do?

He wouldn't blow his fucking cool, Michael reminds himself. So he ignores the ringed tub and the towels wadded on the floor. He steps back into the bedroom and closes the bathroom door so hard the whole room shudders. The pictures of his kids and grandkids, the black-and-white wedding photos of his folks and Audrey's had been knocked askance anyway.

WWJDD. "Audrey," he calls down the dim corridor, "I'm coming."

◇

Audrey is in the kitchen. "They melted plastic onto the range," she says, picking at the stove's coils with a polished nail. She gives herself a manicure every Thursday, the same color of pale pink for the past twenty-two years. When a fleck of the color breaks off and skips across the range, she makes a concerned face but keeps going.

"And look." She holds up a crystal pitcher, a wedding gift from his long-deceased grandmother. "It's chipped. And they cracked the Mr. Coffee." She points to the carafe, and her eyes run over the counter. Michael watches them skim, skitter, and jump.

"What? What is it?" Michael says.

"Oh, it's . . . nothing," Audrey says, in a way that, Michael knows, after forty-eight years of matrimony, means it absolutely is *something*. Her eyes dart again, there and back.

"What? Tell me." His voice is stern, but then he sees what her eyes are unable to avoid: the turned walnut bowl that had previously held their spare keys. Now, save for some gum wrappers, a withered apple, and an oozing brown banana, it is empty.

He feels a curse rising from the grumbling pit of his belly. Of course Michael left a spare key to the Cadillac sitting in the bowl. It's his house, for fuck's sake, and you leave *your* keys, to *your* car that is parked in *your* garage, attached to *your* house, in *your* fucking fruit bowl. He storms across the kitchen, throws open the door to the garage, and faces a big, empty space where his new car had been.

"GODDAMN IT!"

He punches a button, and the garage door begins its creaking ascent. With the light of the afternoon streaming in, he can see into the shadows on the far side of the garage. They also took Audrey's car, an old Camry with a hundred thousand miles and a fritzy air conditioner. Tools gone, lawn mower gone. Michael kicks a bag of mulch because he has to kick something. He kicks it again, the bag giving way like someone's soft middle. Then he stomps back into the kitchen and dials the police.

◇

It's not the Johnstons' fault, he'd never say that. But next-door neighbors Betty and Dave Johnston always did look in on the place when the Taylors were away, and after Betty's fall . . . well. Audrey and Michael sent flowers to Betty's hospital room, and when Dave called to thank them, Michael steered conversation toward their street—he wanted to make sure they'd still be checking in. That's when Dave confessed they'd not be coming around. They were moving into one of those *retirement* developments. Michael didn't know what to say to that. The idea of giving up so much of one's life—possessions, property, even the ability to set one's own damn dinnertime—was terrifying. *You sure about this?* he asked Dave. His neighbor replied that the house was already listed, and he'd hired some college kids to pack up the place.

So Dave and Betty weren't there to hear the home alarm wail or notice when it unceremoniously stopped. They didn't see the perps coming and going, wreaking havoc in the pool. But Michael had to admit that things started going south well before Betty's fall. With the recession came a wave of bad mortgages, homeowners owing more than their properties' worth. Foreclosures. Some people walked away. The house on the other side of them had been empty for a year, nominally on sale but even the broker had stopped coming around. Last spring, not in their development, but not too far away, either, he'd seen a row of houses that had gone to seed: boarded up, gap-toothed with broken windows, pocked with orange eviction notices. Was that coming for them? Michael didn't know; he sure as shit hoped not. Theirs had been a nice neighborhood—kids biking in the streets and splashing in pools. Michael never sees children playing anymore.

Long story short, the Johnstons sold quick, and for a too-low price, to some developer buying up lots like they were Monopoly houses—he had three on their block, four on the next. Dave had heard the guy was fixing to raze the whole neighborhood, but when Michael pressed, Dave changed the subject.

◇

Michael and Audrey wait on the dead grass, holding hands. Michael hopes that by squeezing Audrey's she can get his message: *Hang on, sweetheart. We'll be okay.* The responding officer doesn't use a siren, but the lights on his squad car flash red and blue. Officer Miller looks like he might've played high school football thirty years back. Michael gives him the short version of their rude welcome, and Miller stomps inside. He comes back out in what feels like ninety seconds and tells them they are lucky to still have their plumbing, which strikes Michael as a pretty rotten thing to say.

The lights strobe, red and blue. "Could you turn that off?" Audrey finally asks, her voice sounding pinched. She closes her eyes and squishes up her face like she does when a migraine's coming. Michael squeezes her hand again: *I'll take care of everything.* And this time, he feels her press back, her thumb running over the callus at the base of his palm, pulling along the rim of his embroidered bracelet. *Please*, hers says.

What would Joe DiMaggio do? Take care of fucking business.

Miller continues without enthusiasm. "It could be anyone: your typical drugged-out vagrant, but maybe also a family down on its luck, a vet who's a little out of sorts, some dumb kids from the university. You said there was booze in the house. Any drugs?"

"What?" Michael's mind flashes to the empty vials in the bathroom, pain pills left over from the last time he threw out his back. Those don't count. "No. Nothing."

"So then how do you spot a squatter nowadays?" Audrey asks.

"Yeah," Michael says. "From what you're saying, it's not like they're hoboes trailing a swarm of flies."

Miller sniffs. "They're not. And you don't. Y'all have home-owner's insurance?" the officer says, capping his pen.

Michael's nod feels more like a shrug. "Sure."

"Get ready for a fight. They'll nickel-and-dime you all the way to Kalamazoo. Document everything. Keep your receipts, take photos." Miller hands Michael a card. "Call the station if you folks need anything. We'll keep an eye out for the cars. You said the Cadillac was—"

"Ebony. With a little tint of navy blue."

"That some sort of black?"

"Right. And a sky-blue Toyota Camry, nineteen ninety—"

"Seven." Audrey remembers. Of course she does.

After the patrol car leaves, Audrey and Michael stand there for a minute, just holding hands and blinking at the house. Then Michael heads for the curb—their suitcases haven't budged since the Taylors first arrived, when the cabbie plopped them down with such cheeriness. Audrey stops him, her hand wrapping around his arm with a surprisingly strong grip.

"I don't feel safe here, Mikey." Most days, his wife doesn't look a day over fifty-five, big brown eyes and a cute nose and a smile that hardly sags. Not plastic surgery, just good genes, a little hair dye, and lots of moisturizer. But at that moment, her hair mussed out from its precise bun, her face damp from the heat and showing every one of its wrinkles, she looks frail. Like an old lady. "I don't want to stay here."

As much as it kills him to hear that, Michael can't blame her. "Sure. Right." So he walks back into the stinking kitchen and calls another taxi.

◇

Everyone thinks ballplayers are made of money, but the big salaries—like that ten-year, $150 million contract Jason Goodyear bagged, the biggest in franchise history—are a relatively recent development. Really, everything changed with free agency and the ascension of the mega-agent, guys like Herb Allison, who could bark and bite and get teams to bid against one another until they pushed salaries into *nine* figures. Even seven figures sounds nice to Michael. Hell, he would gladly take six. As a minor league batting coach he makes about $68,000 a year.

In 1965, when Michael signed with the Reds (and in '69, when he moved to the Lions), the major league minimum was twelve thousand bucks. Not exactly the lush life. Only a few dozen All-Stars and a couple of managers who could spin straw into gold went for top dollar. The rest of them, the assistant coaches and third-string outfielders, the career minor leaguers—they were just trying to get by. His minor league contracts were, well, humbling, and while Michael finally got a major league contract in 1974 (that year he'd had a streak in Triple-A that would've made Joltin' Joe proud, batting nearly .500 in August), his bat cooled off, as bats inevitably do, and he was sent back down. He ran through his option years, and when he was released on waivers, he was like the homely girl at the middle school dance: no takers. He switched to coaching then; for a decade he strung together three seasons a year—Triple-A, the Arizona Fall League, and then winter ball in the DR. He missed just about every milestone in his kids' lives, and after he couldn't get home for Katie's state championship (in oboe, not softball), Audrey started on him to quit. *We'll find another way*, she'd said. The amateur clinics had him on the road plenty, but that was still less than three seasons a year. And the pay was better, even if the work was worse.

Michael always assumed he'd send the kids to college. But then the expenses mounted, in unexpected ways. Melissa was uninsured in her twenties, which no one thought twice about until a bad bike crash cost the family six figures. Katie's husband couldn't hold down a job, even as they had one kid after another, four in six years. *There's such a thing as too many*, Michael told Audrey when they heard another was on its way. He helped all the kids with houses because there were grandkids in the picture and he wanted them to be comfortable. And, if he was being honest, part of him still felt guilty for never being around. He knew money wouldn't *solve* that feeling, but it wouldn't make things worse.

◇

When the cab pulls up to the Walshes', Stuart and Helen are waving at the curb, smiles too big to be true. The Walshes have also been with the Lions organization for decades, Stu as a left-handed pitcher and then the team's pitching coach. (Michael and Stu overlapped in Los Angeles only a few months, but these Arizona springs cemented a lifelong friendship.) The Walshes recently upgraded to a new construction on the north side of Scottsdale—three bedrooms plus a pool house, a small in-ground pool and fancy fixtures everywhere—buying at a point that many later identified as the exact bottom of the market. It was a lucky break that would've made Michael mad if it'd happened to anyone but Stu.

Stu and Michael hump the suitcases to the pool house and meet the women inside. Helen has made everyone sandwiches, dainty triangles of ham and cheese for the ladies, a pair of bricks stacked twice as thick for the men. After eating over nervous, thin pleasantries, Helen takes Audrey to the kitchen to make some tea.

Michael doesn't need any chamomile, he needs a highball, which Stu provides from the living room's wet bar. The men sink into leather recliners. The big TV is on some satellite channel, showing the Caribbean series, the DR versus Puerto Rico, the volume low.

The men watch a few pitches before Michael says, "Why'd they have to take the Caddy?" His was a top-of-the-line CTS. Probably a tad ostentatious, but he deserved it, he and Audrey had agreed, for taking care of his family for so long. Deserved it doubly, she'd pointed out, after they'd climbed back from 2008, when their retirement took a sick-feeling twenty-five-point dive. She'd be fine with the Camry another few seasons, she'd insisted. She'd seen how hard he was working—more and more of those awful clinics, barking at high school kids, ten-year-olds even, about how to stride and how to swing and how to wallop the ball so some college scout might notice you—and she knew how much he wanted it.

Michael scoured road tests and reviews in *Motor Trend*. It didn't *make* his decision, but it might've helped that Jason Goodyear started promoting Cadillac right around the All-Star break. Slick TV commercials and glossy magazine ads Audrey would flag, chirping about how he made those cars look handsome. Michael always liked Goody. Maybe because they'd both been left fielders, but more likely because Goody was a decent guy: a quiet, lead-by-example type. Respectful. During spring practice he always wanted Michael to check out his swing, and while they're in the cage he'd make a point of asking about the girls. They were giggly undergrads his rookie spring, and he'd treated them kindly, flirting just enough to make them blush beet-red.

"It's insured, right?" Stu refills Michael's glass. He'd waited for the end-of-year prices, put all of 240 miles on it before they'd had to double back to the Midwest for family obligations and a tween hitting workshop in Evanston.

"Huh? Yeah," Michael says. He has already run the numbers (last year's model, six months used). "But I lost five thousand the minute I drove it off the lot."

"That's the rub." After watching a few pitches on the screen, a high fly that carries to the warning track, Stu clears his throat. "Listen, Mike. Helen and I want you and Audrey to make yourselves at home in the pool house—there's a little kitchenette and everything back there. I know we have a few days before the team shows up, but you two, you should stay through till Salt Lake," he says, "if that'd make it easier." At the end of every March, when Stu and Helen head for Los Angeles and the major league season, Michael and Audrey lock up the house again and drive to Utah. They'd planned to take the Caddy up this year— they'd have to rethink that.

"Thanks, but we'll be here a week, tops."

Stu shakes his head, smiles. "It could be like back when you first got called up, and you and Audrey hadn't found a place in L.A. yet. Remember that?"

Michael watches his friend. Clearly Stu doesn't remember the part right after the three-week slumber party, when the Taylors finally did find a little place in Hollywood and signed a year lease, only to get sent back to Salt Lake five months later.

That was a blow, with the baby and a second on the way. Stu's gaze slides over to the game, his face showing blithe, unknowing comfort.

What would Joe DiMaggio do? He wouldn't take the charity of no one, especially not a friend. "Thanks, Stu, but no one is going to keep me out of my own home."

$\diamond$

Why Joe? Giuseppe Paolo DiMaggio is part of Michael's origin story. In May 1941 one Nelson Taylor, a newlywed New York professional, had an unfortunate run-in with a taxicab, breaking his leg in three places. There was little good news that wartime summer, save for the Streak and Nelson's young wife's attentive nursing. (In recounting his recuperation, Nelson said he rallied some strength every time DiMaggio got a hit—and his raised eyebrows said the rest.) By the end of the season Nelson's leg had healed enough for him to enlist and be assigned to a classified desk in Brooklyn, and in February 1942, the Taylors' first and only child was born.

Michael was a quick fan of baseball, the Yankees, and Joltin' Joe. Even after the Taylors moved to Milwaukee for Nelson's work, young Michael continued to root for the Yankee Clipper. Michael started playing at four (wearing number 5, of course), varsity at fourteen—he was the best player at his high school, hands down. He followed Joe obsessively, calculating his batting average from the box scores in the daily paper. And though DiMaggio's career had ended more than a decade before Michael's professional play began, DiMaggio remained a lodestar. The only reason Michael switched from center to left was that a Double-A coach made it abundantly clear he'd be playing the corner or nowhere at all. And even this necessity felt like some sort of betrayal.

Joe's reputation for a quick temper, his habit of holding a grudge, even his postcareer controversies (marrying Marilyn, divorcing Marilyn, rumors that he was to marry Marilyn again) had not besmirched Michael's view of the Italian American sports star. Who cared if sportswriters called him gristly, if he held a grudge: he had principles, and Michael respected him for it. If anything, in those tragic years Joe'd taken on mythic proportions. Joe as guiding light, Joe as amulet. So when Audrey discovered the mistyped Jesus bracelet in a remainders bin, the extra yellow *D* embroidered into the blue cloth—WWJDD—of course she bought it, and of course Michael knotted it around his wrist.

◇

Michael slips out while Audrey is still asleep. He borrows the Walshes' second car—a peppy little Honda that makes Audrey's old Camry seem that much sadder—and drives to a diner. He orders a short stack and a side of bacon, and spends the meal on hold with the insurance company. When he finally gets a human on the line, the guy tells him they can get someone out to assess the damage the following Tuesday. "It's Wednesday!" Michael bellows, loud enough to startle the sweet-looking waitress refilling his coffee.

He takes the appointment, but knows he isn't going to wait till next week to start fixing his home. No way. He goes straight to the hardware store, buys a new set of deadbolts and door-knobs that lock, chains for the front and back. A new piece of cut glass for the door. A motion-sensor kit to install around the bay windows, front entrance and back. The twerpy store clerk seems to think he should have a professional install it, but Michael tells him to mind his own damn business. He gets a new tool set—decent, but not nearly as nice as the kit that was stolen, which had been a sixtieth birthday present from the Stallions. Cleaning supplies, industrial garbage bags, bleach, and a mop. Two bottles of ant spray. He stops at a drug store for a disposable camera—his visitors had nicked his Nikon, too—then thinks better of it and buys two.

He uses up both cameras and then starts to clean. The loose things first: he gathers empty bottles and junk-food wrappers from every room in the house, finds wadded-up napkins under the beds, in the bookshelves, *behind* the sideboard in the dining room. The discovery of a used needle under the couch makes his skin crawl, and he is a bit more careful about pawing around after that.

Not all of what they left behind is junk: children's underwear, Superman and Transformers briefs, are tucked into the corner of a closet. They might've belonged to one of his grandsons, but Audrey runs a tighter ship than that. In the garage, the washer is full of dank, damp laundry, kid-size T-shirts and the kind of neon-bright tops his preteen granddaughter wears. He stops scrutinizing the load when he finds his hands full of wet lingerie; at that point he throws the whole of it in a trash bag. He goes through one box of bags and starts another.

The cop's idea of it being a family down on its luck? Michael goes from thinking the cop is maybe right to spot-fucking-on when he finds a wide-ruled sheet crumpled up in the living room. He flattens it out—the paper shows the shaky hand of a little kid. *My Thanks Giving* by one Alex S. The kid struggled through a paragraph: *We got a new hose on Thanks Giving. Moms friend Randy got us a turky. Michelle eat too much and got sick. We eat ice cream for desert.*

Michael reads it again and inspects the five-finger turkey. Little hand. The kid probably couldn't get his hand around a regulation bat, much less swing the thing. What would Joe

DiMaggio do? Michael doesn't think Joe would have started a manhunt for some pipsqueak. So Michael balls up the page again and tosses it with the rest of the trash.

◇

The visitors left Michael's bats where they were, in a worn-looking canvas bag in the far corner of the garage, and at the end of that first long day, Michael begs off dinner plans with Audrey and the Walshes, grabs the bag, and heads to the stadium. He's driven halfway to the old complex when he remembers it will be empty, or gone—it is getting turned into a parking garage for the adjacent mall. This spring, the Lions are playing at some brand-new complex, Salt Stick or Salt Lick or something; Michael can't quite remember its name. He doesn't have the keys yet—last week Woody Botter, the GM, sent out a long-winded e-mail about the procedure for getting a new set—so he'll have to track down a maintenance guy or security to open up the cage. He's got his credentials on him, always does. Hopefully somebody will be around, but not too many somebodies—he doesn't want to pretend everything is la-di-da tonight.

Michael isn't quite sure where he's going, but knows the complex is near the new casino on the east side, all of it built on Indian land. Talking Stick Casino is not a place he's been, but it's tall and gaudy and flashing spotlights into the night sky, and so he points the car toward its beacon. He has to loop around the sports complex twice to find the way in, an unlit boulevard that splits two parking lots, one still waiting for its stripes. The landscapers have dropped off the plants for the median but transplanted only a few; the rest loiter in black plastic tubs. For a flash he thinks about taking a couple of the smaller cacti to restart his own battered collection—Audrey loves her succulents—but he shakes the idea from his mind. He is not a thief.

The new stadium is a hulking shadow lit by the occasional exit sign. Through the gates he can see a broad concourse, the spotless counters of vendors who have yet to move in. There's no good view of left field—but he tries to imagine it as he circles the stadium. Big, small? Of all the corners of the field, left is the most malleable, the easiest to shorten or stretch per the site plan. It annoys Michael that while the infield and its dimensions are sacred—the ninety-foot base path; the sixty feet, six inches from the rubber to home; the ninety-five feet between the mound and the grass line—his domain can be doubled or halved, depending on street grids and how many seats some owner is trying to fit. Look at the Green Monster—only 310 to the wall—while the deep part of the old Yankee Stadium was 457. (Another reason Michael admired Joe: in 1937 he hit forty-six home runs in that stadium, even with its farther-than-far left-center wall.) The Lions' Culver City home, a nondescript, moderately nostalgic stadium built in the nineties, has a gigantic left, which is part of why they invested in Goodyear. That man has strong legs and an arm like a rocket launcher.

The first ring of practice fields is dark, but there is a glow beyond them, and he hears something that sounds like a bat making contact. He walks toward the noise. The lights, hanging just inside the upper net, cast webbed shadows onto the paved approach, with a bigger, batter-shaped shadow spilling onto the walkway. *Thwunk.* The next ball is spit out of the machine. The shadow batter swings, a swing Michael recognizes instantly as Jason Goodyear's. Decisive, graceful. Certain.

The left fielder makes solid contact and sends a line drive into the dark of the cage's far net. The hit would've been a stand-up double, maybe a triple with Jason's speed—he's fast, and not afraid to use it. Another pitch, another line drive, this one angling slightly more to the right. He makes it look so easy, Michael thinks. The machine isn't flaming at ninety-five, but these balls aren't under eighty, either. A third, another notch over. He is doing it on purpose, Michael realizes, hitting clockwise across the cage, like a minute hand ticking around the hour. He knows Jason is obsessive about his swing, poring over tape of opposing pitchers and his own performance, asking for advice from everyone, Michael included. But this is something else.

When the bucket is done, Jason sets his bat against the net. It is then that he sees Michael's shadow in the darkness.

"Who's there?" The player tenses. It isn't a genius move to leave yourself so exposed, no one for a half mile in any direction. What would happen if trouble came around? Run for the casino? But men don't think that way, of their vulnerabilities. Michael knows he never did.

"It's Coach Taylor." He steps out of the shadows, shows his palms.

The player's posture relaxes, and his mouth splits into a crooked smile. He is good-looking, a Tom Cruise smile and Paul Newman eyes. *Heartthrob*, that's what Michael's daughters called him, and he remembers the collective sob that happened around the country when Jason's secret wedding to that kindergarten teacher was revealed. Clean cut, too—no visible tattoos, no billboards in his skivvies, no cursing when he strikes out— just a tight-lipped huff and he's right back to the dugout, so that Audrey and Helen's type like him, too. Even if the holier-than-thou bit gets old (his teammates call him "Goody Two-shoes" behind his back), this is a solid man. "Hey, Coach. Thought I had the place to myself tonight."

"Me, too." Michael steps closer. "You're to camp early. Before pitchers and catchers even." He'd heard that Jason's Arizona house had a batting cage built into the backyard, but maybe he'd heard wrong.

Jason shrugs. "Needed a change of scenery, wanted to see this new stadium they've been hollering about. How about you?"

"Audrey and I always try to get down here early. A bit of calm before the storm, you know?" Or the storm before the storm, Michael thinks, remembering the wrecked kitchen, the empty garage.

"I hear that." Jason inspects his hands, the handle of the bat. "How'd I look?"

"Good, as always. Your step is a little shorter than normal, but you probably knew that."

Jason contemplates this, nods. "And how are the girls?"

"Fine. Just saw Katie and her four up in Wisconsin."

"Four, wow. Any more coming?"

"I hope not." They laugh at that.

Jason nods to the bag over Michael's shoulder. "You want in?"

Michael waves the notion away. "No rush. I could watch that swing all night."

"I was just finishing." Jason ducks into the shadows, and Michael can hear him dropping balls into the bucket. "What speed?"

Michael thinks briefly about telling him to set the pitching machine at seventy-five, eighty miles per hour, something a big-leaguer could respect. But then says an honest number. "Fifty-five."

"You got it." Jason adjusts the machine, then walks to home plate. "Good to see you, Coach." The men shake. "My best to the family."

"Thanks, Jason. And to yours." Michael thinks he sees an

unpleasantness flash across the younger man's face, but then it is gone. "See you around." The ballplayer walks into the darkness, in the direction of the blinking casino.

◇

There's something cathartic about swinging a piece of wood at a hurtling knot of leather and yarn. The sting that happens in your palms when you connect, the ball bending ever so slightly at the collision. The reverberations of that rubber center that run up your arms, plugging into your shoulders with a little zing. The sound of it.

As he swings he thinks about what Joe DiMaggio would do with all of this, the wrecked house and the lonely stadium and the desert night blowing cold all of a sudden. His mind drifts to that famous profile in *Esquire*. Late sixties, written after Joe'd been retired for maybe fifteen years. Some writer tracked him down in San Fran, ran him off the end of the wharf practically, played a game of cat and mouse with Joe in his own flipping restaurant. The snook even talked his way into breakfast with DiMaggio's sister at their dead parents' house. But Joe, he stayed classy, like you'd expect out of a guy who always dressed in pressed slacks and a nice silk tie, who drove a Cadillac as soon as his contract with Dodge was done. The whole long article, through all the provocation, Joe never did say a bad thing about Marilyn and only got close to throwing a drink in the guy's face. What'd Joe do? He'd keep it together. Michael takes another swing.

In that same article, they talked about Yankee spring training, where Joe served as batting coach. *There was a time when you couldn't get me out of there*, Joe said of the cages, eyeing them wearily. It gives Michael a small swell of pride to remember that bit, to think how he still feels compelled to swing, capable of it. Not that he is better than Joe, but that he has this one thing, and no one can talk him out of it. Not Audrey, worried about his back; not the management, wanting to start fresh with someone who thinks coaching is *math*; not Jason, too polite to say fifty-five is a little-boy speed. Or maybe, old-man speed. He slaps another ball into the far net.

Michael goes for an hour, feeling good and sore at the end. Walking back through the lot he recognizes Jason's beat-up Jeep, but the left fielder is nowhere to be seen. Why the guy, who pulls down $15 million a year—more than that with sponsorships—still drives a muddy car from the nineties is a mystery. But thinking about cars makes him ache for the Caddy all over again, so he gets in his borrowed Honda and drives away.

◇

When Michael enters the pool house, Audrey scowls at the bag over his shoulder. As anticipated, she isn't happy to discover he's been at the cages—he's thrown out his back a couple of times in the past few years, mostly by doing stupid stuff with the grand-kids, and the doctor says big swings might exacerbate the injury. But she also knows better than to give him an earful when he is in a foul mood. Helen has left him a sandwich on the nightstand.

"I know, honey. I was careful," he lies as he drops the bats in the corner. He sits on the edge of the bed and starts eating in huge, chomping bites. Halfway in, Michael realizes he's not eaten since breakfast.

"You talk to the insurance guy?"

He nods, mouth full.

Audrey watches her husband, concern knitting her brow. "You know, we could hire someone to clean up the place. Professionals, so you can focus on the season." *The season.* The first few weeks of spring are Michael's busiest time of year—more than during the Stallions' season opener in April or anytime down the stretch—because no matter if guys are playing in the Caribbean or mastering their video games all winter, in the first weeks of spring they *have* to get recalibrated to major league pitching. On day one of workouts everyone wants a piece of Michael Taylor—he understands the mechanics of a swing better than any slo-mo camera or instant replay. A guru, they call him in the clubhouse.

He wishes that reputation could help him with the front office and the L.A. job, which has come up twice now since he retired from play. Hell, the last time the batting coach position was open he flew himself to Southern California to make an appeal to the management. When Stephen Smith said no, easy as a pitcher shaking off some call he didn't like—and without even the pretense of conferring with the rest of the ownership—it was as if Michael'd gotten sent down all over again.

Audrey doesn't say more, just watches him eat. When he is finished, has hardly swallowed the last bite, she takes his hand in hers. Her fingers skim over the bracelet and knead into the meat of his palm, where his calluses are red. She presses along the lines of the metatarsals, over and around the joints of each knuckle. Usually, a minute of this kind of rubbing works like a charm, relaxes him into a better place. Not tonight: the joints won't give against her thumbs.

"That's fine, Audrey," Michael says after a minute more. He slips his hand out of hers and closes it into a fist.

◇

The phone bill, thick as a Sears catalog, is waiting for Michael the next morning. Somebody liked calling 900 numbers, one in particular. Wondering what would merit $600 of conversation over the course of a week, Michael dials the number listed on the bill and, in the time it takes to say, *Hello, who is this*, gets an earful of smut that sends his diastolic pressure up by twenty points. The monthly water bill is three times what it is when the grass is alive and they have the pool pumping, a house full of grandkids visiting for spring break.

That day and the next Michael scrubs and sprays, Cloroxes the bathrooms so the whole house smells like the county pool. Saturday he drags the mattresses to the curb and starts ripping up carpet. Sunday he picks out new beds and box springs at Macy's. Monday he gets out the touch-up paint (he keeps cans in the garage) and spackles the strange dents in the drywall.

He checks in daily with the precinct. No news on the home invasion—though in his impatience Michael has bleached and buffed away any possible fingerprints—and not one lead on the Cadillac. The cops seem certain the car is in California, cruising around L.A. in swapped plates. Folks in Los Angeles have no problem buying a hot car, they explain. No one bothers to hypothesize about the fate of Audrey's Camry.

$$\diamondsuit$$

The insurance assessor finally visits. He takes a quick glance at the curbside trash heap, flips through Michael's photos from the disposable cameras, then spends fifteen minutes opening cupboards and looking under furniture, knocking on freshly painted walls. He punches some numbers into his phone, scribbles a few angry-seeming notes on his clipboard, then cuts Michael a check for only slightly more than what he spent at the hardware store that first day.

"What about the mattresses? And the carpet, it's destroyed. Did you see what they did to the pool?"

The assessor keeps a straight face, saying, "Market value. You've had that carpet for ten years, sir." He glances at his paperwork. "The mattress, twenty. Have you heard of depreciation, sir?" It's all Michael can do to not hit him in the nose.

That afternoon they go to visit the Johnstons at their new retirement home, which Michael finds dispiriting despite the cheery paint and big, sunlit windows. He has seen plenty of men age, generations of players go from kids to men to men too old to play (in one interview, Joe had called it "the pressures of age"), but this—the walkers and wheelchairs, the hunched and frail remnants of masculinity—is different. He's still not entirely forgiven Dave and Betty for leaving the neighborhood, but to see them now, Betty looking as feeble as a twig, Dave's wobbly hand supporting her elbow as they walk, he can't find it in him to stay mad.

$$\diamond$$

Michael keeps going to the cage at night. Sometimes Jason is there, always just wrapping up, some nights the place is empty, lit like a stage awaiting his entrance. Hitting does something good for his head, clears it out after he gets so damn hot thinking about what's happened to their home. Focusing on that small sphere rushing toward him, creaming the thing, sending it sailing into the net, where it stops and hangs for a second, jostling around the mesh fabric before falling—Michael likes that. His hands, burning where the knob of the bat bites the heel of his palm: that feels great. The ritual cools him off before he goes back to Audrey and their friends. With them he has to act like everything is fine, like he isn't seething mad. Like he isn't still pissed about how the recession knocked them flat, not angry at how the Lions are trying to force him to retire, not aggrieved at how his kids, all of them over thirty, still can't *find* their bootstraps, much less give them a good yank in the upward direction.

◇

The backyard needs more work and they are still deciding between two carpets for the living room, but even if it is a work in progress, Michael is ready to be home. With no word on the cars, and pitchers and catchers a few days away, Michael proceeds with his auto claim. Market value again. The money isn't enough for another new car, definitely not a Cadillac, but he finds a three-year-old Chrysler 300 in silver that'll do. For Audrey, he picks out another Camry, light blue again, and a year newer than the first.

Audrey requires some cajoling—Michael assures her the new locks are strong and the alarm is loud—but after ten days with the Walshes, she finally agrees to return to their house. They drive in a caravan, both of them tentative with their new vehicles.

"Oh," is all Audrey says when she walks in the door. She goes slowly from room to room, opening drawers, peering into closets. "Oh, oh."

She comes back into the kitchen, where her husband is plating a rotisserie chicken he bought at the Whole Foods. He isn't a cook, does nothing besides the grill, really, but Michael knows how to pull together a decent meal when he needs to. "There's salad in the fridge, too."

"You've done good, Mikey," she says, and smiles. He hands her a glass of wine, no $500 French Bordeaux, but a pinot noir he knows she'll like. She takes a sip, rolls the liquid on her tongue. "The place needed some freshening up, anyway."

They eat outside, the moon bright. After picking the chicken clean and finishing off the bottle of wine, Michael and Audrey make love on their new bed. Some things have changed over the past five decades, but many have not—Audrey still likes it when he nibbles on her earlobe; she still coos like a dove. And Michael still thinks of swinging a bat as he thrusts. The almost-gentle warm-up swipes, then the chops with follow-through, their increasing velocity and strength. It leaves them both breathless. He waits until she is soundly asleep, her breath a slight, reassuring whistle, before he retrieves a bat and sets it next to the bed.

$$\diamond$$

Michael would've been fine to ignore his sixty-ninth birthday, but Audrey insists. "We've got to celebrate the good stuff, Mikey. Besides, once the team shows up you'll be gone morning, noon, and night." She doesn't point out that it has already been this way.

The Saturday before Valentine's Day at Don & Charlie's steakhouse isn't an easy reservation to come by, but Audrey gets them a nice corner table. The waiter treats them like young lovers, placing a rose on the table "for the lady," setting down a dish of heart-shaped butter dollops. Schmaltzy, but Michael doesn't mind. Audrey looks great in the flickering candlelight: her little black dress, her hair pulled back to the nape of her neck, a touch of pink lipstick, something small and sparkling at her throat. The room is swaying with a romantic string soundtrack. God, Michael loves her.

They start with martinis and get a steak for two, the works. Audrey usually eats like a bird, but this night she eats like a hungry bird, giving her husband the bigger half of the steak but enjoying her own pile of meat, red and oozing. They talk about the team. During the off-season Jimmy Cardozo reupped for some big number. Michael's still proud of the work he did with the catcher; Jimmy was a dolt at the plate until he met Michael in Salt Lake. Audrey listens attentively, nodding and chewing, chewing and nodding, sipping on her wine. "Oh, look, Mikey," she says every few minutes, pointing up to some framed sports photo or piece of memorabilia. It is one of the largest private collections in America, hung helter-skelter so something is always popping into view. A big black-and-white photo of Babe Ruth in his home-run stance. A signed Greg Maddux jersey. A pennant from the Brooklyn Dodgers. A whole rack of glinting World Series rings. A picture of Joe in a tailored suit, big shoulders and a tight waist, smiling and shaking the hand of some starched shirt. A shot of Jason Goodyear, holding one of his MVP trophies.

Audrey and Michael split their wine like they do their steaks, and after sharing a bottle of it, Michael is feeling good. They eat a slice of key lime pie for dessert, and Michael leaves the waiter a nice tip. When they get up to leave, Audrey goes to freshen up in the ladies' room, and Michael steps outside for some night air. Since sundown the temperature has dropped twenty degrees, and a breeze, full of acacia blooms, is blowing cool and sweet.

He is enjoying that fine air and the feeling of a premium steak settling in his stomach when what does he see but a Cadillac— his Cadillac—parked illegally in the handicap spot? He walks slowly around the vehicle, his throat getting thick as he reaches the back bumper. His vision clicks across the plate's letters and numbers: they match. The thief even kept the Lions license plate holder—that takes some nerve. Through the window tint he can see the back seat, littered with to-go containers and kids' stuff— more of Alex S.'s homework? It must be hard for that boy to be upended so. Moving from empty home to empty home. But still. Michael's been upended, too. These visitors destroyed his home, his pride, his sense of security.

Michael straightens. What would Joe do? He flits through the options, the car going blurry before him.

Joe might've called the cops, given them an earful. And

Michael could chew out the Scottsdale PD: they couldn't find a stolen car that has been right under their stinking noses the whole time? Not that reporting it would matter—the car belongs to the insurance company now, Michael saddled with a consolation Chrysler and significantly higher monthly premiums.

Or maybe Joe would've walked back into the restaurant and quietly cased the joint. Gone from table to white-linened table and figured out exactly *who* had wrecked his place and stolen his prized possession—and then broken a bottle of Scotch over the guy's head.

No, no. As much as the idea of catching a thief red-handed makes Michael itch, he knows that isn't right—Joe wouldn't have caused that kind of scene. He might have intercepted his dining companion (gorgeous, of course) at the front of the restaurant, and walked her the long way around the lot so she would not have even *noticed* the offending car. He would've gotten her home safe, then driven down to the precinct and ripped the cops good. In person, not over the phone, so the coppers could *see* how much better Joe was than them.

But Joe was a man, too, and every man has his limits. Michael knows the Clipper went through some tough times, bared his teeth, snarled enough to make people wonder what was going on behind that buck-toothed smile. Joe fought with the media, made a scene about Marilyn's funeral, wouldn't let Sinatra come. We're all allowed to lose our tempers when we've been pushed too far, Michael is certain of that. Joe'd done it, and Michael feels himself about to go there, too. The car's paint wavers in the streetlights: black, then blue, then black again. It is too much.

So, with Audrey still inside, Michael walks across the lot to the Chrysler. He opens the trunk, goes to his bag, and pulls out an old bat. A Louisville ash, on the heavy side. He liked to use it against curve balers. Michael returns to the Cadillac and stands in front of the car. He adjusts his grip, steps into his stance, and takes a deep breath before starting into a strong, arcing swing.

The first contact breaks a headlight. The second, square in the middle of the hood, knocks the silver shield out of its seating. Michael can feel the knob of the bat dig into his palm. He knows his hands will be flaring red by the time he is done, but that doesn't stop him.

The third hit takes off the side-view mirror, the fourth shatters the driver's-side window. Michael feels a spray of safety glass ricochet off his blazer and sprinkle down to the asphalt. He swings again and pops out the door to the gas tank. Spiderwebs the back windshield. Keeps hitting the rear of the car until both taillights are shattered and he's knocked the back bumper halfway off. Peels the antenna from the frame, dents in the rear passenger door handle until there is no way that thing will open.

Michael doesn't notice Audrey come out, but then she is there, gaping and gasping like a goldfish out of water. He stops, puts his bat on his shoulder. She doesn't say anything as he walks over to her. The red-wine flush is gone from her cheeks; her skin is the color of bone. Her blue eyes are wide, sparkling with the kind of wet that comes after a sudden blast of Wisconsin's winter wind.

His lovely wife. "You good?" Michael asks her, the blood loud in his ears.

She replies not with words, but with her head bobbing along the high collar of her coat. Maybe she nods yes, maybe she shakes her head no; in that moment, he can't tell the difference.

"Okay, then."

Michael takes Audrey around the waist and starts walking them toward their new car. Others have come out of the restaurant; Michael hears a waiter calling after him. But he doesn't pay him any mind. What is done is done. As Michael weaves between the sports cars and luxury SUVs, he holds the bat in one hand and Audrey in the other. Is he holding her up, or she him? He can't say. But Michael can feel his wife tremble in his grip, and it just makes him hold her tighter.

# SECOND

Remember how I said this was a long game? Let's put it in perspective, consider the history of this place in geological time. Take a look at Salt River Fields' cleat-pocked outfield and imagine this: the ground under Goodyear's feet was once a sea, shallow and warm and dotted with coral reefs, clusters of orangey calcium deposits spread like neon ink-blots across the seafloor. The water was that impossible, startling blue that makes even an Arizona sky look as though it's been mixed with a tubful of gray, and sharks swam through the dugouts, finning to the mound and back.

That should make the pitcher feel better about his visits from the bench: imagine an ancient hammerhead in Coach Stu's place, three hundred incisors and mad at the world. It's the first game of the spring season, and the pitcher, a top prospect from Notre Dame a few years back but rehabbing from Tommy John, looks rattled after even a strong whiff from the batter. So out comes Coach Stu with his slow walk, his hands jammed in his back pockets. The boy nods back at the older man, his glove cupping his chin up to his nose as he mumbles some excuse. The leather, his glove a dark red stain, is high enough to cover the quaver of his lip but not the fear in his eyes. Didn't this kid dominate the ACC? Take the team to Omaha—not the championship, but pretty damn close? Wasn't he looking good in Salt Lake, didn't the PT and the team physio say he was strong? It's the second inning, and he's quaking like seagrass under a big wave. The scar from his surgery is a bright seam around his elbow, you can't help noticing it.

Today, Arizona is littered with shark teeth, dentin-and-enamel fangs lost in the sand. Some are as small as the top joint on your pinkie, others the length of a tall man's index. You don't have to go scratching too far below the surface to find one. With a bit of spit and a thumb rub, it'll still glow white as bone. What's past is prologue, a murderer once said. It goes without saying, but there's some drama in baseball, too.

Enter stage left, Tamara Rowland. Mind you, I'm not pinning all that's to come on Tami—she'd argue, *Wrong place, wrong time, rotten luck.* And she'd have a point. In our profession, we try to be objective, and I'd like to give Tami the benefit of the doubt. Jason had plenty of mess before their first gin and diet, and he made more than a few bozo moves on his own. The scope of the mess is still unclear, but I know for a fact that Jason has been in Arizona for three weeks and he's never once used the front door to his Arizona home, even as Liana gets up and goes to school every day, teaching a bunch of snot-nosed first graders at Sandpiper Elementary. And it wasn't just Michael's memory, there *is* a batting cage in Jason's backyard—so why is he working out at Salt River?

Last season he was fine, but this winter the line started going shaky. Three months of paparazzi photos, and not one with Liana by his side. Sightings in Vegas, look-alikes in Atlantic City. His California house is on the market, as is a flood of memorabilia. Nobody's connected the dots, but I have a mind to.

Look, I said "we" and "our" like I'm still part of the corps, like they didn't buy me out when the paper took its most recent nosedive that sad day, two Februarys ago. *Isn't half my pension concession enough?* I'd said, not wanting to turn over my creased and cracked credential, the laminate so familiar it felt like a second skin. But my new boss, some dot-commer who looked younger than my son, shook his head no. He could not condone misrepresentation, he said with a holier-than-thou sniff.

What does a sportswriter do without his badge? Loiter around the parking lot, that's what, watching for players to come out of the clubhouse, hoping he can launch a question over the heads of the shortstop-size kids waiting for signatures, their uncapped Sharpies waving (don't wear a white shirt). He's not a hell of a lot different from Tamara Rowland, truth be told—yesterday, I spied her sitting in the shade, a few yards away from my own perch.

And in watching Tami take the stage, I can assure you it isn't "wrong place, wrong time" as it is happening. To get Jason Goodyear in her thrall, to share a meal with him, to have their bodies close, to imagine them even closer is a thrill. She's not thinking about ripple effects, not thinking about dominos—she's mooning over his sapphire eyes then hoping for dinner then watching the landscape in the moonlight then wondering at how much cash is in the till. But there are those encounters, in baseball and in life, that send every sort of tailspin into motion, and with their meeting, Tami might just've sent our man whirling.

PROSPECTS

Tamara Rowland knows only the rookies hang out by the exit. Done-up divorcées, new-to-Scottsdale cocktail waitresses, ladies in from Single-A-affiliate sorts of towns—places so small they don't know any better. Tami could find half a dozen of them squeezed into the line of four-footers, grubby-fingered little boys with dirt under their nails and summer freckles just starting to blush. Nearby, but probably not attentive enough, the kids' bored-looking fathers hang back in the shade, thumbing phones and tugging on their belts. Tami knows not to be distracted by these men: doesn't matter if they're handsome in that midlist-Hollywood way or if they've got a whiff of Silicon Valley about them—these guys are still mentally in California, booking dot-com deals or toothpaste commercials, thinking about something, someone, far away. After all, the boys-only trip to watch Lions spring training is as much a gift to the woman waiting back home (a quiet house for three straight days, a weekend for brunch with girlfriends, a free afternoon to call her mom) as it is a dose of father-son bonding.

Also queued up by the players' exit: the too-pushy teen and preteen boys, pudgy middle schoolers and undersize underclassmen who bike over from the local schools, just as soon as the final bell rings. Zitty, awkward guys who'll never make it, definitely not with girls, and unlikely even into the ranks of the JV squad. Equipment manager, maybe. Without better prospects, they throw their hearts into this, baseball fandom, and the signatures they might catch as athletes depart the stadium. Tami feels for these boys, remembers how touch-and-go it was with her son Connor, before he'd shot up and thinned out and learned that no woman likes a guy who makes fart noises for fun.

The only group that can overcome the bad vibes of loitering at the players' exit are the sorority girls from ASU. A couple of times a season she'll spot a lithe pack of them, watch them giggle and wiggle their way up to the front. If the air could go out of a sky the way it goes out of a room when a busty Kappa Alpha walks in the door, that'd be happening in this Arizona parking lot, the aforementioned teen boys going twitchy at their proximity to young, nubile sex. These girls, tan in their tiny denim shorts and bleach-white spaghetti-strap tanks, pay the fanboys no mind. They know what they're dealing: quicker than a ninety-eight-mile-per-hour fastball, a blond coed will get any ballplayer's attention. There's no hope for anyone else the days *they* come to the stadium. These girls could be standing behind the outfield Port-O-Lets, covered in sod and chew juice, and the players would still stop and notice. Not that she likes it, but Tami understands it's the natural order of things.

Now Tami won't deny that she's waited for a player to emerge from the locker room; of course she has. She learned this game the same way anyone does: by misjudging balls, by swinging and missing. But the woman who just waits there, right along the rope, thinking that her doe eyes will make him notice: that's a rookie mistake. Everyone else has learned better.

◇

People from up north think that all desert is the same, but Arizona mornings are different from those in Texas, and Tami loves the way the sun creeps over the McDowell Mountains with its sparkly fingers of white-gold light. Her place is a half mile from where the foothills go steep, but the elevation is enough that it cools off every night until early April—another difference she is thankful for. So on this late February morning, it's still chilly when she gets up. She pulls her kimono tighter across her chest as she pads downstairs.

Hers is a nice kitchen: granite-topped island, triple-bay stainless sink, pendant lighting, an intricate backsplash. Tami grabs a grapefruit from the fridge, a knife from the drawer. The inside is always brighter than she expects. Halves, quarters, eighths.

The phone rings. Tami thinks Texas could be calling, if something bad happened to one of the boys, or one of their boys, or that little girl, Adelaide. But she's not on the top of anyone's speed dials, hasn't been for a while. It's probably Joanne. She's a troublingly early riser, a habit that's only gotten worse since menopause.

"What are you up to today?" Bingo—Joanne. She's got this low, husky voice. Old guys—coaches and veteran pitchers and the like—go crazy for it.

"Oh, I don't know," Tami responds. For a while before meeting Ronnie, Tami had a half-time gig working over at Taliesin West. Mostly the register in the gift shop, but she'd lead tours, too, when the volunteer docents couldn't manage to make it in. *That's no problem, ma'am, someone will cover for you*, she'd say when they called to cancel twenty minutes before their shifts. And, *Of course, dear, we'll see you in May. Have a lovely time in Paris*, when their vacations got in the way of the "mandatory" eight hours a month of volunteering. Talk about *Snots*-dale, Tami thinks, remembering those haughty women swaddled in their linens and silks. She knows as much about Frank Lloyd Wright as any of those wrinkled old bags. The difference between her and them? Less linen, and she has to *work* for her money.

"You working?" she says, licking a sticky finger. Yesterday she got her nails done, a bright pink called Bachelorette Bash.

"At two," Joanne says. Neither particularly wanted careers down here—who moves to the desert for a job?—so they lean on their alimonies and try to keep their overhead low. But when things got tight for Joanne's ex, which meant they got tight for Joanne, she landed three days a week at the Whole Foods on Pima. Thirty percent off everything but the meat. It's great for Joanne and her battery of life-preserving supplements. Tami told Joanne that she could do better, that no one would miss a little something more, but Joanne got all flustered and said she's too good for funny business. Tami knew she meant *too scared*, but didn't push. Joanne keeps Tami in grapefruit.

She spreads the wedges around a plate and walks over to a set of French doors. "I was thinking I'd go see the Lions game. Check out the new stadium." This season, the Los Angeles Lions are moving from Scottsdale Municipal—one of the dumpier places a major league team could spend their spring season—into a brand-new complex, just down the road from Tami. Salt River Fields, they're calling it.

"Really?" Joanne says.

Tami knows that tone. When Joanne finishes something, she's onto another team, no matter what. Doesn't want to get a "reputation" anywhere. She started with a scarred-up Giants catcher, then went to Peoria. That's where the two women met, loitering around the Mariners lot, both of them trying to look too good to be there. Joanne spent the spring with a veteran reliever. The year after that, she was in Mesa and met a DH who could put just about anything in play (never mind that he could barely shuffle up the base path). With fifteen Cactus League teams, she figures there are squads enough. Tami's not sure what her friend sees in these codgers, near as old as them and back to making the major league minimum. And the drives! It is thirty-five minutes to Peoria *without* traffic; the Lions' new compound, built on Pima-Maricopa land, is seven minutes, door to turnstile.

"Do you think that's such a good idea?"

Tami also knows from her friend's strained voice that Joanne's eyebrows are trying to make their way up her forehead. Back when she was Mrs. Thomson, she'd had a good deal of work done. It looks nice, except for when she's trying to move something. Tami's lucky that way—nothing's gotten too draggy or droopy.

"It'll be fine," she says. "Besides, Ronnie's not *on* the team. He just financed the stadium. He doesn't count toward your silly one-a-team rule."

"What about Hal Moyers?" A few seasons ago, Tami had a fling with the Lions' veteran curve baller, at least until his wife got wind and stormed in from Los Angeles. He was on a short leash after that.

Tami is surprised, and not surprised, that Joanne remembers Hal. "That was ages ago. Water under the bridge."

"That's what you think. But ballplayers—motherfucker." Tami hears a clatter of kitchenware, and then Joanne is muttering far from the phone. "Gotta go," she says. Joanne's always been a klutz.

Tami sets down the phone and steps into the backyard. Ronnie never got around to landscaping, but he dug for a pool and paved a not-small patio. Tami bought a few pieces at an estate sale, a café table and a couple of chairs that make her think of Paris. The yard looks pretty nice, if her eyes don't wander over to the pool-size hole or the pile of red-orange dirt where the landscaping is supposed to start.

No, it's not bad, she thinks as she settles into her breakfast. It's the last week of February, there's a game on this afternoon, and as the sun reaches over the McDowells, the tiles begin to warm under her bare feet.

$$\diamond$$

Tami's not racist, but she knows better than to go for the Hispanic players. Not that she doesn't like *them*, but they won't like *her*. Those guys will pick a younger woman, sometimes even young enough to get them into trouble. She got Anaheim's Latin American scout drunk once, and all he wanted to talk about was how his top prospects kept getting themselves into teen pussy, and team counsel was on his ass. Apparently the age of consent is twelve in Panama, fourteen in Paraguay. And they're babies themselves, the DR prospects signing the day they turn sixteen if they're any sort of talent. Shit, she'd made a boatload of bad decisions at sixteen.

And she doesn't mean to stereotype, but the few black guys still playing professional baseball (the numbers have dwindled since the Rickey Henderson years), aren't usually interested in women like her. They'll go to the "urban" clubs in the rehabbed warehouse blocks north of the train station to find edgy sorority sisters and dancers for the Suns. There are exceptions, of course. Tami had a nice time with a Padre originally from Arkansas; he had a thing for chicken-bone blondes with big hair. She hadn't worn her hair like that since Lubbock, but teasing it came back like riding a bike.

No, as a single woman in her midforties, Tami's best shot is with the white guys. Not Joanne's masters of the clubhouse—too old for her—or the deer-in-the-headlights rookies, young enough to be a son, but guys a few years in, going through a hard patch. Maybe they're struggling on the field or coming back from an injury. Wading through a divorce or adjusting to a trade. Mourning a dead parent or worrying over a sick kid. Vulnerable, somehow or other. Those are the ones to try for; they're the ones who need it. Sometimes they remind Tami of her Danny, how after a game there was nothing he wanted more than to lay his head in her lap. It's nice to be needed like that.

◇

Tami knows an old wino, Troy, who worked the left field gate at Scottsdale Municipal; after flashing him a smile and doing her best shoulder-shimmy hello, maybe throwing in an I'm-glad-to-see-you-too hug, he always let her in. Someone was feeling generous and hired him at Salt River Fields, and when she steps up to the gate, he acts like it's the world's biggest coincidence they've found each other here. No harm in acting like she's bowled over, too.

She picks a section by the right field line, close to the rolled-up tarp, and takes in the new stadium. Nice grandstand, pleasant-looking general-admission lawn (not that she'd *ever* sit in the grass), McDowell Mountains on the horizon. Good sight lines from the seats on either side. The architect used a bunch of exposed steel beams and curved a minimalist canopy around home, details that made it feel modern and maybe even a bit slick. She sits down with her latte and the spring season program. Jason Goodyear and Trey Townsend, the team's two Gold Glove outfielders, are smiling back at her, with a banner across the front about them being "the golden boys" of the L.A. Lions. Clever. Jason Goodyear, with his hunky good looks and shoulders that suggested he could be the bottom of a cheer pyramid all by himself, would be her kind of guy, except that he was dating movie stars, right up until he married that teacher. Phoenix girl, if she remembers right, some sort of collegiate athlete. And she's tried with Trey—they were at the same cocktail bar one night several seasons back, him sitting with that partial owner, Stephen Smith—but she wasn't as interesting as the itch on his ankle.

Flipping through the program, she sees plenty of names she recognizes. Some go back to that improbable postseason run in 2008. She'd watched from the edge of her seat, the time with Hal recent enough she felt invested. Lots of new faces, too. She'll have them memorized by the end of the day. "A gift," her daddy'd called her memory for a lineup.

There's still an hour thirty to first pitch. The field's morning watering is sparkling the sod in a pretty way. Tami loves this time before the game, being surrounded by the *thwack* of hard leather on soft, the wooden ping of a practice bat making contact. Baseball sounds, carrying across the field—not for a rapt audience, not because the game is on the line, but just because these motions are essential. Throwing and catching are like sleeping and eating for these men: natural, necessary. Now, of course she likes a nail-biter as much as anyone, but this warm-up is something else. Elemental.

She glances over to the boxes on the other side of home, but it's too far to see anything distinct, much less if Ronnie's there.

Down on the grass, Greg Carver is throwing easy balls with the catcher Jimmy Cardozo. She first saw Carver throw last week, during a bullpen session. A right-handed fastballer, twenty-seven and lanky. Just coming back from Tommy John. Tami wasn't the only one standing by the fence; some snowbird in a plaid polo was watching, too, his fingers looped through the chain link. He smiled at her—dentures—when she approached. Some of these retirees just about live for the spring.

There was a bucket of balls next to the mound, a queue that went back past second. At home plate, the stand-in batter never took his bat off his shoulder. The pitching coach—Stu Walsh, a lefty Tami remembers playing back when *she* was a little girl—stood just behind the mound, his face stony under his ball cap, whispering notes to a guy with a clipboard. Every pitcher had eight balls to make an impression.

The retiree said Carver had been a high draft in 2005. Was climbing like normal till his elbow went kapow. The Lions still hoped to make a starter out of him, but during his long convalescence, Victor Vásquez, a prospect from the DR, had come up quicker than anyone expected. Now, the old man explained, the team had a fight on its hands. The last spot in the rotation. He seemed to relish the conflict, the possibility of someone's dreams being quashed. She noticed he was wearing a wedding ring, and also caught him staring at her tits.

At the bullpen session Carver threw seven strikes in a row, a few of them looking ninety-five. Walsh seemed unimpressed, right up until the last throw went wild, sailing so fast and high that it sent the batter scrambling onto all fours. At that, Walsh cursed under his breath—but not so quiet that Tami could not hear—and pointed Carver to the back of the line.

Now, watching Carver ready another throw, Tami wonders how he's doing. Walsh's scrutiny, the swarm of aspiring arms, coaches cutting a dozen athletes every Thursday. Does that sort of pressure help or hurt? And how is his arm feeling, finally pitching again? A cloud passes over his face and he rockets another to Cardozo, a fast and perfect strike. The catcher hoots and breaks into a gap-toothed grin.

"Tami. How are you?" She just about jumps out of her skin

at his voice, the baritone popping up behind her like a surprise foul ball.

She turns. "Hi, Ronnie."

The first time Tami saw Ronald Duncan, over at Scottsdale Municipal, she thought he was a scout. He was sitting next to a couple of front-office guys. Tan, with an open-neck team polo and a head of handsome gray, leaning into the game with a notebook on his lap. She'd already had a round with a twenty-eight-year-old from Seattle who'd left camp early with a hamstring injury; why not spread her wings and try something new?

She'd had Troy pass him a note in the seventh inning, and when Ronnie came up to her that night at the wine bar, he didn't correct her assumption about being with the organization. By the time Tami figured out he wasn't—Ronnie was a developer, that notebook was full of property values, nothing at all on pitch velocity—they were most of the way through dinner and getting along well enough.

Scottsdale has always had its rich ($25 million compounds in the hills, golf courses that cost fifty dollars a hole), but during the boom a lot of folks in the middle were looking up, stars and dollar signs in their eyes. Ronnie made a fortune on those kind: people eager for better schools and fancier zip codes and more expensive groceries. Nobody seemed to care if the houses were shoddy in their bones—the plumbing unreliable, the windows leaky, closets framed off plumb—so long as the driveways were long, the pools deep, the ceilings high.

By summer, Tami'd quit Taliesin and Ronnie was focused on Salt River—by his math it was not worth working on other projects until the market improved or the contractors got so desperate they undercut themselves by half again. *Waiting game*, he was fond of saying, tapping his temple and flashing a white-toothed grin. Meanwhile, Ronnie'd weaseled his way out of most of the rest of his bad situations before the shit really hit the oscillating fan. He was one of the few local developers who could claim that, who didn't eat his hat. As for Salt River, the tribe had plenty of money, and was expecting plenty more revenue from the casino, so construction proceeded apace. Ronnie expedited paperwork, smoothed out construction contracts, "liaised" with city hall (probably greased some palms, too, but Tami's not one to ask questions). He visited the site every Tuesday, hard-hat tours from when it was a rat maze of inlaid irrigation pipes to a horseshoe of concrete slabs to a steely skeleton to done (not once inviting Tami to join, either).

"That coffee?" He raises his left eyebrow like he guesses it's not. It was a thing they did sometimes, slipped whiskey into coffee cups and walked around the fancy outdoor mall. Camouflaged rum cocktails in soda cans and visited those cowboy art galleries downtown. Drinking on the links. He was a member at three of the better golf clubs in town—a developer's perk—and she wasn't a bad shot. They'd giggle like teenagers, and somehow those sunburned days slipped by.

"Yes, Ronnie." It comes out sharper than she means it to.

"Fine." He makes himself comfortable in the seat next to hers. "How's the house?"

"You made me quit, remember?" she says, thinking of Frank Lloyd Wright's winter compound. Ronnie didn't like it when she wasn't available, sneered at the word *retail* like it was something stinking on the bottom of his shoe—and sniffed at *nonprofit* like it didn't smell much better. When they split up, Tami called the HR gal at the house and told her she was available to come back. *No spots open*, the woman said. Tami asked if she could sub. *I'll make a note of it*, she said, her tone bristly enough that Tami wondered if she knew about the missing scarves, the solid-silver cufflinks.

"Not that house. Mine."

By the time they'd met, Ronnie had gotten rid of almost all the lots in Sandia Hills, his tanking 180-home development, making the half-built homes and empty foundations another man's headache. But the model home (five bedrooms and four baths, fancy appliances, marble) was still on his rolls. Tami was a proud woman, *is* a proud woman, but she had been living in a real craphole of a one-bedroom in South Scottsdale and she can spot a gift horse from a quarter mile. No word on it since they split, but really, she's doing *him* a favor, making sure no one breaks in, steals the appliances, and strips the pipes. There's been a lot of craziness going on.

"Right." A bunch of players jog up the warning track, slow and easy. "It's fine."

Ronnie follows her gaze. "Scouting another player?"

She can feel her brow wrinkle. "How's the project over on Paradise going?" Paradise East is his latest, or his last, and it might actually lose him a big chunk of money. The prospect makes her a smidge happy—she always hated his ego, how he strutted around town. "Make any more sales?"

The men are jogging backward now, toward home in a bumbling cluster. They tell fielders not to run backward—you'll get your feet tangled up—but they also say to never take your eye off the ball. One of those things is more important than the other.

"How are Jeremy and Connor?" he asks. His eyes are also on the players, but he knows exactly where to hit.

"The same. Fine." Tami hardly speaks with her sons anymore. Holidays she hears from them, birthdays if she's lucky. They made it pretty clear they were done with her as soon as they had a choice in the matter.

"What do your boys think about you going for guys their

age?" Two players collide and land on their duffs, cleats in the air.

"You don't know anything about my boys." Tami wishes she'd never told him about it, her want for ballplayers. It was stupid. Wined-up pillow talk. He'd wanted to know what turned her on—probably was waiting to hear her say tanned real estate execs with bleached teeth—but she'd told him the truth: power, potential, and a well-developed upper back. She laid it all out, the stuff about the possibility and drive of these men, before she even realized what she was saying, before she understood that something so honest could hurt, him and her both. They laughed about it at the time, but something changed. They were never particularly *nice* to each other, but after that night he stepped up his jabs, his mean-spirited asides. By January, it felt like a full-contact sport. Love was never really on the table with Ronnie—companionship was, sex was, and there was something comfortable about having someone handsome by her side. Less so when that someone was sneering. So when, two weeks before pitchers and catchers, she suggested they split, he didn't seem very broken up about it. Just said, "Figures."

Ronnie stands. In retrospect, Tami can see they were both lonely, that more than anything else. He says, "I hope you have a good season, Tami."

She doesn't watch him leave; she's looking for the guy who caused the pileup. It's William Goslin, the baby-faced rookie. The boy rises slowly and brushes himself off. His cheeks are flushed red.

She finishes her coffee and watches the team ease through the rest of their pregame stretches and rounds of toss. They act so casual, all loping limbs and toothy grins. As the crowd fills in around her, the players' movements focus into sharpened points: the infield does whip-fast throws around the horn, the outfield tosses sail high and higher. Before she knows it, everyone is standing for the national anthem, and then the first batter steps up to the plate.

◇

When did she start loving baseball? Well, her daddy'd take her and her brothers to the minor league stadium in Lubbock a few times a season, spoil them sick with soda and peanuts. Tami learned how to keep score at age seven. By eight she could spot a strong arm the way an architect senses a perfect site, the way a divorcée tastes want on her tongue. Was it intuition? A sixth sense? She's not sure. It was just a feeling she had.

Danny was a rocketballer, one of the best prospects in the state. She was cheering then, team captain, and even though the school didn't generally send the squad to baseball games, Tami insisted they go, and that meant they went, stomped around on top of the dugout, waving their pompoms at the crowd and flashing their panties at every player coming off the field. Danny got recruited into a D-I program, and Tami was so proud, she married the guy. Tami's mom had to sign her marriage certificate, Tami being seventeen, and the woman groused about it plenty. That signature was the last nice thing Charlene Rowland ever did for her daughter.

Tami didn't finish at Lubbock High, being a year behind Danny, but that hardly seemed to matter. They just wanted to be together, make a home and start Danny onto the kind of career that ended in Cooperstown. Step one was All-American, which he got his freshman year. Step two was baby Jeremy, born the following winter. But Danny's golden arm and Tami's good feelings about it didn't mean shit once he blew out his elbow his sophomore season. The young family was counting on a contract—step three. Instead, he was sidelined for two seasons.

When Danny finally did come back, or tried, they had two sons and he had to switch to relief. Danny got signed in the twenty-first round of the 1989 draft. He topped out at Double-A, the Midland Rockdogs. To Tami, playing Double-A felt like two left feet, walking around in circles.

When Danny and Tami decided to call it quits—he had an unpredictable temper and the sex drive of a salted slug—the boys chose to stay with their father. Tami got it: she wasn't one of those affectionate moms, and Danny let the boys walk all over him. Plus, Danny's momma and sister lived nearby and spoiled those boys rotten. So Tami got a job and an apartment, did what she could to see them as much as she could. Meanwhile, she started spending time with a big right-hander named Terrance Flanagan, who was on his way back down from a few good-ish years in the majors. They eventually married, when Tami was thirty-three. Objectively, she knew she wasn't any sort of old, but those fifteen years since she'd left Lubbock High felt like a lifetime, or three.

Terrance was the one who introduced her to Frank. They were at some holiday party in Dallas, a friend of Terrance's who'd done well—so well he'd bought a Wright original. The Gillin House, it was called, though she didn't know that then. What she knew was that she was gobsmacked by the dimensions and details, the harmonious aura of the place. The scale, the materials—the diving board matched the mantel, for Christ's sake. While everyone else swilled champagne, she gave herself a tour. The building pushed and pulled her in and out of rooms like there were magnets in the doorframes, until she found herself standing directly below a big copper dome—and oh, how *that* had made her heart sing. Tami didn't have any training in design, unless she counted the pattern-making in home ec, but after that she read whatever she could find, borrowed books from the library and read chapters while standing in the Borders. She even drove to Amarillo to see another of his Texas houses.

Meanwhile, Terrance became a development coach, which was fine by Tami—so long as she got to stay near the game. But when, after eight years of holy matrimony, he started messing around with her best friend, well, that was less fine. Road affairs are one thing, a way to blow off steam, but Terrance's infidelity hit too close to home. Plus, they wanted to get married. Her boys were older, Jeremy finishing at A&M, Connor working in Corpus. She didn't need to stick around for them.

Everything was sorted in a conference room over the course of an afternoon. The settlement got her to Arizona, a place she'd circled on her map back when Danny first told her about the Cactus League. (For all those years she'd spent married to ballplayers, all those springs they'd disappeared to Arizona for six weeks, not once had anyone invited her along.) She circled it again when she realized Frank Lloyd Wright's winter retreat, Taliesin West, was in Scottsdale. And they were hiring. For once in her life, everything was landing just right.

◇

In a lot of ways, baseball players are like other men. Some of them are dummies, some of them are mad, some of them are suspicious, shallow, arrogant. Some are so driven they'll just about forget there's a woman in the room, even if she's dressed up sexy or screaming her lungs out, even if she's the mother of their children. But the difference separating ballplayers from everyone else is that they care about something tremendously, and have since they were little. It's thrilling, and Tami feeds off it. Most people will never touch that kind of drive. Most people, whether they're living in small towns or big cities or sprawl, spend their lives dealing with crying babies and stupid jobs, whatever life throws at them. Baseball players, they do the throwing.

After everything bad with Danny and Terrance, after trying to grow old with these men and having it go plain wrong, Tami doesn't want to give anyone too much. She can't stake everything, not again. But these six weeks of spring can mean so much: they make the team, they get sent down, they get sent home. What happens here can shape the rest of a career in baseball, and it's a rare man who can keep his head down and plow through that kind of uncertainty. For everyone else, this is where she can help. She is ready when they need reassurances; she has a calm, steady smile and a warm hand to rest on an aching thigh. No, she doesn't regret telling Ronnie God's honest truth about it: she loves a ballplayer.

◇

Greg Carver starts the game. He looks strong, but when he begins to lose it, his arm slips quickly—two doubles in three at bats. The guy seems startled when the catcher pops up and comes to the mound, and shakes him off with a gesture so overdone that Tami can see it from right field. Then he walks a batter, and Walsh calls in a reliever. Carver quits the mound with his head down.

It's a nice afternoon, and she doesn't have anywhere to be, so after the game, she hangs around the players' lot, not up against the fence but over by the handicap spots, where there's a bench in the shade. She wants to see who's driving what this season. It says a lot, whether a player's got a snazzy rental or owns something nondescript. If he opts for tastefully expensive that means one thing, vanity plates mean something else. And she's looking for wives and girlfriends. Players won't rat on other players about any funny business, but baseball wives are another story. Melissa Moyers taught her that lesson plenty well.

Tami sees a few plain-looking players come out first, relief pitchers and guys who probably have only another week or two until they're cut. Jason Goodyear signs a few balls and then goes for a dusty old Jeep with a faded black-and-gold Lions bumper sticker—strange that he's still driving *that* after all these years and bazillions of dollars. Makes her feel better about her shitty Chevy (Tami's car is fifteen years old, a convertible that won't convert, so at first whiff of rain or a dust storm, she has to go skittering for a garage). More outfielders, Townsend and that new right fielder, Corey Matthews, leave together, climbing into a slick blue Audi. The fireplug catcher, Jimmy Cardozo, walks out with Carver, the latter's arm still wrapped in ice. Maybe him, she thinks. They drive off—Jimmy at the wheel—in a rented red Mustang. Ronnie strides across the parking lot, heading for his Mercedes. Suddenly there is something very, very important in the bottom of her purse.

◇

Her eyes snap open. The house is still, eerily so. She turns to her alarm clock and sees nothing. The button on the bedside lamp doesn't respond. She feels her way to the window, trying her best to avoid the linen chest.

The vacant, half-built houses around her are always dark, but the streetlights outside are burning bright. What happened? And then it hits her, hard as a beaner: Ronnie cut the power.

He could have given her some warning. He could have asked her to transfer the bills to her name or said time was up on her free utilities. Instead, he watched the game from his front-row box, drove across town in that small-prick car of his, and called the power company: *Shut her off.*

How much does it cost to restart power? This happened once in Midland, and it was an arm and a leg, on top of the balance. She's never seen a bill; when they were together it was a given he'd cover all that. She weighs her options. Put it on a card and hope? Try to quickly hawk something? The last piece she sold—a glazed tile that had been festering on a back shelf of the conservation lab so long she doubted anyone would miss it—got her through three months. But she's got no inventory, just a couple of silver doodads from the gift shop. With a tightness in her chest, she knows there's nothing to do about it until the morning, so she edges her way back into bed.

A few hours later, she's in her cavelike kitchen on hold with the power company. The agent tells her the primary account holder, a Mr. Duncan, called yesterday and said that address no longer needed service. It's $150 to turn things back on, another $100 to transfer the account to her name. The balance, too. Tami's seething on the inside, but she tries to stay calm. With some smooth-talking she gets him down to $175, gives him her credit card number, and, miracle of miracles, the charge clears.

She takes a cold shower in the dim bathroom, the place feeling more like the moon than her house in the skylight's strange cast. Naked and dripping, she watches herself dry off in the mirror. She's still pretty, still trim. But she misses those days of stepping into the bathroom to take a piss in the morning and being startled by how beautiful that woman in the mirror was. Half asleep, one of Danny's baggy T-shirts hanging nearly to her knees, it didn't matter: she was gorgeous, and not even trying. She could eat whatever she wanted, drink all the drinks, let her hair go wild. The curve of her ass, the way her breasts sat on her ribs—she loved her body then. Even after the boys, and they breastfed like wolves, she looked good—maybe even better.

That beauty was something she had for so long that she forgot about it. Then poof. Divorced (the second time) at forty-one, moving across the desert, hanging on to some vague idea of herself—but what part, exactly? It isn't her youth, she knows wanting that is foolhardy. She can't look like she did at twenty-two, she won't. Is there timeless beauty in her? No, that is something they say about ladies who have gone to seed. She's still beautiful, and not in that magnanimous way. But even as she convinces herself of this, in the mirror she can see how her ass has begun to sag, how her breasts swing low.

She twists one towel around her blond hair, wraps another across her chest. She knows this much: there's no more surprise-herself beauty.

In the dark she feels her way through mascara and powdering her nose, then gets dressed in a pink Juicy sweat suit. She should have grapefruit, but opening the fridge will hurry up the spoiling inside. It's better to go out, wet hair and all.

Bacon, eggs, home fries, an English muffin—she orders the kind of greasy-spoon breakfast she used to be able to eat without thinking twice, and Lord, does it taste good. The woman on the other side of the counter, managing the crowd all on her own, reminds Tami of herself, how she used to feel running around, looking after those boys and worrying about Danny. Young, but old. Worn out. That was the other part of her twenties—it was an awful time. For a few years there she existed on the constant verge of tears. She remembers driving down the highway, feeling like she might as well just lie down in the parking lot of the next truck stop and wait for a big rig to roll right over her pretty little body, put her out of her misery. Now, the money's just as tight, things with her boys are different but still not good, and she's alone again. Getting older, pickling, puckering. *Pruning*, that's what Joanne called it. Joanne, who gave her this Juicy sweat suit—there's some irony for you. It's another set of problems now, not better or worse, just different. But most of the time, Tami doesn't want to lie down in a parking lot.

She finishes her coffee and wants more, but knows better than to rush that poor woman. She'll come back around soon enough.

◇

"Who you watching?" An older man—the dapper, golf-club sort—slides into the seat next to hers. Most of the stands are still empty before the 1:05 start. Tami came early, stopping at a gas station, where she picked up a few adult beverages. Cheaper than buying them at the stadium by a long shot, and today could use an assist. Power won't be back on until five.

"No one in particular." Tami is not interested in making a new friend. She looks back at her program.

"Vásquez's pitching today." Not that she asked. The man points an arthritic finger to the warm-up mound. "I think he's gonna be good."

"Mm-hmm."

"Five bucks says Hal Moyers doesn't make it through the year. That's his replacement."

Tami thinks Hal will last—and not just because she's seen him naked. "That's interesting."

The man starts flipping through a program, and she takes the opportunity to transfer a second wine cooler from her hand-bag into a stadium cup with a quick slosh. The organist must've shown up—fanfare plays over and over, each time moving higher up the keys. *Dun-nuh-nuh-na, duh-na!* She starts to feel the booze at her temples with each *thwack* of the ball hitting the catcher's mitt. It feels good.

"What do you think of that Goose kid?" The golfer flashes a page in the program. The nineteen-year-old first baseman is Goose's great-grand-nephew, the man says. Tami shrugs; she'd read the same article yesterday. Last game, nerves got him in the field—he bungled two easy plays—and he was underwhelming at the plate. He probably shouldn't even be at camp this spring. He's too far gone for her kind of help—besides, he is too young. "He'll find his stride," she says. "I bet he'll find the exit quicker." The man is happy with himself for that, and Tami lets him laugh.

◇

It's a sloppy game for everyone but Vásquez, who pitches superbly, nothing like a twenty-year-old making his spring training debut. Afterward she hustles home, changes into a strappy floral-print dress, and is styling her hair into something that looks less crazy when the house's lights buzz back on. She winces at her bare-looking face. She skipped most of her rigmarole this morning—moisturizer, cover-up, foundation, eyeliner, eye shadow, mascara, and blush, then her eyebrows and this expensive lip gloss that makes her mouth tingle—but does the litany now, finishing with a puff of perfume onto her breastbone. She's only ten minutes late to meet Deidre, who is waiting for her at the bar of Don & Charlie's. Last fall, Deidre hooked up with a Suns assistant coach. (Tami never got into basketball, but Deidre spent her twenties as a cheerleader for the Sacramento Kings and says she feels about sweatbands the way Tami does about stirrups.) His night-game schedule has made her all but nocturnal, so happy hours are Tami's best shot at seeing her friend, at least until the playoffs. When Deidre spots Tami the woman does a quick, high whistle and waves.

There's a white-tablecloth dining room in the back, but up in the lounge, things are more casual. Red-nosed regulars have snagged all the stools, which leaves the rest of the crowd standing around, jostling one another. As per usual in spring, there're stag parties from the West Coast throwing back one last round before their night flights, golf-tripping corporate types reliving their best holes, and retirees taking a nip before early bedtimes. When a player comes in—and there are a dozen, scattered through the building—heads turn and voices dim. Unless they're wearing diamond-studded everything or have an entourage of Playboy Bunnies (both of these things have happened in springs past), the room absorbs them quickly enough.

Not many women around, which is also usual. It's part of why Tami and Deidre like it. Another reason: between long-weekend vacationers and the businessman travelers, only the stiff-lipped bartenders, a couple of world-weary sportswriters, and some septuagenarians recognize them and what they're up to. Tami's not worried about the old folks or the writers, they've got their own problems, and as for the bartenders . . . the women make sure they're well taken care of by whomever is taking care of them.

"How was the tournament?" Tami asks, still a bit breathless, both from rushing over and because the place is chock-full of memorabilia, stuff that should be in Cooperstown, not getting sticky with beer in suburban Phoenix. Mickey Mantle balls, pennants dating back to the teens, baseball cards displayed like dead butterflies. Stepping inside always makes Tami's skin go hot.

Deidre twirls the tiny red straw in her drink and casts her eyes around the room before replying. "Boring." Deidre's spent the day on the links, watching her boyfriend play in some charity tournament. Then, a broad smile spreads across her face. "But he's getting me a car."

Tami nearly spits her drink. "For watching him play golf?"

"No, silly. For being me." Deidre regularly insists she didn't set out to be a gold digger, but she's doing pretty well at pulling up nuggets. Tami's opinion is that the guy needs to have money enough for nice dinners, maybe some jewelry, but she's not hunting for a new convertible, so long as her crap car keeps running to the stadium and back. She wasn't hunting for a house, either, until Ronnie dropped one in her lap.

It takes a moment to recognize Jason Goodyear in his street clothes, a fashionably faded T-shirt and slim blue jeans, a blank red ball cap pulled low over his brow. A certain amount of anonymity in that, not being decked out in team gear. (Danny would make himself conspicuous on campus, although hardly anyone cared about him, even when they went to Omaha.) He's flanked by Trey Townsend and Corey Matthews, the two other outfielders looking like brothers in matching dark blazers and khaki pants.

Tami feels her heart trilling with the new arrivals—this always happens when she sees a player out in the world. "Omigod, Dee."

"What?" Deidre turns. "Hmm, he's handsome in real life, too." She scrunches up her nose. "I heard he just got divorced, poor baby."

"What?" Tami doesn't mean to sound shrill, but the question comes out like a squeak. "You're sure?"

Deidre nods. "I told you, Tami, you have to join Twitter."

Tami puts her hand on Deidre's shoulder. "Deidre." Tami's talking to her friend, but watching the outfielders walking toward the bar, toward them. Her stomach does a somersault. He's getting divorced?

"I know, I know." Deidre rolls her eyes. "You want a Tamara Special."

Tami hates that she calls it this, that they've done this so many times it has a name at all. But her friend is right. Yes, a Tamara Special.

Deidre sets down her tumbler, straightens the straps on her dress, and gives Tami her "I'm ready" nod. The men are getting closer; Tami can feel the zaps of their electricity on her bare arms. She opens her mouth, mumbles some nonsense, and Deidre breaks into near-hysterical laughter. "Oh my *gawd*, Tami! That's the funniest thing I've heard all week." Just as he's passing by, she grabs Jason Goodyear by the arm and pulls him to her. He stiffens momentarily, then loosens when he realizes it's just another done-up divorcée.

"This woman," she says, pointing at Tami, "she's a riot. Tell it again, Tami."

Tami demurs, eyes on the floor. "It wasn't that good, Dee. Leave the guy alone."

Jason starts to turn away, but Deidre tugs at his elbow again. "Well, stick around for a drink, at least? Maybe if we loosen her up she'll let us hear it. Woo. Haven't laughed that hard in years." Jason looks over Tami's shoulder to his teammates. She can see the question in his face: *Two old broads?* Tami wonders if Trey Townsend recognizes her. Unlikely. Her efforts that night had been a blip, a nothing moment on his carousel of springs.

They must've signaled for him to go for it, because in the next moment, his face softens and his blue eyes light up. "Why not?" His voice is deeper than she expected, just a few steps from a rumble. There's a bit of brashness there, which she also didn't expect. Who knows—maybe she looks better than she feels.

"Great." Deidre gives his arm a little squeeze. "Oh," she says, feigning surprise. "You a body builder or something?"

"A baseball player." Half his mouth curls up, something like a smirk. What does that smile mean? Is it prideful or embarrassed? Tami's not sure, only knows that she's never seen it. On the field he's all steely determination; most of his ad campaigns employ that same serious-competitor persona. The thin line of his mouth and the square, set jaw, the narrowed eyes of supreme focus. And in interviews he's all, *Yes, sir; no, ma'am*, polite as a piece of toast, smiling for the camera when the cue cards tell him to.

"Whoa! I thought it was time for basketball!" Deidre's staring at Tami when she says this, but Jason doesn't notice. He's trying to make eye contact with the bartender.

He glances back to Deidre. "Well, it's preseason. We are in town for spring training." He says it slowly, loudly, like he's talking to a kindergartener or someone very old. Or very drunk. "I'm with the Lions. From Los Angeles?"

"Fabulous!" she all but screeches. "You hear that, Tami? A baseball player!"

"What are you having?" Tami cuts in, which he welcomes by stepping back, letting her slip ahead of him. In the switch his hand brushes along her hip and she very nearly shudders. Jason Goodyear has the reputation of being as clean as a choirboy, quiet as a mouse. But what was that?

"Gin and tonic," he says. Then he adds, a bit bashfully, "Diet, if they have it."

Tami gets the bartender's attention. He knows what the women are up to, but also knows one round will turn into three or four, fat tips each step of the way. For that reason, they comp the women these first rounds as often as not.

"What'll it be?" he asks.

"Gin and diets, two. And . . . Dee?"

But she's turned around and is talking with the young right fielder, who looks nervous at the attention. Tami shrugs and smiles to Jason. He smiles back, and this time, she doesn't doubt it.

◇

When she tells him she was married to a pitcher in Texas, she can see his shoulders relax, his jaw loosen. She's one of them. Like flipping a switch, his vocabulary nosedives into baseball jargon. He talks about his batting practice routine, about watching tape obsessively through the winter. He's not bragging, but there's a swagger in his assuredness, and it makes the skin on her chest flush. He prattles off his OBP and RBIs, last year's numbers and goals for the next. The bar clears out—Deidre and the other outfielders are long gone—and Tami, so hungry her stomach feels like a woozy walnut in a sea of gin, suggests they eat. Remarkably, he agrees.

She's been to the dining room only a few times, always when someone else was buying. Waiters in tuxedos weave between the tables with steaming plates and gleaming knives. Their server seems snippy that Jason won't remove his hat, but he's also too polite to tell him to do so. They order steak for two, and when he says *two* Tami can feel her pulse throb in her neck. What does this man look like at rest? What does he look like happy? What does he look like turned on?

The Caesars come and Tami asks about college—at the bar he mentioned he'd had some. She didn't realize he'd been at the University of Iowa during the school's one championship season; they talk about Omaha and the College World Series. She'd been once with Danny—not on the team bus, but following it up Interstate 35 in their VW Rabbit, baby Jeremy hollering in the back for most of the ten-hour drive. They'd been eliminated in the first round of the tournament.

The waiter reaches for their empty plates. "Are you going to finish?" she asks. He looks down, brow knit in confusion. "College, I mean."

As soon as it comes out she realizes the mistake, how she sounds like some nagging relative. She can feel a wince, and when she tells herself to smile through it, the result is some sort of grimace. She reaches for her wine.

But then he says, "Maybe," without any hesitation, and she's released, all that fussiness and worry gone in a puff of smoke. Thank the wine and his quiet charisma for that. "I think I might start over."

"Oh?" He keeps doing this thing with his eyes—maybe it's more eyelashes, or eyebrows, she can't figure it out yet—but it's one of the most suggestive, sexy looks she's ever experienced. "My agent, Herb Allison—you've heard of him?"

She nods, of course she has.

"He's a big architecture buff, got me into it. I think I might do architectural preservation." The steak arrives, bloody and glistening and almost the size of a second baseman's glove.

"Really." Her heart is racing, her head spinning. She never thought she'd be so lucky, to find an athlete who cared about her other passion. "Architecture?"

He butchers their meat, pushing the smaller piece onto her plate before stabbing the rest onto his. "Herb, he's got one of those Test Case—sorry, Case Study—houses, and convinced me to buy another, just down the street. It's amazing to inhabit that kind of space. I mean, we all care about our homes, right? But when you're preserving something of architectural significance—"

"It's like it's not really yours," she says, thinking first of Taliesin but then of her own house, how it looked so spooky without its lights. She notices a tremor as she reaches for her wine and hopes he doesn't see it. "You're more of a steward."

"Exactly. It's a money pit, but it's worth it." It was. He's chewing like a midwestern boy, elbows on the table, and it makes her smile. "Anyway, I was thinking I could set up a preservation trust, for stadiums or something. Do you think I need a degree for that?"

"Maybe not." Tami never went to school for Frank Lloyd

Wright—she got her GED and took some community college classes, but nothing close to an architectural history course—and she knows as much about organic modernism as anyone working at the house. But then Jason is talking about LACMA's new pavilion and visiting Frank Gehry's studio and the Philharmonic's concert hall, about parabolic arcs and things that have nothing to do with Tami, with this moment. She needs him to come back to her, to Arizona. "You've been to Taliesin West, then? I mean, sure Gehry's great, but the *other* Frank. He's the original."

He shakes his head. "I keep meaning to, but every season I just get too busy, games and practice and strength training and then Lian—" He stops himself before he finishes her name. Tami didn't know it, but that must be her. Lianne? Liana? What happens to his face just then is like the outfield grass when a thick cloud passes overhead, blocking the sun. A brief darkness, his eye jumping from sapphire to navy. Then it's gone. He takes another bite, swallows. "By the time I'm done at the stadium, it's always closed for the day."

"And how long have you been with the team?" She gives him a playful glare, praying that his gloom won't return.

"I know. Too long to keep using that excuse."

"You sound very occupied. I mean, focused. On your training." Her foot slips out of her shoe and a toe finds his calf, that ball of muscle. He's filling their wineglasses and a splash jumps out of his cup, making a purplish stain on the white linen. "I like that."

◇

Over the rest of the meal he asks about her. She worries he's trying to separate himself back to some safe distance with generic getting-to-know-you questions, but as he persists, she senses it's not a buzzkill but something else, some midwestern earnestness that's been bred into his kind. If you like a woman, you ask her about her hometown, her mother's people. If her mother's people are wicked—and Charlene's family was—back up and try again; ask about her father. It's so different from Ronnie—the only time he asked about her family was to hold it against her. Typically she'd gloss over Danny, Terrance, and the boys, but if Jason's in the middle of a breakup, he should hear it. Life goes on. He nods thoughtfully when she talks about divorce; that sexy man she saw earlier pushed aside by a kindhearted one.

She reaches recent history, her time in Arizona. "I work up at Taliesin, actually." It's not deliberate, her decision to use the present tense, but it does sound better. "Gift shop, mostly, but I'll guide tours if they need me. Know all that stuff, just in case."

While they're waiting for the check, he says some nice stuff about how good a listener she is—which seems silly because she's the one who talked through most of their bottle of wine— and that he likes her dress. She finds his knee under the tablecloth and says thank you, that he's a good listener, too. That she's excited for him, for the possibility of starting fresh.

"What do you mean by that?" he bristles. Only once tonight has his wife, or ex-wife, come up—and then it was his doing, a darting near miss.

"I—I—I," Tami stutters, sure she has ruined everything. The cloud is back, his eyes a dark sea. "I just think the spring is great for new beginnings. A new season, a fresh leaf." She keeps stammering about the opportunities of the coming year, trying to hurry backward from whatever dangerous line she just about crossed.

Something works, and when she looks up at him again, she can see he's moved away from that angry knot. The waiter delivers the check. Tami makes a cursory reach for it, but Jason pulls the leather folder from the table. "Please, let me." She can't help noticing he pays with hundred-dollar bills, and as he does, a poker chip falls out onto the table. He doesn't ask for change, but the chip—$1,000—he jams back into his pocket.

◇

She's probably too drunk to get behind the wheel, but she offers and he agrees—he'd ridden to the restaurant with teammates. She's embarrassed to have such an important, such a famous, such a *handsome* man in her crappy old car, but then she remembers his dusty Jeep.

As he slides into the passenger seat, he grins at the duct tape on the Chevrolet's interior panels. "Your car has seen better days."

She smirks at him. "So have I. We can't all drive Cadillacs."

He harrumphs at that. "Those boats? Me and my lucky Jeep, two hundred thou and going strong." With the alcohol, he's loosened, reminding her of nothing so much as a giant puppy, big paws and a waggling tail. She loves it. He lets his body sink back against the seat. "Where are we going?"

"You'll see. Put on your seat belt."

"Yes, Mom."

This sets them both snickering, and Tami reaches over the gearshift to check his lap. Her fingers grip the seat belt holster, but also brush down his thigh, the solid slab of muscle. "Very good." They titter some more.

The road's practically empty this late. They rush past ritzy lodges with triple-height columns and giant, red-tiled haciendas with sprawling crabgrass lawns. He finds some classic rock station and starts singing along. He's awful, but it makes her feel the buzz and prick of want, which spreads from a thick spot in her throat, up, down, everywhere.

The song ends, and she turns the announcer down to a low hum. "I know there are a lot of women in this town trying to take advantage of athletes." He's watching the palm trees flick by in a fronded colonnade. The resorts on both sides are getting bigger and bigger, but each steps farther back from the edge of the road, so it looks like everything is the same, like they're not moving at all. "I'm not."

"What are you doing then?" He turns to look at her. His face isn't happy or determined; it's something else entirely, a look she doesn't recognize. Bewilderment? Dismissal? Is that sadness? She wants him to smile again, so she does, so wide she feels her teeth clench.

"I'm here to help." He snorts. That half smile again. Tami presses into the accelerator. "Laugh all you want. You'll see."

◇

Another ten minutes north, and the roadside development drops down to a smattering of homes. He surveys the new emptiness, the scrubby land that starts just past the shoulder. The cacti are tall here, taller than a man. "Are we still in Scottsdale?"

"Technically, North Scottsdale," she says. "It's not much farther."

They curve up to the compound entrance, the sandstone sign lit from below. Above, Frank Lloyd Wright's low-slung buildings are dark shapes against a craggy backdrop of mountains. Tami knows a service road, five hundred feet past the main entrance, with a gate they rarely lock.

They take the long way around the compound, rutted roads carved into the mountainside. The moon casts everything in strange greens and browns, purples in places you wouldn't expect. Once, this whole landscape was filled with tents and lean-tos, Frank's disciples camping in the desert, hoping to gain, by proximity, some expertise from the great master. Hundreds came during the Depression, paying for the opportunity to quarry stones and put them in place, the already-old man directing them with the tip of his cane. The steady flow continued for decades, long after Wright's passing, first his widow and then his apprentices directing studies. But as the rest of architecture came to believe in technology, to prefer homes not with canvas louvers but with windows that shut, the stream of students slowed to a trickle. Now, only a handful come each year. Tami's heard a few stalwarts still camp far up the hill, in those last places from which you can't see the power lines and the perpetual glow of the city. Those holdouts won't bother them tonight.

She parks the car next to a stand of acacias. Jason comes around and opens her door with a wobbly bow, and she thanks him. The electricity has returned, zapping between them, and she runs a finger across his abs. "Follow me."

The pavilion, the cluster of cabins, the theater and studio and Frank's residence are dark shapes blocking the sparkle of Scottsdale and Phoenix beyond. "On our left is Wright's studio," she starts, waving at the building with her best Vanna White. "Construction began in 1937. He designed the Guggenheim in there." Jason walks up to the casement windows and peers into the room lit by a lone desk lamp. He must still be drunk, but in his admiration he's turned a reverent that seems nearly sober. "Notice how that whole wall up there, the ceiling, is just treated canvas. Makes for great diffuse natural light when the morning sun hits it. Less great in the weather. Water . . . *resistant*." They start toward the next building, another angular shadow coming up like the crag of a mountain. *Idiosyncratic modern*, that's what the tour ladies call it.

Her finger points to a low rock along the path, a red square inscribed into its face. "Notice the red tile. That's his signature." Jason squats to see it better: a big *F*, two *L*'s, a *W* that melts into something diagonal. This tile is a replica, the difference between it and the original discernable only to connoisseurs, but she doesn't mention it.

"And over here we have the cabaret theater. Built later, in 1949, it has seating for fifty." She tries the door but it's locked. She never had the key to this one. "You'd have had to stoop through the entryway. That was a big principle for him, compression and release. Also, he was short." She winks, he smiles. Her heart is thumping in her chest.

The wavering of the reflecting pond sends out blue light from around the corner. Jason surges ahead, eager to see it. "And the main house," she says, anticipating the moment it will fill his field of vision. The Prow—that's what Wright called the grand entrance, its angular pool and regal stairs. She can see Jason's whole body lift at the sight. "The elevated first floor, just past that pool, was the Garden Room, where Wright received guests. His private library and bedroom were upstairs."

That's the last building; past it is a long, low wall separating the house from the terraced slope of hill. She steps toward the ledge, imagining the labor it took to quarry and cut these stones, to transport and arrange them just so. Jason follows, and they settle down atop the wall, their legs swinging over the edge. "When Frank Lloyd Wright built this compound, he planned the sightlines so that he couldn't see anything but the open valley. No lights, no power lines, no development save for the road coming up to the house. Originally, he didn't even want electricity up here."

"So much for that," Jason says and he hiccups, the tinge of alcohol coming back into his voice. He surveys the city blinking below them. Tami does, too. Somewhere, not too far from the base of the hill, is Ronnie's latest development, Paradise East. She tries to spot it, knowing the particular orange of construction lights is different from the white of streetlights, the yellow of cars, the blue of screens. Jason's hand, its callused fingers, finds the small of her back and she forgets all about Ronnie.

"Growth," she says. "Even the best architect couldn't stop that."

Jason is watching her; she can feel his eyes on her face. Is he going to kiss her? But instead he says, "Do you like it here?"

"Taliesin is my favorite place in the state," she says quickly. "On the planet, maybe."

"No, Scottsdale. Arizona, I mean. Restarting here."

Suddenly, she feels about an inch from bursting into tears, from telling him how hard it is to be poor in a place like this, the fancy houses and flashy cars, the rich bitches and mean men like Ronnie. But she tamps down the feeling, cursing herself for nearly letting it surface. That's not why they're here. This is about *him*, about her helping *him*. "I like the springs here. The weather, the blooming cactus. Spring training. This season gives me hope."

He's looking out at the twinkling horizon. "You got enough to share? I'm feeling pretty low."

"You?" She shakes her head. "No hope about it." She remembers the banner across the spring program—"the golden boys"—and can hardly believe that same man is now sitting next to her in the dark, so close she can feel his body shifting. "Whatever's going on, you're going to be fine."

"If you say so." The two are quiet for a minute, more.

"Do you want to talk about it?" Tami asks.

He shakes his head. "I just can't turn it off, you know? I always want to win."

"There's nothing wrong with being competitive. That's why you're where you are."

He shrugs. "Exactly. You ever hear of 'thrill-seeking behavior'?"

She hasn't, and she tries to imagine what that means. The thrill of stepping up to the plate? Of course he has that, and the batting average to prove it. Or does he mean something more explicit, some thrill more dangerous? It's not fast cars—he still drives that old Jeep. Is it pushing his body to its limits? He'd get caught if he was doping. Is it women? Is she just the latest lady in some string of calculable risks? "Is that why you're getting divorced?"

He nods. "Liana—my ex—she finally called me on it. I guess I figured no one would, because, well . . ."

"You're you."

"Yeah." His hand drifts from her back. Tami waits to feel his fingers again. She closes her eyes, anticipating the touch. Nothing. She opens them: he's cupping his shoulder in his palm, frowning like it's bothering him.

"You sore?" she asks.

He keeps rubbing. "Just a little stiff."

"Maybe you need to loosen it up." Danny always had to throw on his days off; she caught. She slides off the wall and picks up a stone the size of an apricot. "Try this."

He throws the rock impossibly far. They finally hear the soft thud of it smacking some cactus.

"Impressive." She feeds him another. This one he frowns at, winds up, and—crack. The streetlight on the switchback below them goes out with a spark.

"Whoops."

"Oh, it's okay. It'll give the biddies something to worry about tomorrow." She settles back onto the ledge. But the busted light sends her mind running. "Can you hit that one?" she asks, pointing a finger at the next lamp down the road.

He tosses a third, but it bounces off the top of the lamppost. He shakes his head, disappointed in himself. "I can make that." It would sound boastful, but she knows the man can throw a strike from the warning track to home plate. She feeds him another stone and this time the light goes dark with a crack. His whole posture changes, his chest rising like he's the tallest man on earth. And Tami, too: that shaky feeling she had when he asked her about Scottsdale is gone. Now there's a giddiness under her breastbone. Is this the thrill Jason was talking about?

"Can you hit that?" She points at the red glow of a camera mounted above the entrance to the gift shop. She's made a point of avoiding its scope on their tour.

It sounds like a gun going off, the way the camera snaps off its mooring.

"Wow, okay," she says. That's the only camera monitoring the store. Her heartbeat picks up, remembering the keys she still has, buried deep in her bag. "Hang on a sec. I have to—" But he's already launching another stone at a nearby overhead light. No matter Frank's plan, they added flood lighting in the 1980s. Had to—disability compliance, safety regulations or something. This willful destruction probably would've tickled the old guy. Back to the land, to nature's intention. To his.

Jason sidearms a stone and takes out a knee-height walkway light. "Not those," she says, shaking her head. "Those are originals. Or from the fifties, at least."

"Oh, okay." He nods like he understands, like he's not glassy-eyed and swaying. He's rooting for another rock when she touches his shoulder. "I'll be right back."

◇

She lets herself into the shop, wraps her hand in one of those geometric silk scarves all the docents wear around their necks, and starts pecking at the register. They haven't changed the code, and while it has only $200 in twenties and fives and tens, she finds the jewelry case key is still under the cash drawer. She clears out the bracelets, takes a handful of cufflinks and Wright-inspired watches and the silver letter openers. As she grabs a fistful of rings she hears another hit, but it sounds different from the quick snap of plastic and metal and glass, the extinguishing of filaments. It comes from somewhere behind her, toward Wright's studio and the parked car. This one is loud, a boom thick enough to echo up the hills. Then everything goes dark: the green numbers on the register, the balustrade lights, the remaining overhead floods. Even the lamp glowing in Wright's studio—the one the tour guides insist they keep on all night, like some sort of beacon—stutters off.

"Jason?" she calls into the dark. "Are you all right?" She hears nothing, sees nothing. Then she catches a movement in the window. She starts, but realizes it is only her own reflection, a dark shadow against the creeping glow of the city. She watches herself for a moment, until the horizon goes bright with red and blue.

# THIRD

Let me remind you of our timeline. We're a few games into the season, a few billion years into Arizona's geological history. At this point, like a determined left-hander learning to switch-hit, the ocean floor rose. At first, the batter's success is sporadic and slow, but then—the crotchety old hitting coach barking instructions, yelling at the batter about his feet, his grip, his eye, his goddamn eye—the player gets the hang of it, and the net of the batting cage's far boundary starts to push out in a steady pulse. *Contact, contact, contact*, says the crack of the bat, says the creak of rising land. *What the fuck did you do*, Herb Allison yells into the phone when Jason calls from the precinct at 2:00 a.m. *What the hell*, Woody Botter hollers when Jason walks into the clubhouse the next morning, looking as rough as a rosin bag after a rainstorm. *He did what?* Liana asks when a reporter, waiting at the edge of her property, shouts out a question about her husband's trespassing charge. *No comment*, she corrects herself, hustling into her car and off to school. That's their promise, hers and Jason's. That wasn't just Twitter gossip Deidre heard: the picture-perfect marriage to the elementary school teacher? A source, and not just a wined-up left fielder, confirmed they're split. She gets the house with the brand-new batting cage in the backyard. She gets every penny promised in the generous prenup, so long as she keeps saying: *No comment.*

Up, the seabed climbed, until the Arizona landscape looked more like East Africa, a loose and grassy savannah, dust-brown and baked. Up, the seabed climbed, until the last corals were gone, the fish scratched from the order. They were replaced by mastodons, by giant ground sloths, by bullpen-size beavers. And dinosaurs: a duck-billed hadrosaur darts between the bases as a long-necked sauropod ambles the concourse like a lazy peanut vendor. But no lions yet—the MGM lion, the team's inspiration, would need more time to cook. And no humans. A few million years would have to pass before the giant footsteps of the titanothere could be shrunk down to a man's size twelve, to say nothing of Jason Goodyear's forthcoming signature line. I'd tell Jason to think about *that* the next time he sinks a boot in the warning track after a downpour. Look at the tiny impression your cleat makes, Goody. Think of those ancient footsteps, and remember: you are a speck.

Not that he needs any more lectures right about now, especially not from a sportswriter whom he only ever addressed in press conferences as "the older fellow with the 'stache." How quick does a face like mine fade? Does a guy like him notice when a guy like me goes missing, when half the press corps is wiped out in eighteen months, replaced by tweet-happy rooks whose only experience is bumbling through the scores on college radio? Theirs make my early dispatches seem like Chekhov; the new form makes this story, the long route, feel that much more necessary.

But I digress. As the land rose, the Pacific plate pulled west and northwest, taking the taffy-soft plateau of Arizona's continental shelf with it. Stretching, stretching, stretching, until the crust was so thin that a mountain range was able to push up through it like an arc of pimples on a teenage rookie's oily skin. That thrust of rock was followed by a flow of basaltic lava down the slope as smooth as motor oil, lava that laid a new floor across the plateau.

I know what you're thinking: Why the history lesson, chief? What does a new mountain have to do with a major league club? Rocks for jocks? Think about this: If the earth's skin is so thin, imagine that of a man. If the planet's minute shifting can thrust a whole continent off kilter, imagine the skin of a person, even a strong one. Thin as a gum wrapper, as tissue.

That "no crying in baseball" line is nice but a load of bull: plenty of us walk around on the verge of tears. Goodyear, strong man that he is. On the verge before, after, and during that encounter with Tamara, as he stood by the sparking transformer, as he talked to the cops. Still on the edge when his agent chewed him out at the station that night, and the next morning, when his GM did, too. He's on the brink of it every damn morning this spring actually, every time he wakes up and finds himself alone.

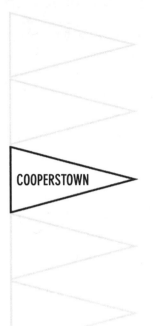

COOPERSTOWN

"So, back in September, I was watching a client on the Red Sox and I fell down a flight of stairs at Fenway Park. I blame the merlot. Very nice vintage." Herb Allison pauses. Dr. Timothy Jewell, proprietor of Diamond Physical Therapy, and Sara Jones, Dr. Jewell's assistant, take the cue to nod politely. It's clear Herb has told this story before; he knows where to put in the breaks, where to raise his eyebrows, where to smile. He makes a chopping motion with his hand, which stirs the small white dog sitting in his lap; the animal looks around with impassive eyes. "Snapped my left femur, clean in two. Had to have emergency surgery in Boston then two more at Mayo—the Scottsdale one, no way I'd go to Bumblefuck, Minnesota. You guys aren't from up there, are you?"

The two shake their heads no.

"Good. A few screws and a titanium rod later, this is what we've got." He pats his leg. "They told me to take eight weeks before starting 'vigorous physical therapy.'" Herb curls his fingers into scare quotes. "I hope you know what the fuck that means, because I sure don't." He smiles so wide his eyes scrunch up.

Sara takes notes as fast as she can.

"I meant to start *before* the holidays," Herb continues, "but Marlene said you couldn't see me until after the New Year. It's okay, things got busy for me and Kirby." He indicates the dog. "End-of-year paperwork, MLB winter meetings. Shit like that."

"Marlene?" It's the first time Sara has spoken since Herb rolled in to Diamond. Dr. Jewell glares at her.

"His wife," Dr. Jewell says sharply.

"Ex-wife," Herb corrects.

Dr. Jewell starts to stammer an apology, but Herb holds up a hand. "Don't worry about it. Trust the universe, et cetera. Anyway, Marlene found your practice and suggested it might be a good fit. Said you were very client-focused, very discreet."

"We are, Mr. Allison."

"So here I am."

"And we're very glad for that, Mr. Allison. Aren't we, Sara?"

"What?" The question interrupts her writing, and her pen skids off the notepad. "Yes, sir. Very—glad."

Dr. Jewell hardly leans in as he says, "Don't mind her, Mr. Allison. Sometimes Sara's head's in the clouds, but she's our longest-serving PTA." The doctor smiles, drops his voice. "And the prettiest, too."

"PTA? That got something to do with school?" Herb frowns.

"Physical therapy assistant." The doctor sits straight, speaks louder. "Sara's got real commitment. She's been working with us, what, seven years?" Sara smiles. It's common knowledge that Dr. Jewell hires the attractive applicants, rather than the brightest ones. That's why *she* got the job all those years ago.

It was not her grades at ASU, surely. Not her references, spotty
at best. And *not* her work ethic, which has landed her on probation with Dr. Jewell more times than she can count. It's not that
she doesn't like the job; she does. But things come up. Things
are always coming up.

"Eight."

"Ah." Herb looks her up and down, taking in her blond hair,
blue eyes, full lips. Her nice long neck. Also noticing her foundation, thick enough to cover up the circles under her eyes, the
eyeliner trying to make her look younger than she is. And even
through the boxy pastel scrubs it's clear she possesses a lithe,
athletic body. He nods. "Sounds like a winner."

◇

Herb Allison is assigned to Sara for his three-a-week appointments, and he quickly establishes himself as difficult. His leg
has healed enough that he can walk, shakily and with the aid of
a cane, but he tires easily and prefers to come and go from Diamond in an elaborate motorized wheelchair. It's a customized
contraption, expensive enough to suggest he isn't planning to
quit it anytime soon. (*It does stairs!* he proudly boasted after his
first appointment, when Sara and Dr. Jewell walked him out. He
jumped the curb to prove the point.)

Herb spends half of any given session yelling into his cell—
his curses can make even Sara's ears burn—and the rest of it
tapping away at the phone's screen, muttering to himself. Every so often his tone shifts to obsequiousness, "Hey, baby,"
and, "Hiya, champ." He's so engrossed that she often has to
ask twice, sometimes three times, for him to lift his leg or move
from one machine to the next. All the while, his yippy bichon
frise, Kirby Puckett, weaves between his owner's wheels and

amid the weight equipment like the animal *wants* to get its tail flattened.

His third week, as she is angling his mended leg, trying for ninety degrees at the knee, she hits a tough spot. Herb, in momentary anguish, drops his phone. It clatters to the floor. "Jesus, that hurts."

Sara can hear the tinny voice of someone on the other end: *Herb? Herb! You there? Can you hear me?*

She passes the phone back and starts the stretch again, more carefully. The leg is so narrow under the shiny fabric of his track suit—half the size of its right twin. "You said you just broke your leg?" While she'd expect muscle atrophy with an injury like this, his seems extreme.

Herb, already back on the phone, holds up his palm. "I'm here, Jason. What were you saying? Right. And I'm telling you, divorce is the best thing that could happen to your career at this point. Advertisers will love that you're back on the market— maybe we'll even do one of those shirts-off campaigns . . . I know, you won't ever show your ass. But your abs, that's another . . . Liana, she seems reasonable. Just make sure she signs that NDA, then give her whatever the fuck she wants . . . Cash flow issues? *You're* having cash flow issues?" He snorts. "Fuck you."

Dr. Jewell is across the room, gingerly extracting an augmentation patient from the seated fly machine. Sara catches him frowning her way and drops her gaze. First tenet of Diamond Physical Therapy: discretion. Dr. Jewell's built a very successful practice by offering a range of services to clients recovering from procedures they would rather not discuss. Vain wives, prideful husbands, public figures recuperating from private injuries: Diamond is a place where no one gawks at elaborate braces or bright incisions. Dr. Jewell wants his patients to be comfortable, to be put at ease by a firm touch and a pleasing countenance. *Not* to be given the third degree, especially not by the help. Sara just needs to know what has to get fixed—in Herb's case, strength and range of motion in that broken left leg. The muscle weakness, the atrophy, the slightly slurred speech and uncontrollable outbursts—those symptoms are none of her business.

"How are we doing over here?" Dr. Jewell says, striding toward them.

"Mr. Allison is doing very well," Sara says. "Good progress."

"Glad to hear it." The doctor watches the pair suspiciously.

Sara's eyes go wide at something happening over Dr. Jewell's shoulder. "No! Bad dog!" The doctor turns just in time to see the white scrap of a dog taking a leak against the recumbent bike.

"Ha! Ha ha!" Herb's nearly heaving, he's laughing so hard. He exhales into the phone. "Jason, let me call you back," he says and hangs up. The dog trots over, tongue lolling. "Kirby, you little shit."

Sara sets down her client's leg. "I'll get the Lysol."

◇

During his next session, his cell phone conversation is even more heated than usual. From what Sara can gather—and it would be hard *not* to hear the names and numbers, he's talking so loud—he is about to finalize an endorsement contract for somebody named Moyers. Something about vitamins, men of a certain age.

"Fuck me," he says as he ends a call and starts tapping on the screen. "Those geezer-pill pushers are playing hardball."

"Is he a baseball player, your client?" she asks him. They're working on range of motion again today, Herb's heel cupped in her palm.

Herb looks up from the tiny screen, brows knit together. "Is he a *what*?"

"You said something about 'left hander.' That's baseball, right?"

"Yes, that's baseball."

"Is that your favorite sport?"

"Dear, it doesn't matter if it's my favorite sport or if it feels like oral surgery—or like what you're doing to my foot right now, for that matter. An agent's commission is capped at three percent in football. Basketball, too. Why the fuck would I get involved for three percent?"

She stares at him blankly.

"Exactly." He looks down, pecks at the phone's screen for another minute, and slides the puck into his shirt pocket with a smug smile. "Now Hal and this Centrum deal, for instance. My cut's two hundred."

"Mm-hmm." Sara flexes his foot then points his toe. Flex and point.

"Thousand."

"Oh." His foot is suddenly very heavy in her hand. The number, *two hundred thousand*, is impossible to her, and she tries to click through what such an amount could mean: Her long-ago student loans, gone in a flash. Rent for twenty-five years. Her mom's surgery, paid five times over. A mound of coke, as big as Camelback Mountain, Davis sliding down it, his gleeful, little-boy grin. *No*, she shakes the image from her head. Not that.

◇

Sara is drinking coffee in her apartment when her phone rings, a Southern California number she doesn't recognize. She considers whether she should pick it up. It *could* be Davis, but she can't figure why he'd be calling from California. After three rings, she answers.

"This is Sara," she says.

"Sara, Herb Allison here."

Her mind clicks through faces and names until it lands on the right combination: Broken leg, little dog. The giant wheel-chair. *It does stairs!* Two hundred thousand. Handsome, in an old-guy way. "Good morning, Mr. Allison."

"Bad news, kid." No one's called her "kid" in years. She's nearly thirty, and if she's being honest with herself, her lifestyle since moving to Phoenix hasn't done her any favors. Most mornings, like today, she feels old. "Marlene is leaving me."

"Oh . . . I'm sorry." The line is quiet. "But I thought you were already, uh, divorced?"

"We were. I mean, we are. But she's going back to L.A. You understand?"

"Sure," Sara says, though she doesn't.

"I don't blame her. Spread her wings, all that bullshit. I gave her a doozy of a settlement, too. Fuck, I'm letting her *live* in my house, just to have someone keep an eye on the place. You couldn't imagine the burden of having a Richard Neutra. I've got wackos climbing in the windows just to get a look at the built-ins."

"I had no idea," Sara says. She doesn't know what a Richard Neutra is, but hopes he can't tell.

"He's an architect, dear."

"I knew that."

"You didn't. But don't worry about it. Listen, Sara, I didn't call to talk midcentury design. I need help."

The offer: Sara would live in the guest suite—a large bedroom, private bath, separate entrance if she felt so inclined. She would be responsible for transporting him to and from appointments in his vehicle—she's noticed the Escalade, with its customized lift, coming and going from Diamond. She'd shop for groceries and prepare meals, all expenses covered. She'd generally maintain the household. "I can do bills from the chair," he says. "And running the business is no problem, or all the usual problems. But someone's got to make sure me and Kirby get fed." As if on cue, the dog yips in the background. "And once spring baseball gets going, you'd come with me to games. I splurged on a suite at the new Lions complex."

Sara has never been to a baseball game, but she can guess what he wants to hear. "That sounds nice."

"It is. Don't worry, it's not like I need someone to wipe my ass," he continues. "I mean, not anymore, thank God. To be honest, that's probably the straw that fucked the camel, regarding Marlene and me." Sara tries to imagine this woman, but can't. "The leg's doing better, as you know. But it'd be nice to have an able body around the house."

"I don't know, Mr. Allison," Sara says, her mind racing. She wants to ask for the details again, they sound so impossible, so good. A nice place to stay, no expenses . . . "I've been with Dr. Jewell a long time and—"

"What's he paying you?"

"What?"

"How much? I'll double it. On top of room and board."

Truth be told, Dr. Jewell has underpaid her from the start, but she's been afraid to complain. In all the ups and downs, the bad boyfriends and good times, the weeks she'd call in "sick" for spur-of-the-moment trips to Mexico or Burning Man, and for all the hangovers that really did keep her in bed, Dr. Jewell forgave her. He'd dock her pay and cancel vacation hours, talk down to her plenty—and he never once has given her a raise—but he forgave her screwups.

She rounds up to save face. "Thirty-two thousand."

Herb Allison lets out a sharp *ha*. "Cheap bastard. I like it. I'll start you at sixty-five. Upward potential, if you know what I mean." Sara does not know what he means, but dollar signs are dancing in her vision.

"What about my place?" Sara asks, looking around the cramped and dingy kitchen. "I can't just leave."

"Sure you can. Quit the lease. I'll cover any fees for early termination, have my guys get you a storage unit." She's heard Herb use this tone on the phone, but to be on the other end of it: even with its gruffness, somehow he sounds like she's the one doing him a favor. "Movers to haul your stuff, too."

"Why me?"

"You? I like you, kid."

"But you hardly know me!"

"You seem like you can roll with the punches. And I've got a guy." He means a service that does background checks on all potential clients, to make sure he doesn't make any unwise investments. "No domestic assaults or child porn on my roster, no way. Try to stay away from the drunk drivers, too. At least the habitual ones." It was easy enough to run her name. "Sara Ashley Jones, daughter of Cathy and blank. Born February 27, 1981—big birthday coming up, my dear—raised in Flagstaff. First in your family to go to college—congrats for that—though your grades were nothing to write home about. Started out with Jewell eight years ago, which we knew, stable employment since. Your credit score is shit, but—"

"Some of it was for school," she interrupts.

She hears a rustle of papers. "Whopper loans, I see that. But I'm looking at thirty-five K of uninsured cosmetic medical treatments for one Cathy Jones."

Her face burns, remembering that.

"What was it, her tits?"

"She just said she *needed* a medical procedure."

Herb coughs. "What you *need* to do is become a better judge of character."

He couldn't possibly realize how deep that digs. "Are you all done with that Davis guy?"

"What?" Coffee sloshes around in her stomach. How could he know about Davis?

"That thug you were seeing. I've got controlled substances in the house—pain meds and the like—and I can't have any addicts around. Convicts, neither. I'm not saying no gentlemen callers. But not him."

"Right," Sara says, though she is more confused than ever. Her on-again, off-again boyfriend isn't exactly a Cub Scout, but in three years of dating he'd never said anything about jail time.

"It's a lovely house, as cookie cutters go," Herb says. "Just a few years old, right on the Troon North course. Did I mention there's a hot tub?"

Herb prattles on about the patio and the view. When he reaches the chef-quality kitchen, a new message pops up on Sara's computer. Davis, again. Still. Subject line: "I'm Sorry."

Sara's heart starts to gallop. Last week, three nights straight, he loitered outside her apartment. Stayed the whole night, rushed her in the morning, looking like a zombie and sputtering out apologies that sounded too rehearsed to be true. Was she supposed to forgive him for what happened on New Year's Eve, easy as that? She can't forget how *scared* she was. And how mad. Then he vanished again—another bender? Now these e-mails, more every day. She sort of expects him to be standing in the parking lot.

Sara interrupts Herb's description of the dishwasher. "When can I move in?"

"Atta girl! Room's ready now."

Sara deletes Davis's message without reading it. *Sorry,* her ass. "I'll be there tomorrow."

◇

"I wanted to go back to L.A. for the PT, but Marlene thought Arizona would do me good," Herb explains as he tours Sara through the house. He doesn't mention, so neither does Sara, the single-floor layout, the wide doorways and low counters, the grab bars in the bathrooms. "Desert air or some nonsense. Besides, my chair is too wide for Neutra's doorways. The man's a genius, but hardly ADA compliant."

They'd had the Realtor furnish the place, he continues. "It's no Case Study, but it'll have to do." Sara thinks it looks beautiful, like one of those posh Southwestern resorts she and Davis would sneak into for the pools. Suede couches and cowboy-blanket throws, formal-looking cacti in beautifully glazed pots.

There are no trinkets, no refrigerator magnets, no photos— almost no photos. Sara finds two on the side buffet in the dining room. One is of the dog standing outside a regal-looking red-brick building. The other is of a brown-haired girl, smiling up from the seat of a stadium.

She watches the photos all of dinner. She'd charred their chicken, and, after many apologies, called in Thai and opened a bottle of merlot. At the meal's close, far enough into the bottle to muster the courage, Sara asks about them.

"That's the Baseball Hall of Fame," Herb explains, pointing his fork toward the dog. "Cooperstown." Sara'd really wanted to know about the girl, but she nods like she's interested. "I wanted Kirby to pay his respects to his namesake."

"Namesake?"

"Kirby Puckett?" He blinks, unbelieving. "Do you live under a rock?"

Sara shrugs, her shoulders getting loose with alcohol. "I don't follow baseball."

"He died of a stroke, not two miles from here. Forty-five years old."

"Oh."

"Nineteen seventy-nine, *I* discovered him"—Herb pokes his chest for emphasis—"in the Chicago projects. High school All-American but poor as dirt, he wouldn't mind me saying. Living in a three-room apartment with his parents and nine siblings. Nine! *I* got him a college scholarship, and then, four years later, third pick in the draft. He was my first big contract—and the easiest ever. Stayed with Minnesota his entire fucking career." He makes a face. "'Just keep me in Minneapolis, Herb, just keep me in M-N'—who ever thought they'd hear *that* sentence?"

Sara smiles. "Not me." She's never been north of Las Vegas, and can't imagine life up there, all covered in snow, the millions of lakes and dairy cows.

"He didn't make me much, but of course I couldn't quit the Puck." He looks into his wineglass, lost in reminiscence. "You've really never heard of him?"

"I guess he sounds familiar."

"All-Star ten years in a row. Career batting average of three eighteen. Made the Hall of Fame his first year of eligibility. You know, every agent wants to get a guy into Cooperstown. But most guys have to wait a lot longer. Fuck, I wasn't even fifty." He shakes his head at the memory. "You know, he was the second-youngest ballplayer to pass away having already been enshrined in the Hall of Fame."

"Who was the youngest?" Sara says, her curiosity piqued.

"Lou Gehrig." Herb drains his wine, nods at her to pour him more. "You've heard of *him*, right?"

◇

The first weeks are strange, like one of those arranged marriages: two people who hardly know each other suddenly sharing everything. She makes him breakfast, lunch, and dinner, figuring out the kinds of foods he likes and trying her best at them. She figures out where Marlene stowed the paper towels and potholders, gets acquainted with the linen cabinets and the locations of the power outlets. The place still smells like fresh paint in some corners, and it's about a hundred times bigger and a thousand times nicer than her cruddy studio. She's not heard a peep from her landlord—Herb took care of that, gave her keys to the storage unit where he'd had moving guys stash her beat-up furniture—though the pleading e-mails from Davis keep coming in, every day.

And they go places together: Herb visits Diamond three times a week, the barber every Thursday, a psychologist on Tuesdays. She types the addresses of his appointments into the Escalade's GPS, then has to negotiate as the car's British-woman directions send her one way and Herb points her in another. Herb's gotten a new PTA at Dr. Jewell's, a pretty brunette whom Sara doesn't recognize. Dr. Jewell shot her a mean stare the first time she dropped off Herb, so now Sara waits in the car, AC blasting. Once, she went to a café at the far end of the strip mall, but after a few minutes with her latte she thought she saw Davis, so she gulped down her coffee and drove the Escalade in loops around Scottsdale's golf courses, feeling guilty about the gas.

Marlene calls daily; she and Herb seem still to be friends. Sara is always the one to answer: at first their conversations are tight and antagonistic, like Marlene is trying to poke holes in

Sara's story. As if plateauing as a PTA, the crap apartment, and her going-nowhere life were some ludicrous fiction, a façade for something more nefarious. Don't you think I'd give myself a better story if I were making it up? Sara wants to ask; she holds her tongue. But the conversation always slides to Herb: *His speech okay?* Sara says he's a mumbler unless he's yelling, but she's learned to lean in. *His fingers?* Not falling off, she'll say, though she's noticed he's no good at buttons. More than once he's appeared in the kitchen "ready to go" with just the button over his sternum secure.

Aside from buttoning buttons she doesn't dress him—but Sara does do his laundry, picking up piles of sweat-sour undershirts and crumpled khakis, faint wheelchair tracks ribbed across the fabric. One afternoon, throwing a load of whites into the high-efficiency washer, she has a revelation: Davis, her mother—everyone has been taking advantage of her. She did all of Davis's laundry, and she even had to scrounge the quarters. Her mother, too: convincing Sara to come back to Flagstaff for "holiday," just so she could spend her week of vacation time scrubbing the house, buying food, and running her mother's long-postponed errands. They'd spent $600 of Sara's money in one afternoon at Walmart. *Thank you so much, Sar-bear. I don't know what I'd do without you.* How long would Cathy keep playing the poor single-mom card? It had always worked on Sara, but as she sets the washer running she considers that maybe her dad, whoever he was, had a good reason for quitting Cathy Jones.

Back in the kitchen she starts on dinner, attempting to debone a whole raw chicken with a paring knife. Her cooking is still poor, but she is making improvements; Herb surreptitiously leaves cookbooks for her to find, the easiest recipes marked with pink Post-its. Herb had scolded: *Be a better judge of character.* Is he taking advantage of her, too? It doesn't feel that way, but it's strange, this cohabitation, her playing chauffeur and maid and confidante to this lonely man. She gives up on the slippery knife and starts ripping at the carcass with her hands.

Her phone chirps, and with a dry pinkie she deletes Davis's most recent message without reading past the first apologetic line.

◇

While Kirby Puckett may have been Herb's first client, now more of them are with the Los Angeles Lions than any other franchise, and he feels a certain affinity for the team. He wants to support his athletes—Goodyear, Cardozo, Moyers, and Goslin, a handful of relief pitchers Sara cannot keep straight—if not the front office (whom he considers stingy bastards), and the new stadium looks like a good place to watch a game, so that spring he plans to attend several Lions games a week.

Opening day, Sara parks in a handicap spot just next to the players' entrance. She and Herb eventually find the accessible gate and the elevator to the suites. Theirs is next door to the organist's, and through the wall she can hear someone hitting woodblocks.

As they settle in, Herb points out favorite clients, prattling off the details of their contracts and his plans for their next negotiation. Sara smiles; it's like he's speaking Greek. Then he's reabsorbed into his technology, tapping at his phone, typing things into a laptop mounted on the arm of his chair. But somehow he seems never to miss a play, hooting and hollering with each feat of athleticism.

Sara has heard of three strikes, but knows little else of the rules. Even in her confusion, she enjoys the players' movements, how they bend and dip to collect batted balls, the spinning motion of the pitcher, the prance of the base runners. Like ballet, she thinks. She'd wanted to be a ballerina, but her mom vetoed that, like she did most things. *How we gonna afford that, Sarbear?* So Sara learned what she could, gleaning toe positions from the girls whose mothers *would* pay for classes, recording *The Nutcracker* off the public television station at Christmastime. In a roundabout way, ballet's what pushed Sara into PT—she learned after one quarter of ASU dance classes she was no Martha Graham, but she wanted to do *something* with bodies, to help them achieve their potential.

Sara doesn't mention all the connections she's making between baseball and ballet. She doesn't say that the outfielders run with huge strides like grands jetés. That the infielders are all coiled energy, ready to leap into action with another saut de basque. And that pitching is just one barrel turn after another. Then there's the catcher: he pulls players in and pushes others back like he's choreographing the whole troupe.

But she does note aloud that the base runner just did a pirouette on his way into second.

"You do ballet?" Herb's ears perk up. "My Julie did that for years."

"Is that your daughter?" Sara says. "The little girl in the photo?"

Herb nods. "The same. She's twenty now."

"Where is she?" she asks.

"In college. Pitzer, last I heard, though academics aren't exactly her priority. You know about that."

Sara makes a face like she doesn't.

"Anyway, her mother—my first ex, Linda, will give her absolutely anything she wants."

"How long were you together?"

"Linda and I?" He pauses to think. "Three-year contract, then she asked for a trade."

◇

Early mornings, at twilight, when the temperature is bearable, she tries to encourage Herb to walk—well, roll—outside with her, around the golf course or over at the nature preserve. But Herb always waves her off, glued to some screen. *Too busy*, he says. And he's working all the time, pecking at his phone or typing on his laptop, barking into a headset. At home he has a complicated setup of monitors and speakerphones; several TVs stream different games and sports talk shows.

He might be too busy to exercise, but he never misses a meal and makes a point of having a nice dinner. Herb likes a certain kind of restaurant—the kind Sara could never afford—and they dine out several times a week. Up and down Scottsdale Boulevard, everyone knows Herb, or knows *of* him: the maître d' who is ready to clear a path through the dining room to accommodate his chair, the bartender who pours him a Belvedere vodka martini upon first sight, the waiter who hurries to their table to talk about the specials. Sara is aware of people watching them as they settle into their secluded booth. Part of that is wonder at Herb's elaborate chair, but is it also wonder at her? How pretty she looks, her little black dress, her shimmering eyes and red lips. Is she the new girlfriend? No one will say it, but she knows they're thinking of sex, her naked body and Herb's. How in the world that might happen, this feeble old man and her dancer's frame.

People can think what they want. She's helping him. She's young now, next to Herb, rather than the old one in the room, as she was at those parties with Davis. It made her crazy how no one cared that Davis was twenty-eight going on fifty-four, with his crow's feet and premature gray, but *she* was the old maid. Dr. Jewell, too—if it were up to him, she'd have frozen time at twenty-four. She's still mad at her mother for the surgery, but in the last year she's started to understand why she did it, why she felt she had to. If Sara feels this way, so worn out at twenty-nine, what will forty-five be like? Or Herb's fifty-two? She watches as he slurps at his martini, hunched and looking even older than that. His eyes squint with pleasure.

◇

On Sara's thirtieth birthday, Herb has a huge bouquet of flowers delivered. At the stadium, between innings, there's a birthday announcement on the scoreboard, the organist next door playing "Happy Birthday."

When they get home Herb hands her a hundred-dollar bill and tells her to buy steaks—he'll show her how to grill them. Sara cruises down Hayden faster than she should, pushing the car up to fifty on the long stretches between lights. As soon as she passes a golf course on her left, another country club begins on her right. A sign for another old folks' home, "supported living" they call it, is on the left, the barracks-style housing only slightly softened by its red-tiled roof and faux-adobe walls. If Herb were in the car right now, he'd shudder and make the international sign for choking, his tongue flapping out the side of his mouth. He does it every time they pass an old folks' home. *Oh, stop it*, Sara always tells him. *You're not even sixty.* He shakes his head. *You know what to do*, he says, *if it comes to that*.

She returns with two sustainably raised porterhouse steaks, organic asparagus, and a loaf of ciabatta. Eighteen bucks change in her pocket. Herb never asks for the leftover cash, but even so, she clings to the bills like she's holding on to a secret. Her mother taught her that—*It's yours until it isn't*. Cathy's ferocity, the scheming and deception Sara grew up with, hardly seems necessary now, but Sara can't seem to shake it, her mother's hand. She touches the bulge of bills in her pocket.

Her mother doesn't call—Cathy's been forgetting birthdays for a decade—but Davis does, and Sara lets it ring. Last year, her twenty-ninth celebration started with a bottle of wine and romantic candlelight, them going to eat at a restaurant that neither could afford. She woke up the next morning with a nosebleed, a black eye, and $400 missing from her bank account. She had to call in sick for a week, lying to Dr. Jewell that she had the stomach flu. She didn't want to see Davis but didn't have much of a choice; he brought her food and apologized nonstop until he'd convinced her of the choreography of what had happened, describing some unlikely, expensive accident.

That was the nail in the coffin, she'd told herself at the time. But somehow he'd hung in there, begging his way back into her good graces. It's not like he was a total drag: He was handsome, funny, could talk to anyone. On their good days together she was the queen of the world, and he gave her the sort of attention that made her hum with contentment. And there was the sex, which was truly remarkable. What couple didn't have some problems?

Then, on New Year's Eve, he did it again. Promised a big night out, persuaded her up to the ATM, and coaxed her to withdraw the last five hundred in her account. Which he turned right around and spent on coke. She hadn't wanted any, just champagne. Davis, however, went on a rip, leaving her stranded in some far corner of Phoenix, all her cash gone, with just one good-for-nothing credit card tucked into her bra. Eventually she bummed a ride home, broke into her own apartment (her keys were in his car), and slept for two days, getting up every three hours to call Davis. No answer, no answer, until his phone died outright. Then it started going straight to voice mail, a chipper version of her boyfriend promising to call her back soon. At a certain point she stopped leaving messages. On the third morning she cleaned herself up as best she could, washed her hair, and covered the dark circles under her eyes with makeup. She found a spare set of car keys in a kitchen drawer and headed off to work. It was that first day back at Diamond Physical Therapy that she'd met Herb.

$\diamond$

"Sara, wake up." Herb is a silhouette in her bedroom doorway, his chair's shape making him look massive.

"Huh? What time is it?" Dinner had gone long, into a second bottle of wine. Herb was in a good mood, chatty about endorsements. Apparently, he was a few days away from sealing a deal with Nike. "*The Goodyear*," he'd said, hands in the air like he was envisioning the marquee. He said it was the first time they'd named a shoe after a ballplayer since Griffey—Sara nodded like she knew what that meant. She didn't mind that she didn't—she just liked having the light of Herb's attention cast on her, his mood so unabashedly cheery. They'd even had a small cake—how he'd snuck that in without her knowing was a mystery. Her wish, as she blew out the candle, was that they could stay like this forever, chatty and happy and each other's everything. She didn't need the fancy dinners, the little black dresses: just this. That he wouldn't go back to Los Angeles, not for the regular season, not ever. Earlier she'd overheard him talking to Marlene about accessible rentals in Culver City, and it nearly made her cry.

"Two thirty-seven." He'd been barking at Letterman when she said goodnight. "We have to go down to the precinct."

"The precinct?" She thinks of Davis, of her own stupid behavior, the many times they could've gotten caught. They should've. Davis carried drugs on him more often than not, made a game of skipping out on bills at fancy restaurants. Had something to do with dealing, but she never knew exactly what. Never asked.

"You have a hearing problem?" Herb snaps.

She thinks of the three big glasses of wine she had with dinner, wonders if her head is still buzzing. She swings her legs off the side of the bed. Only a little; she's fine to drive. "What's going on?"

"Just meet me at the car." He reverses his chair out of the doorway.

The city is quiet as well, the roads all but empty. Theirs is the only car at the intersection of Hayden and Shea, each street seven lanes across and typically jam-packed. Sara waits for the light to turn green. "Can you tell me what's going on?"

"No."

"But—"

"Sara, now is not the time." The light changes. "Please, just go."

The police station is a comparative commotion, a squad car pulling out, its lights on but sirens off, a half dozen more patrol cars parked in the lot. Sara pulls into a handicap spot. She's always been so scared of this place. "Can I come in?" She means to help him, but realizes that's not how it sounds.

"Looking for your boyfriend?" Herb shoves his phone into his breast pocket.

"No, I—" The chance to see the inside, to walk in and then walk right back out sounds strangely alluring, but Herb's scowl suggests she drop it. "Never mind."

She helps Herb disembark, and she's still standing next to the vehicle, folding up his ramp, as he rolls over the curb and up to the front door of the station. He hits the automatic open button. Nothing happens. He hits it again, with a mumbled curse loud enough for her to hear. Then, "Sara! A little help here?"

She closes the door, walks toward him. When she holds open the door she feels the blast of air-conditioning. Herb says, "I'll be out in five."

Sara returns to the car, fiddles with the radio. Herb only listens to sports talk; now she settles on a stoned-sounding DJ talking about the transformational power of love and the potential of kindness between tracks from Mariah Carey and Cher. Ten minutes later a tall, hunched figure with a red ball cap low over his face steps out and holds the door. Herb appears, rolling at full speed, and sails off the curb, so that Sara's barely out of the car by the time he's alongside it. "Get over here!" he barks at the red-capped figure. "I told you to be quick!"

Sara feels a presence beside her; the figure with the ball cap is now at her arm. He is visibly drunk, swaying slightly, the smell of gin radiating off him. He looks vaguely familiar, but—

"Don't get too excited, Sara," Herb says, rolling onto the lift. "At the moment he's too drunk to be charming. Or to remember anything you say to him." The man gives her a half-cocked grin, a bit woozy, a bit apologetic. Very handsome. "Jason, you get in the back."

Once they're out of the lot, she finds the man in the rearview mirror. He's squinting like he's watching something very far away. "Where to?" she says.

"The stadium," the man says. His voice is wavering, but clipped like he's trying to cover it up.

"Fuck you, Goody. What, you're gonna hit some balls at this hour?"

"No, I'm staying at—"

"Sara, take him home. Jason, we'll put you in Marlene's room, and deal with this bullshit in the morning."

◇

"Sara, get up." Herb is in the doorway again. This time, at least, light streams through the window, suggesting a more reasonable hour. "You're always hassling me to go for a hike? Well, let's go." He's already down the hall, and she hears him bellow, "Jason, you fuck, up and at 'em! Hike o'clock!"

Sara hurries into her exercise gear. In the kitchen Herb is eating a banana. He passes her one, and she pours them both coffee. The clock says seven—they've all gotten four hours of sleep. Jason steps into the kitchen next, gray-faced and staggering. He's in a pair of Herb's too-short sweats, a faded Lions T-shirt that is tight at the shoulders. Even so, in the bright of morning Sara recognizes him. Not from the field, but from his advertising campaigns, billboards and bus stops around Phoenix metro. And she's seen that handsome face on the front page of the grocery tabloids. For some reason she'd assumed he played football.

"Did you shower?" Herb sniffs, makes a face. Jason still smells like booze, now also the tang of sweat. "Never mind, you'll sweat out the rest." Kirby does a figure eight between the athlete's legs before hopping into Herb's lap. "At least someone's happy this morning," Herb says, patting the dog on the head.

Their bad moods aside, the morning is glorious, the sky impossibly blue, the air crisp. Sara drives them to the nature preserve, and at the trailhead they stop at a large, laminated map. "How about this one?" Sara points out a route. The legend says it's two miles up and back. "I can't tell if it's paved, though."

"No bother," Herb says, patting the arm of his wheelchair. "This puppy can do anything. Jason?" Jason's staring at the lines like they're dancing. Herb puts a hand on his arm. "This is for your own good."

Within five minutes, the trail's settled into a steady climb, not steep but far from flat. Kirby dashes ahead, yipping happily. Then comes Sara, then a trudging Jason. He's forgotten his ball cap, doesn't have sunglasses, and without either, he squints like he's staring down a spotlight. Herb downshifts to bounce over the rocks, weaving between the jutting arms of cacti, one eye glancing down to his phone. "You get a signal up here?" Herb asks. Bright pink flowers explode from the tips of cacti.

Sara shrugs. "Phone's in the car."

"Jason, you?" Herb holds the cell above his head.

"I don't know where my phone is. I haven't seen it since—"

"Where did you have dinner last night?" Sara is trying to be helpful. "Maybe you forgot it there."

"Or maybe it's in that hussy's car." Herb rolls over a stone and it kicks up, pinging a cactus with a *thwunk*. "Do I need to worry about this lady, this Tamara? You met her at Don & Charlie's?"

"Yes, I mean no."

"No, you didn't meet her there, or no, I don't need to worry about her?"

"You don't need to worry about her. Just a nice lady, a bit down on her luck."

"Nothing a little larceny and property damage can't solve."

Sara looks over her shoulder. She can't tell if the look on Jason's face is in response to Herb's barb, or because Herb, gaunt and exhausted, his wheelchair like a fortress around him, looks so unwell. He's even paler, skinnier, and more ragged in the bright morning light. "It's historic register, for fuck's sake. You could've burned it down, you know that?"

Jason kicks a stone off the path.

"The other Taliesin burned to the ground. Seven people, dead!"

"I said I was sorry. It's not like I killed anyone."

"Just your shoe contract. What will Nike do if they hear about this?"

A jogger approaches. From the way his face lights up, it's clear he recognizes Jason. He slows, raises his phone. "No pictures!" Herb barks, and the runner scampers away. Herb looks at Jason again. "So do I? Have to worry about you?"

"I don't know. Things aren't good."

Up ahead, the dog starts a panicked barking. "Oh my god!" Sara yells. A rattlesnake is coiled in the center of the trail, between her and Kirby Puckett. "Kirby's trapped!" The trembling dog skitters back and forth, the snake watching his every move, its hiss low and sinister. "It won't let him pass."

Behind her another noise, a low whirring, becomes louder, closer. "Sara, move!" Jason shouts.

She can feel the machine swoosh by as she dives off the path. Herb is full-bore accelerating up the trail, a growl coming through his clenched teeth. The snake's head whips from Kirby to Herb and the quickly approaching machine, its thrumming engine and massive wheels.

The tires flatten the snake, one smashing its head, one bisecting its body. The back wheels do the same. Kirby jumps into Herb's lap, panting with relief.

"We done here?"

Jason may show no fear on the field, but right now it looks like he might be sick. He nods, then reaches to help Sara up. She's landed on a cactus, the spikes of which have printed a red constellation up her arm. Jason plucks the pink flower from its crown and hands it to her. "A small consolation."

"Don't even think about it, Jason." Herb, Kirby still in his lap, has pivoted the chair and is rumbling back toward them. "Sara's mine."

◇

When they hit asphalt again, Herb's phone chirps and chirps again, then makes another buzzing noise Sara doesn't recognize. "Oh, fuck." Herb scrolls down the screen. "Jason! I thought you said there wasn't any press!"

"There wasn't." Jason and Sara are following a few feet behind Herb, not arm and arm but with their shoulders close, Sara's cactus flower tucked behind her ear. Sweat makes a dark V on his chest and dark circles under his arms, and his face is pinking without his hat. Her cactus arm isn't quite bleeding anymore, but the thorns' punctures make tiny bubbles of blood that Jason periodically swipes with the hem of his shirt.

"'Golden handcuffs for the Gold Glove'?" Herb shouts, loud enough to make them wince. "'Goodyear has a bad night'? What the fuck!"

His phone rings. Herb rolls his eyes and accepts the call. "Woody, hello! Long time no—Jason? Yes, he's with me. No, I don't have any idea why the fuck he did such a bozo thing. No felony charges, just a misdemeanor—that's good, right?"

As Jason wipes the blood from her arm again, she sees a flash of the tattoo on his chest: it looks like a playing card, a jack, on his left pec. "Thanks," she mouths.

Herb's eyes are locked on Jason, and he talks slowly, trying to tamp down the anger in his voice. "Yes, Woody, I understand. I'll get him to the stadium pronto. And I guarantee, on Kirby Puckett's grave, this is the beginning and the end of the funny business with Jason Goodyear."

But what Sara sees on Jason's haggard face just then suggests that that's anything but true. She might not be a good judge of character, but after all she's been through, she's very good at spotting a man in trouble, and Jason Goodyear, blood-streaked and sunburned, is still in the middle of some serious shit. She hands him back the cactus flower and, without another word, he crushes it in his fist.

# FOURTH

As the tectonic plate's weak spot pulled west, another line of mountains cracked through the seam, then again, and again, until Arizona was neatly striated: mountain, valley, mountain, valley. Temporally, it was not unlike the Lions' own draft system—big player, journeyman, big player, journeyman, the positions cycling through apogee and ho-hum every few years. But if you look across the land, consider the topography at the start of 2011, the Lions outfield is synced up into a moment of peak, peak, peak; Goodyear plus Trey Townsend (several years apart in age, but both 2010 Gold Gloves), plus Corey Matthews, a high draft from UNC. Matthews reported to Single-A Carolina in August, spent the fall in Arizona, and played winter ball in the DR. His stats were good in Chapel Hill, but reports from coaches—all that different letterhead, the Carolina Clappers and the Arizona Arroyos and the Gigantes del Cibao stacked in a pile on Botter's desk—are that he's been making unbelievable progress, the kind of development that poises him to do the improbable: jump to the majors in his first full season. Which would mean that across the Lions outfield: mountain, mountain, mountain.

Back in the day, some of those Arizona slopes were two miles tall. Taller than that even, to start, but like an octogenarian back in uniform for the old-timers' game, we all lose a few inches. Hell, I'm two inches and eight pounds shy of my peak, which I hit during my junior year of college, when I was just a tick younger than Corey. The school was in need of a catcher (the recruit had a broken arm) and I, being Little League friends with the team's ace, was called on to catch. We were D-II and no one expected much, though we won more games than we lost when I was behind the plate. After the season I went back to my English major and to slowly shrinking, but that time on the field, a couple of months of orchestrating the team from behind the plate, I think it always gave me a leg up with the athletes. Looked like one of them, at least until I started looking like one of their coaches. Aging's a bitch.

But I was talking about mountains. Take a look at the McDowell Mountains, bordering Scottsdale to the east—that's a fine example. They started as nearly perfect basaltic cones. But wind picked up the valley floor and blew dirt in the mountains' faces; the softest stone slipped away with the insult. Not everything has the steely nerve of Stephen Smith, the fortitude to remain flawless under attack. Stephen can stay strong, but mountains, lesser men, they crack and crumble. Today, the McDowells are all jagged, and the tallest of them: four thousand feet.

There was another element at play in the mountains' demise: water. So much water. Hard to believe it on a day as blue-skied as this one, the stiff-armed saguaros the only green beyond the stretch of Salt River Fields' irrigation, I know. But it did rain, for days and weeks and years. And that falling water traveled in flashes down the new mountainsides, pushing for an extra base with all the momentum it could muster. With each rain, the water was widening the base path, picking up stones and carrying them down, carving until there was a clear route, one that cut deeper and quicker than any other. Water flowed into a divot that became a crevice, a crevice that became a canyon, a canyon that became the bed of the new Salt River. And the Salt River became a path to follow, all the way to the now-far ocean.

By dust and by deluge, diminishment. It is inevitable, in mountains and in men. But over the following week, as news of his run-in at Taliesin spreads, Jason's team sweeps into action, holding up so many umbrellas over his head. A whole bevy of folks, attempting to keep him dry. Damage control, they call it, trying to hold up the mountainside. Jason has never been one to seek the diva treatment, doesn't like an entourage or attention, the kind of thing most people expect out of celebrity athletes. He's a good leader in the clubhouse, stoic but kind, highly motivational or slightly goofy as the situation requires, but he hardly socializes off the field—which makes this spring's babysitting, the rabid-with-concern attention, that much more frustrating. He holds his own umbrella. No, better yet, he wears a raincoat.

In the postgame press conferences, manager Dorsey Paine deflects journalists' questions about his trespassing charge, *No comment, No comment, Give it a rest already.* Then Dorsey goes back to the clubhouse and waits for Jason to wash up: the two of them are going out to dinner, whether Jason likes it or not—they're eating together every night this week, *Boss's orders,* Dorsey apologizes—the boss being a very ticked-off Woody Botter, the GM. (Trey Townsend, his outfield neighbor, is the only guy on the team who seems to enjoy time with the bosses, and no one quite trusts him for that. Everyone else thinks it's bad luck or brown-nosing to get to know the owners, but Trey's relationship with Stephen Smith is its own strange and special thing.)

Meanwhile, another umbrella or three are being spun by Herb Allison, who tries to mend fences with Nike (unlikely) and Taliesin (they gratefully accept a $100,000 pledge). He calls his star every morning, sending Sara to the stadium with bran muffins and coffee for a 7:00 a.m. rendezvous. Sometimes Jason's waiting for her at the players' entrance, like they agreed, and sometimes he's not—when he was fifteen minutes late on Wednesday she went exploring, trying one walkway and then the next until she spotted him coming out of a supply shed with a bashful look. She promised him then she'd say nothing to Herb, but didn't feel as good about her promise on Friday when she spotted him, late again, at 7:20, crossing the footbridge from the casino to the stadium complex. *Your coffee's getting cold*, she said when she passed him the cup, which they both knew meant *Fuck you*.

At least Jason has umbrellas, people trying to preserve his image and performance, attempting to keep him dry and protect that perfect, conical peak. When no one's protecting you, or when they're protecting the mountain next door: you'll get soaked, and worse. With enough water, enough wind, enough relentless force, the earth of your slopes will start to slide away.

# WEDGE SHOT

The waiter weaves across the shady patio and deposits the men's margaritas, double pours of the elder's favorite reserve gold blend, onto the table, then stands at prim attention. The older man inspects: a tan, almost milky tint. He licks the salt along the rim and tilts the drink toward his lips.

Stephen Smith closes his eyes: yes. It's sour, then a line of sweetness, then the round, toothsome taste of the aged agave fills his mouth with swelling, subtle heat. He flashes a smile of straight bright teeth at the waiter and watches the man's retreat between the planters of aloe.

Stephen and Trey Townsend, the Los Angeles Lions center fielder, have caught each other up on their holidays and starts to the year. Trey spends the off-season in Grosse Pointe, and is hardly in touch when he winters in Michigan, so this happy hour feels like more than an afternoon chat—it's a reunion after several months apart. It's strange to Stephen to have a friend so present for half the year, then nothing, a light blinked off. Stephen takes another sip.

"So how's the new outfielder?" They've already chatted about his impressions of the new stadium, his off-season training. Trey looks fit; he always takes care of his physique.

Trey takes a sip, licks his lips. "Which one?"

"Come on, Trey." Now Stephen looks squarely at his companion. "You know, the right fielder. Our second pick, behind that kid first baseman, oh jeez, gimme a sec . . . Goslin." The partial owner of the Los Angeles Lions is not good with names, not even those names for which he has paid millions. Numbers, he's good at those, a walking calculator. Faces, absolutely—he could nail any precinct lineup with one eye closed, or, more important to his profession, the fabric of any blazer by one glance at the lapel. But names are hard. His daughter's seventh-grade teacher, that old Triple-A batting coach who simply refuses to retire, the waiter who always serves him at this, his favorite restaurant in Scottsdale. All blanks.

Trey shrugs, his shoulders announcing themselves under his collar. Navy blue, meant to minimize his bulk and complement his skin. Stephen notices the familiar sheep logo embroidered over the breast, but doesn't remind his friend that he'd taught Trey that, years ago: *Wear dark colors, conservative brands, to make yourself seem less imposing in mixed, or otherwise sensitive, company.* These two black men, drinking expensive tequila together an hour before the Arizona sunset, are not a mixed crowd—something Stephen very much appreciates after walking into so many all-white boardrooms, after hosting so many press conferences wherein the sea of reporters was mostly all white. Nor, Stephen thinks, is he a "sensitive" audience for Trey. They've moved far beyond the owner-player, boss-employee relationship; they are friends. Is it just that Trey has internalized the lesson, as he has so many of Stephen's offerings and advice? That now, this presentation—and following Stephen's direction—are what come naturally?

"Matthews. Corey Matthews," Trey says at last. He takes his drink without salt—Trey claims the sodium bloats him up, which in turn may slow him down. And Stephen does not want anything to slow down his center fielder. *I want my boys at their best!* is his line on the occasional clubhouse visit, always delivered with forced jocularity. Though *boys*—with Trey he should say *men*. Man. Trey's younger than Stephen by enough to make the owner feel old, but the outfielder's been with the organization for a dozen years, which puts him solidly on Stephen's side of thirty. "You've seen about as much as me."

"Oh, I doubt that." Stephen presses the rim's last salt crystals into the roof of his mouth, holding them there until they are gone. He licks his lips and smiles. His wife, Mona, tells him he looks like a Cheshire cat when he smiles. Usually, she says this with suspicion, like it's a bad thing to act self-assured. "The locker room?" Stephen's eyebrows raise suggestively.

He thinks he sees Trey blush, but his complexion reveals almost as little as his expression, which remains a stern sort of poker. He's been stiff all afternoon, or even stiffer than normal. Not unhappy to see Stephen but something . . . "I suppose," he starts, staring at his drink as if he could see the young man there. "Good physique, if a bit slight," he continues, deliberate in his words. "Though he says he did plenty of strength training during the fall league. Why?"

"Just curious." Stephen waves his hand like he's flicking something away. "I watched a few clips, but still haven't seen him in the flesh." Emphasis on "flesh." Stephen has read the scouting reports, has reviewed game highlights from Cibao and the first week of Cactus League play, but he's had no luck in seeing

the prospect in person. The week had been a bear: a board of
trustees meeting and a financial report review in Santa Monica, a ribbon cutting for a store in San Diego. Then Mona
needed him to go to a cocktail reception at LACMA *and*
on a double date to some flashy new Thai place downtown. And
his daughter, Alexis, begged him to attend her basketball
game Wednesday night, which Stephen did even as he hated it:
ten gawky girls, klutzy and maddeningly slow, playing like
the hardwood was coated with molasses. He loves his daughter, cute but awkward in the seventh grade, yet after five
minutes—no, after sixty seconds—on the court he can tell
she will never be an athlete, not a real one, and it pains him
to watch her try. Just because she is tall like him, lithe like
him, darker than the other girls on the prep-school team—her
skin tone is almost exactly halfway between his and Mona's—
does not mean she's got, or will ever have, game. All this
busyness in Southern California meant he'd missed the whole
first week of spring training, the stadium inauguration, the
debut of their new acquisitions.

He'd taken the noon shuttle from L.A. yesterday, dropped
his bags at their North Scottsdale home, and was over at the
stadium in time for an evening matchup against the Athletics—
but some sloppy old-timer was in right. Today the Lions were
split squad—forty guys at home, forty driving over to the
western Phoenix suburbs to play the Padres—and Stephen had
picked wrong; he watched some minor leaguer bungle his way
through the game. He could've called Paine to ask the field
manager who was going where, but he didn't want to sound
*too* eager after any given player. No help in the team's owner
picking favorites before they've done their culling. His coaches
already have their work cut out for them: there are eighty guys

suiting up every morning in the Lions' black and gold. The starters have their names in gold thread across their backs, while others just sport numbers—reminders that half of them will be sent to the minors, another dozen'll be let loose entirely, not even worth a custom jersey. By the end of March, there will be twenty-five men left. Stephen wants his coaches to coach, to improve the best athletes and to release the men who have to be let go. It's something he learned in business school: empower your employees and they will rise to the occasion.

Trey swirls his drink, cracks his neck, and pops each knuckle, left to right. He skips the thumbs today, though Stephen has seen him crack those, too—the sick crunch of it loud enough to make him grimace. Trey's body is deteriorating; both men know it but are unwilling to say as much. They can wait to have that conversation; there are three more years on his contract.

But those hands: in them are three Gold Gloves, including one last season, and he did it so elegantly as to make it look effortless. If he weren't on a team—in an outfield—with Jason Goodyear, Trey'd be their star. Stephen is proud of this, the almost.

Trey must know that Stephen is watching him as he plays with his napkin, but he doesn't acknowledge it. This, too, has always been part of their relationship: Stephen's attention, Trey's demurral. The push and resistance, pull and restraint, the one heaving the two until—once and only once—Stephen's efforts broke the jam and they were swaying together. That one time the two men coupled, after a big walk-off win, Mona and Alexis in Hawaii, is another thing that Trey never acknowledges, even as the men continue their friendship, these postgame happy hours and rounds of spring golf. Not a word.

After another moment of quiet, Stephen asks, "Is he as fast

as they say?" Last season at UNC Corey'd stolen something like fifty-seven bases in sixty-two games.

Trey wipes his mouth with the back of his hand. It's a strangely casual gesture coming from a man so measured, so precise. Maybe that is something of the winter Trey, the man Stephen knows so little about. "He's fast," he says. "Stole two last week. In the field—" Trey pauses, presses his lips together in that way he does when he's trying to be tactful. Sweet Trey, Stephen thinks. Most players these days are raunchy or disrespectful or mean-spirited, or all three. But not Trey. He so appreciates this man's efforts.

"In the field he . . ." Stephen prompts, leaning forward.

"I guess you could say he dances a bit, under the ball. *Reaches* more than he needs to." Trey lifts his hand over his head and does some kind of twist with his wrist. A delicate gesture, despite his arm being thick with muscle. That juxtaposition moves something in Stephen's core, a sensation not unlike the small and sudden drop of an elevator at the start of its descent. "Ta-da, you know?"

Stephen smiles. This man, this soft-spoken man he has known for a decade, more, has never said anything harsher than that he would prefer not to eat raw fish. (The first time they went for sushi together, Trey took one look at their two-person nigiri dinner and ordered himself the chicken teriyaki.) The outfielder looks uncomfortable now, fiddling with his glass, the tequila hardly touched. Because he said something mean? Or is it something about Stephen, something he's said? Stephen takes another sip of his drink; his is already half gone.

Trey clears his throat. "Just a touch showy, if you know what I mean."

"Trey"—Stephen guffaws, he can't help it—"I think that's the meanest thing I've ever heard you say." Trey's eyes find a spot on the ground. "Well, then," Stephen raises his glass. "To the new brother on the ball club."

◇

Saturday morning Stephen sleeps in, which means waking at dawn rather than in the dark. Mona has called three times since they last spoke, which was at 4:00 p.m. California time the previous day. There is only one voice mail; on it her voice so angry it sounds nearly percussive. He has forgotten—they both have forgotten, but he is the only one out of state and unable to easily correct the oversight—some important charity function this weekend. A fundraiser at Alexis's school, one that he had promised to attend. *Our names are on the freakin' invitation, Stevie*—that was part of the message. Unless he gets his tail back to California ASAP, Mona will have to attend alone and she does *not* want to do that.

She has also sent several texts. Four vehemently disappointed in him, including a threat to bring Marco, her stud personal trainer, to the gala as her date. One message in the middle of the stream shows mild concern; Mona must've briefly considered that an accident was preventing her husband from replying (rather than the three—or was it four?—margaritas he'd consumed with Trey, the two of them staying on the patio until well after dinner), but then she returned to the thumbed invectives. *Asshole. Selfish bastard. You love the team more than your family.* Stephen scrolls through the messages and deletes the thread, all the way back to Tuesday and a moment she was feeling generous. *Have a nice afternoon.* Theirs has always been a complicated relationship, made infinitely more so in November 1994. It was the MLB strike and a Lions investor wanted to wash his hands of his stake; he was asking the bargain price of $6 million. Back then, Mona had still loved baseball; as a native

Angeleno she'd cheered for the Lions since their inaugural season. Their partial share was meant to be an anniversary gift, a "diamond" for his wife. A project for them to do together.

*You're lucky you didn't ask me if I wanted it*, she likes to tell her husband. *I wouldn't have let you buy the team, Stevie.*

*Let me?* Stephen is, always, taken aback by her presumption. *Let. You.* She stretches out the words. *Not even a single share.*

And Stephen had misjudged her reaction; he did not anticipate her quick-boil resentment. *You've ruined baseball for me, dear.* She resents the time spent on those men, the friendships grown. When he talks to her about *performance* and *competition* and *fraternity*, about all the things that make him love owning the Lions, she looks at him like he is speaking gibberish.

But he didn't regret the purchase, not at all. Over the past seventeen years he's inched his way up. Far from the majority stake, but a big enough percentage that people pay attention to what he has to say. Nothing gets done without his okay. And as a *black* owner—that's another kind of notoriety. He's even been on *SportsCenter*, talking about the importance of diversity in sports leadership. Mona likes to remind him that his cable TV debut had occurred during the slowest of sports weeks, the doldrums between the NBA finals and the MLB All-Star Game. She thinks she's being cute, saying something so sly. She is a beautiful woman still, at fifty, petite and regal, but she hasn't been *cute* for decades, not since their undergraduate days at UCLA. And her smile is no longer as endearing as it was: now it has gray teeth, thinner lips, meanness at its corners.

He turns on the morning news and does sixty minutes on the elliptical in the den, then showers, eats a yogurt, and goes to the field early. He asks around the clubhouse and someone tells him the outfielders are doing wind sprints on practice field six. He studies a map of the new complex, then heads down a fresh asphalt path, small, round cacti lining the edges. A crew guy, zooming along in a dusty golf cart, stops abruptly, with a little squeak of the brakes.

"Joe Templeton, groundskeeper," the driver says, stepping from the cab and extending his hand. Stephen doubts the man knows his name, but at least he recognizes that Stephen must be important in his navy blazer and khakis. Stephen's always overcompensated in his dress. As if an expensive pair of loafers and a good chortle could make up for the poverty of his youth, the prejudice of a nation. But since Obama's inauguration Stephen's noticed a certain uptick—more respect from service workers, more interest from Mona's mainly white circle of friends. Maybe things are changing.

Stephen introduces himself, and Templeton offers him a lift. He declines: he wants to walk, to take in the new complex at his own speed. Templeton wishes Stephen a good day, and the golf cart whirs off in the opposite direction. Stephen likes the Arizona morning: it's brighter than those in L.A., or maybe just clearer, no smog or salty sea air dampening the resolution. The peaks are sharp on the eastern horizon, and Camelback Mountain pops in the west like a giant stone ungulate.

At practice field six Stephen sees a number of faces he recognizes. Jason Goodyear is jogging along the warning track. The new kid, Corey Matthews, is running across the outfield green. He touches the chalk of the foul line and then pops up and pivots, his knees pistons pumping toward the invisible finish line fifty yards out. Trey was right: good speed in those legs. The boy jogs back, high knees for half, then heels up for the remainder. Trey is in the near grass with a cluster of other players, the men stretching, their legs splayed into wide Vs. Stephen nods hello as he approaches—all of the men polite, deferential, *Hello, sir*, and *Good morning, boss*—and squats on his heels by Trey's side. "Want to introduce me?" Stephen says.

Trey slides one heel into his crotch, reaches for the opposite toe. "If you need it." The rookie crouches at the foul line and explodes up again. He runs with his head down, his hat's bill nearly perpendicular to the ground, until he reaches his imagined finish, pivots, and starts the jog back. He kicks his legs out like a drum major. Of course he can introduce himself.

Stephen stands. "Corey!" he calls. The boy looks up and makes a quick diagonal toward them. Trey rises as well, brushing off his rear.

Stephen puts out his hand. "Stephen Smith. Partial owner of the Lions."

Corey takes his hat off, shakes Stephen's hand. Nice grip, but the older man is startled by how young he looks. Smooth cheeks; hairless, glistening arms. Breathless. "Pleasure to meet you, sir."

◇

The team has a doubleheader across Saturday afternoon and evening. Corey plays in the first, sharing the outfield with Trey and Goodyear. The rookie bounces on his toes between pitches, streaking the outfield whenever a pop fly carries past the infield dirt. He *is* a dancer, Stephen thinks, and such a contrast to Trey, who remains planted to his piece of sod, calculating trajectories and speeds, until the last possible moment—only once his analysis is complete does he approach the ball, traveling with such efficiency he's like some antiballistic defensive shield calibrated to the center-field grass. In the toss between innings Corey throws a few lazy balls to the bullpen, then, at the catcher's urging, tries a long ball to home plate. His throw to home is respectable, one bounce, and ends up in the box, but nothing like the rockets Trey and Goodyear can launch.

Across the game the young right fielder takes a couple of big swings, but ultimately goes one for three with a walk and a dribbly single he earns not by hitting but by hauling ass. That run to first, and one magnificent sprint in right, all the way to the right-field foul post and scaling halfway up the wall to make a catch on what was ultimately a foul ball, are the only opportunities Stephen has to enjoy his impressive speed.

Some of the front office guys are going out to eat, but Stephen, feeling slightly fatigued by the heat—it cracked ninety today—decides to go home. He picks up tacos from his favorite hole in the wall and drives the rest of the way with the smell of cumin filling his car. Once there, he opens a favorite vintage of California sauvignon blanc and calls the house, knowing Mona will already be at the event, clutching desperately on the arm of her handsome trainer or their daughter's basketball coach or some other boring and attractive man. Stephen leaves her an apology on voice mail and finds a movie on Netflix.

◇

Most players take the spring's rare free day to sleep in or call their mothers, to get a massage or sit in a sauna or do something equally relaxing. But when Stephen asked at the practice field on Friday morning, Trey and Corey said they'd be happy to give Stephen their day off for a round of golf.

Monday morning Stephen packs his Callaway irons, slips a bottle of Scotch in the bag's side pouch, and goes to the diner downtown, where he flirts with the waitress and orders pancakes. He sends some e-mails over breakfast, texts Mona the morning *I love you* (while she still won't answer his calls, she is replying to texts; the dinner had gone well, no thanks to him), and calls his assistant to make sure no fires started over the weekend. He tells her he'll be out of pocket until the afternoon.

The dry-cleaning chain he married into would have been comfortably profitable if he'd just kept its business steady, but when he took it over from Mona's father he transformed it into Southern California's first organic dry cleaner. Now they just about print money. That he'd climbed from a steamer paying his way through UCLA to the owner of a hundred-shop franchise was no small feat, and occasionally he lets himself feel a touch proud. At these moments he is aware of the jump start of his father-in-law's gift, but also slightly dismissive of it. Look at what he has done.

The outfielders arrive together, in Trey's Audi, which is the same make and model as Stephen's, the next model year. As they approach, Stephen flips through the similarities between the outfielders like so many pressed coats on the dry cleaner's rack. They are dressed the same—unpleated khakis and dark polo shirts. Trey's got fifteen pounds of muscle on the kid, maybe another ten of middle-age settling, but their gait—they're walking the same. When they spot Stephen standing next to the golf cart, they even wave the same way, pivoting from the elbow.

Stephen is startled by this twinning. This young man before him is not the boy he saw in postgame interviews after UNC won its division, not the brash player grinning for the cameras from under a Lions cap on draft day. Now he looks just like Trey. Trey, who looks just like Stephen. Some of that may be coincidence, but some is concerted effort. Stephen should know: he'd had to remake himself for Mona's family, a new wardrobe and posture and way of speaking. Then, he'd had to steer Trey through the same. It took two seasons to lose his coarseness, to eliminate the kind of crass and crude manners that would get him nowhere fast. And he was so skittish, so startled, when he first arrived in Los Angeles. Trey could hardly say one syllable without stuttering it into four, and he looked at the world like everything—not just the rattlesnakes and desert spiders, but also the third baseman and the laundered uniforms deposited in his locker each morning and the signing bonus—might bite him in the ass. On Stephen's part it took patience, perseverance—Christ, it took shopping trips to Neiman to get him in some decent off-field attire, banishing those ratty Michigan T-shirts—to cure him of all that.

But the boy—they'd only met that once, out on field six. Could Corey react, absorb, and adapt to meeting Stephen Smith so quickly? Is he that fast of a study, a savant at manners? Young baseball players are rarely smart at anything but baseball; Stephen's first impression of Corey was the same. But perhaps Trey is some sort of conduit, sharing earlier lessons, passing them along to the boy as they sit on the bench, as they get dressed in the clubhouse (Stephen, again, imagines the young man's physique, his bare shoulders and waist), in the toss between innings. That seems plausible, but why would Trey lie about having gotten to know the boy?

The men stride toward the cart. Stephen has always seen himself in Trey, and appreciated the tribute, but if the mimicker is mimicked, the mirror mirrored—where does that leave Stephen, the original image? His head swims; his knees feel suddenly weak.

"You all right, boss?" Trey asks, looking concerned.

"Huh, what?"

"Your eyebrow was doing that thing." He signals the furrow between Stephen's brows.

"Right." Stephen massages the skin of his temples apart with his fingers.

After a moment more of pleasantries, back slaps, and allusions to the amber-colored fun they'll have on the links, they turn to the golf cart. There are three iced coffees in the drinks tray, two sets of clubs—Stephen's, plus one borrowed set he selected for Corey, based on the boy's height and weight—in the rear. "We can share one cart, yes?" The men nod, and Trey adds his bag to the pile. "Great," Stephen says. "I'll drive."

◇

Stephen thinks someone who could connect with a curving, ninety-mile-an-hour pitch would understand the mechanics of swinging a golf club. Sure, Corey grew up in a tough part of Chicago, a place where golf occasionally popped up on ABC's Saturday sports programming and nowhere else. But shouldn't a guy who hit twenty-five homers his last college season get the physics of sending a ball in a long-hang arc? The boy miffs and miffs again, not even striking the dimpled surface. Stephen tries to describe the step-by-step. Corey listens attentively, nods as eagerly as a junior engineer his first day at the power plant. No luck. Trey explains the geometry of it, velocity and trajectory. Corey pretends he knows what a double-pendulum swing is, but Stephen can see the utter confusion behind his calm.

The trio proceeds, but hole after hole he blunders—balls into the woods, into the pond, even ricocheting one off the top of a passing golf cart. He'd have done better had he thrown it. Corey loses so many that they send him back to the clubhouse to get a basket of dinged driving-range balls and allot him three shots off each tee before Trey and Stephen begin play in earnest. Their earnestness: a gentlemen's wager of $500 on the round, a sum that, when agreed upon, made a little slip of exclamation sneak out of Corey's mouth. Stephen remembers something similar in Trey's first season, how he could not believe it when Stephen opened, and drank dry, a $400 bottle of wine. Stephen had had the same reaction any number of times, including his first visit to his in-law's, the dripping opulence of their cut-glass chandeliers and brocade drapes.

The men are neck and neck until Stephen goofs the fourteenth hole, sending an easy ball into the water. When Trey sees his victory is all but assured, he loosens up. At the next hole a miracle: Corey's first swing carries all the way down the fairway. Trey slaps his ass as if it'd been a game-ending RBI, which makes a resonate *fwack* sound, and all three men pause before continuing their hoorahs.

It's two-thirty when they're back to the clubhouse, the Scotch nearly empty, all three of them flush with sun and alcohol. The dining room carries the quiet clatter of recovering from a rush; the last lunch plates are being cleared. A waitress sits at a banquette, prepping silverware for dinner.

While lunch service is technically over, the hostess has the good sense to put them at a big table by the bay window, looking out toward the McDowell Range. The trio agrees to drink red and orders accordingly—a steak salad for Stephen, chicken Caesar for Trey, and a thirty-dollar burger, Wagyu beef and blue cheese, for Corey. Corey, with sidelong glances, copies the older outfielder as best he can: the way he holds his wineglass, the napkin on the lap.

But the boy, who just twenty minutes before had been jovial, seems startled into quiet now. Is it the fine china? Stephen wonders. The pressed tablecloths? The players steal glances at each other, looks like Ping-Pong balls, fast and light and already moving again by the time Stephen notices.

Wanting to put Corey at ease, Stephen encourages him to ask about anything. *Anything.* Eyebrows up for emphasis. Corey's first question—about the pretty women (he uses a coarser term) who loiter around the players' parking lot—makes Stephen's face hot. "I haven't noticed them," Stephen says, even though, of course, he has. Maybe not at Salt River, but they're the same at every park. The women act as a distraction to the players;

has any man ever said, *I met my wife in a parking lot?* No. He'll have to ask at the stadium—maybe that golf-cart-driving groundskeeper—to keep an eye out for them, shoo them off as tactfully as possible.

The boy looks disappointed, as is Stephen, but he tries to hide the emotion from his face. He doesn't mind direct questions, but the boy should know better, should learn how to conduct himself around elders and administration. There will be plenty of stuffier stuffed shirts in his future, plenty of guys—*white guys*, Stephen clarifies in his mind—who will give Corey one half of one chance to make the right impression. No one says *sluts* at a golf club.

Corey tries again: "Did you hear about what happened to Goody?"

"The divorce?" Stephen nods. Mona had read about it in some gossip column; he could tell she relished in sharing the bad news. "Yes, it's unfortunate. Love's hard."

The boy shakes his head. "Naw, man. I'm talking about the police incident." Trey coughs into his fist, and Stephen's throat constricts. No, he definitely has *not* heard their $150 million investment had a run-in with the law. And why hadn't he been informed? By Dorsey or Woody or Goodyear himself? And why not by Trey? He tries to keep his face calm and make eye contact with Trey, a *Did you know about this?* glance, but the center fielder is watching out the window, where a hawk makes loops in the sky.

"How'd it—what the—" Stephen stutters, stops. Begins again. "When?"

"Last week, I guess. It's cool," Corey shrugs. "Misdemeanor. Trespassing or some shit. I mean, he's a white guy. A famous one. He'll be fine."

Trey snorts.

"Trey?" Stephen is feeling light-headed. Over margaritas the two men discussed Jason's recent divorce, how the usually stoic athlete has seemed shaky this spring, slumping at the plate. But Trey said he was pushing himself harder than ever, spending even more time alone at the training complex. Trey also said he was keeping an eye on Jason, not that the two were particularly close (and both have reputations of standing at a remove), but because the two do share an outfield. But obviously—getting arrested for trespassing! nearly burning down Frank Lloyd Wright's house!— Trey had not been watching his teammate closely enough.

"I thought you knew," Trey says.

The boy fidgets, realizing at least some dimension of his mistake.

Stephen waits for his voice to steady before beginning again, speaking to Corey. "I'll make sure to follow up with Jason. Thank you for telling me."

Corey is visibly relieved when his burger arrives. He slips into the posture of a slouching teenager, the boy he was until just recently, and leans forward, one arm on the table, almost protective of his food.

"Whoa, Corey. No one's going to take your burger," Stephen says with a laugh. Corey swallows deeply before he looks up, and Stephen smiles, full of teeth. *Cheshire.*

Stephen tries to restart the conversation. "Where are you living this spring, Corey?" It's an innocuous question—he recalls that sections of the low-rise condos on the municipal golf course are rented to young players each spring, one building for the infield, another for pitchers, a third for the outfield prospects. But the boy stammers, hems. Haws.

After some leaning, Corey admits he spent the first week of

camp in a bug-infested motel on the south side of town. *Spent*, past tense.

"What happened to the condos on the city course?" Stephen asks, trying to swallow his new doubt. Where is he staying now?

"They didn't happen this year," Corey explains. At least not any he was invited to join. The team'd gotten a block of rooms at the Best Western, one guy was staying at the casino, and a couple of the relief pitchers rented a loft in downtown Phoenix. Corey curls his nose at the thought. "Why would I want to live in a dirty-ass old warehouse?"

It is finally revealed: he is staying in Trey's casita. Stephen's ears prick—was the boy already staying with Trey when the men had their margaritas? Why would Trey withhold such a thing? Stephen can read nothing on the other man's face except for the flush of alcohol, how his eyes are slightly glassy. No, there's something else in them: he can also see some smugness. Maybe it's the five crisp hundred-dollar bills buoying him, or some satisfaction of keeping Goodyear a secret all week. Or could it be this boy, their new friendship? Stephen is surprised by the anger that rumbles in his stomach.

Stephen's swirling thoughts are interrupted by Trey. "Hey, boss." Stephen's hand goes to his forehead, the crease there, but Trey shakes his head and pushes his empty wineglass toward Stephen's plate. "Nah, not that. Hook me up with more wine?"

◇

Mona Smith is coming for a long weekend, without Alexis—she's got a school slumber party at a museum or the zoo or somewhere else Stephen thinks sounds unhygienic—and his wife insists they have people over Thursday. He points out that Thursday's the first cut meeting of spring; she says it's all the more reason to host. She likes the Lions' management's wives, she says, misses them, wants to see them. The men can have their meeting, and the women will catch up. She promises to stay out of their hair. Stephen points out that only a few of the wives are in town, and that she'd see plenty of them if she ever came to a regular-season game. *I come to plenty, Stevie,* she says, same as always, though last season Stephen could count her attendance on one hand. This time he does not push the matter, as he is still far from her good graces. Besides, at this point in the spring there aren't any surprises. They're just letting a few nonroster invites go home early, guys who had good numbers in the development league but who, once they started playing with the big leaguers, clearly didn't have the stuff. The weekly meetings will continue—and become increasing difficult—until the end of spring.

The group assembles on the Smiths' patio at seven-thirty; the coaches, management, and owners agree on their list of dismissals and warnings in all of fifteen minutes. Then, more people fill into the patio: Ronnie Duncan, the real estate developer who helped them with the stadium, a few neighbors Stephen's not seen since last fall. He likes this house, this neighborhood— it's full of suntanned cardiologists and chummy estate lawyers, men who have made millions off the snowbirds of Scottsdale.

There are a smattering of athletes in attendance, too. Conventional wisdom is that it's bad form for management to socialize with the athletes. It's like a teacher fraternizing with her students or a homeowner hanging out with the help. Trey, of course, is an exception; everyone's come to expect him at Stephen's side. The new right fielder, Corey Matthews, is there, too, awkward and quiet and looking like Trey's mini-me in the corner. José Oliveira, a left-handed ace who's aging himself out of the league, and his much-younger wife, Hillary, were invited because Mona likes Hillary more often than not, and she says she feels some kinship, both of them white women married to brown men. *She knows what it's like*, Mona says whenever the Oliveiras come up. *What what's like?* Stephen asks. *The Dominican Republic is nothing like Watts.* That always stops Mona in her tracks.

Jason Goodyear is there, too. Divorce is nothing new—major league ballplayers are notoriously fast to marry and quick to split, so much so that the team counsel has a standard pre-nup on file—and when Dorsey questioned Jason at the start of camp, the left fielder had told the team's manager that he was handling it fine, that the club didn't have anything to worry about. *Get it out of your system this spring*, the man had told Jason. *April 1, I need you good.* Then Dorsey left Jason to sulk, as was his right, and told Trey to keep an eye on him. At least, that's the story he conveyed to Stephen, who called in a rage after his golf outing. It made him sick, he bellowed. He was feeling livid and maybe slightly drunk. What if he'd burned the place down? And why hadn't anybody told him? *Nobody asked*, was Dorsey's too-sharp reply, like Stephen was the idiot for missing the news. *Don't let your eyes off him*, Stephen had shouted before hanging up.

So every day this week, Dorsey Paine has picked up Jason at the stadium after the game, the left fielder showered and changed and waiting in the clubhouse. Tuesday they went for burgers, Wednesday to some sports bar to watch college basket-ball. Tonight, he brought Jason to Stephen's house, where the first thing the owner did was to grab Goodyear into a bear hug and then punch him in the kidney. *You fucking idiot*, he'd said under his breath, even as he was grinning.

It's eight-thirty when Stephen comes into the kitchen to get more ice for the Scotch. He sees that Mona's already drunk, waving around a smudged glass of white wine. He counts the empties by the sink—the women are four bottles into a case of nice sauvignon. If they're going to swill something, he wishes they'd pick a fifty-dollar vintage. But rather than say anything snide and risk Mona's ire, he just retrieves his ice and retreats. Mona, in the middle of some complicated, adoring story about Alexis's basketball team, ignores her husband.

Stephen heads down the darkened hall, proceeding toward the tiki torches of the patio, when a thick outline fills the doorway, backlit against flickering orange. That saunter, those shoulders: Trey. The low rumble of men at one end of the hall and the high chitter of women at the other enter the corridor and collide in the air above them. Both men slow as they move together, as the space between them shrinks.

Stephen is not sure he has forgiven Trey for Monday's revelations, what felt like two betrayals. But he also is not sure how to stay angry at the man. The past decade, outside of his family, it is this friendship that he holds most dear. They have shared so much.

"The wife thatta way?" Even Trey's inflection is Stephen's, down to the now-deliberate extra syllables, WASPy affects picked up by one man, then passed to the other. It's like a mynah bird spouting its new vocabulary. But all at once Stephen is uncertain if he should be proud of his pupil or if the creature is mocking him with its chirps. If the mimicker mimics—

Stephen shakes the thought from his mind. This is Trey. *Trey.* His friend, his confidant. In another world, if this hallway were endless, not opening onto wives and colleagues, he would take this man in his arms. So why would Trey speak to him with malice? Stephen has no answer, just as he can think of no reason Trey would do something as deceitful as not telling him about the boy. Monday must have been a mistake, some disturbance in the air.

He tilts his head back toward the kitchen. "Yes. But she's in one of *those* moods." They chuckle, understanding. "Consider yourself warned."

Once Trey's down the hall Stephen backtracks, stopping a few feet shy of the kitchen, still in the shadow of the corridor. He listens from the dark as Trey thanks Mona for her hospitality and begins an excuse about heading home. Stephen peers around the doorjamb just in time to see her grab his bicep, her fingers not even close to making it around his arm, but squeezing her bony hand like she's determined to make it happen, regardless. The ice in Stephen's bucket rattles and he worries someone might hear him, but no one turns.

Mona pulls him toward a woman Stephen doesn't know, a new neighbor or someone's recent girlfriend. "This one's his favorite," Mona tells the brunette. Mona has loosened her grip and puts a hand on Trey's back. She does the same to Stephen when presenting him at parties. The pressure of her palm makes him feel like some sort of puppet. Mona's creation, her captive, like saying, *Here, here is a thing that I have.* "Stevie's favorite on the whole team."

The new woman mumbles some pleasantry that doesn't carry, but Trey responds as clear as day, somewhat louder than his normal voice. "Mr. Smith has been a great friend over the years."

"Why don't you ever bring a girl around, Trey? You're so handsome," Mona says, scrutinizing his face, pressing into his back. "Dontcha think?" If his posture could possibly get any straighter, it does. The new woman clucks in agreement, looks him up and down admiringly.

Trey clears his throat. "It's not easy to find the right one, Mrs. Smith. The right girl, I mean."

"Puh-lease. It's *Mona* for my husband's best friend. What's so hard? Try one, and if it doesn't work, try another. I mean, look at

Jason—you get knocked down and you get right back up again. I heard he was canoodling with some barfly the night he—"

"Being on the road all the time is tough. And I have . . . particular tastes."

"Tastes." A flash passes over Mona's face, and she indicates she wants to whisper something in his ear. She is trying for height, stretching on her tiptoes, but Trey still has to lean down for her to reach him. She squeezes his arm again, a hard cinch.

"Did he fuck you?" She hisses it, but the question carries over the chinking of wineglasses, cuts through the rumble of men's voices behind him. Its venom is a sharp, quick sting, and before Stephen realizes it he's back in the kitchen, the ice bucket clattering on the counter as he puts a hand on Mona's, their rings clicking, and pries her fingers off of Trey. With his other hand he pats Trey's shoulder; short, hard raps trying to steer him toward the doorway. "Mona, dear, be careful." Stephen lets Mona's grip curl tighter, and he clenches his teeth to keep from grimacing. "That's his throwing arm." He chuckles like it's funny. Stephen pulls their hands below the counter and squeezes back. She welps softly and eases her grip. "You doing well, Trey?" Stephen asks, ignoring the rustle under the counter. "You need anything else? Another Scotch?" Another rap lands on the player's back.

He shakes his head. "No, thanks."

Below the counter Mona finds the inside of her husband's thigh, her fingers exploring the surface of his chinos in a way that makes Stephen squirm. Suddenly, her hand pauses and her face lights up. "Who wants to go swimming?"

◇

In the time it takes the women to assemble on the patio Stephen has had another two fingers of Scotch and convinced himself

Mona's forgotten the whole idea and instead gone back to sucking on olives and squeaking in the kitchen. But then his wife announces herself in the doorway, howling like a banshee. She's donned a short robe, most of the length of her legs at the mercy of the tiki torches' light. She leads the conga line of barefoot women, some of them wrapped in towels, others in sarongs, in a strut across the patio, waving arms and kicking legs. The colors and prints look vaguely familiar to Stephen, swimsuits and cruise wear and poolside cover-ups he has bought his wife over the years.

"Fellas, any takers?" Mona drops her robe at the edge of the pool and steps down the underwater stairs, doing her best sea-nymph impression. Her legs tremble with booze and the change in buoyancy. Behind her, another pair of women walk in, tentatively in step like amateur synchronized swimmers. "We brought trunks!" another guest—Helen Walsh, the pitching coach's wife—yells and waves a pair like a flag. Stephen's trunks. He recognizes others in the stack: they've raided his closet. "Stevie," Mona says from the pool, submerged up to her shoulders, her body a ghostly mint color, "you don't mind, do you?"

"Sounds fun." Stuart Walsh is drunk enough to think it's a good idea to get in. He grabs the pair out of his wife's hand. "I'll be right back."

Within ten minutes there are a dozen people in the pool. Pandemonium, splashing and the kinds of shrieks you'd expect out of preteens on the hottest day of summer. The Walshes are playing a game of chicken with Ronnie and his new girlfriend. Goodyear's in the shallow end with Dorsey, the athlete sulking and the manager well on his way to being drunk. Stephen can't help noticing the athlete's one visible tattoo, a jack of diamonds inked over his heart. Strange, that; Jason didn't strike him as the card-playing type. Unless the diamond is some double entendre, a baseball diamond instead of a felt table. What would that mean?

"Stevie, take off those pants!" Mona splashes to make her point, spraying an arc of water over the lip of the pool, to where Trey, Corey, and Stephen sit in a semicircle of lounge chairs. They are smoking cigars, hardly talking. Actually, just Trey and Stephen smoke; Corey has declined and continues to smack on a large wad of gum. That won't do, Stephen thinks, but it's better than chewing tobacco—he's known enough players who've had the cancer cut out of their jaws with a demented jigsaw.

The pool's splatter gets Stephen's loafers wet. "Mona, dear, you've given away all my trunks."

"Pish-posh. You too old to skinny-dip?"

"Yes, I believe I am."

She treads water for a few moments, lets her mouth dip below the waterline before kicking herself back up with a humph. "Trey, how about you?" Trey is quick to shake his head; thank you, but no. "Or your new friend?"

The boy looks startled, as if he'd rather be mistaken for patio furniture, but she is bobbing and sputtering, waiting for an answer.

"Corey. His name is Corey, Mona," Stephen says.

"Right. Corey. You know how to swim?" She dips down and pops back up, blinking at him. Her mascara has smeared an inch down her cheeks.

"Jesus, Mona," Stephen says. "That sounds racist." He's been correcting her for decades, though her bullheaded comments are less frequent now (their daughter, after all). Usually alcohol is involved, and it's almost always sparked by ignorance. "Asking a black man if he knows how to swim."

"What? It's a simple question. Maybe he doesn't."

"I do," Corey says.

"What was that, son?" she says, spitting a spray of pool water from her mouth.

"I do. Know how to swim."

"Well, good." She smiles. "Hop in, then." The boy is already kicking off his shoes, unbuckling his belt, pulling his shirt out from his waistband.

"You're not going in." Trey's voice is anxious, somewhere between a question and a command.

"Why not?" Corey's chest, hairless and ridged with muscles, is more striking than Stephen had imagined. Trey, also staring at the boy, looks stricken.

The ferocity in Corey's eyes and the pleading in Trey's: suddenly, Stephen sees everything, all that has happened between these two men. He sees a physical bond, an emotional one. These men have been together, or else Trey desperately wishes it so. The locker room, indeed.

His heart sinks. He thought Trey was better than this, more like him. Adaptable to the point of mimicry, flexible into the realm of acrobatics. But still composed of the kind of fortitude that would keep him from ever looking so desperate, so vulnerable, as the center fielder does in this instant. To be like Stephen, you have to be strong, stronger than everyone else. You go out and get—take—what you need. Never ask, unless you know the answer will be yes. Never plead. *You're not going in?* The boy steps out of his pants, revealing short boxer briefs and long, lean legs. Even as Trey crumples, Stephen can see: this boy is fierce.

Stephen knows what he has to do.

As Corey steps down the ladder into the pool's deep end, as Trey sulks back behind a potted aloe with the last puffs of his cigar, as Mona dives below the surface, kicking hard, Stephen marches around the pool to where Dorsey Paine is guffawing in the shallow end.

"Where's Woody?" Stephen looks around the pool patio; he doesn't see the general manager anywhere.

"Headed home early. Said he has a call with New York in the morning." Dorsey shrugs and reaches for a sweating bottle of Corona on the pool's ledge, but Stephen pushes the bottle with his foot. It slips into the water and begins to sink.

"Hey!" Dorsey complains. The lime floats loose from the neck and bobs back to the surface of the water. Jason, still silent, grabs it and sets it back on the lip of the pool. He retrieves the bottle, too. "What gives?" Dorsey asks.

Stephen, crouched next to the men, looks at the left fielder, at his chest. "Jason, will you give us a minute?"

When he's out of earshot, Stephen starts, his voice a whisper. "Trey Townsend."

"What about Trey?"

"He has, what, three years left on his contract?" Corey climbs out of the pool, dripping wet, Adonis-meets-Venus under the desert moon.

"I'd have to check with Woody, but that sounds right." Could Trey not see that they are all the same? That the three of them are a continuum, not an either/or? One arc proceeds Corey, Trey, Stephen, if they are going by age. By net worth: Corey, Stephen, Trey. Or by potential: Stephen, Trey, Corey. Even as the order of each progression changes, as the trajectory shifts, they are all strung together. Or, they should be.

Stephen had not asked too much of Trey. Just his appreciation, his loyalty. Instead, he'd folded so easily toward this new one, this washboard-stomached, rough-edged boy. And, as quickly as that, Stephen has lost him. He has lost his favorite. Trey comes forward with a towel, but the boy bats it away.

Stephen crosses his arms. "I want him gone by opening day."

"Really?" Dorsey says.

"Tell Woody to make it happen."

Just then, a great, guttural scream rings out. Everyone turns as Corey Matthews, standing at the end of the diving board, leaps up and gathers his lithe body into a tight ball. The guests, Mona, Stephen, Trey—they all watch as he soars through the air, as he quickly, perfectly, drops out of the blue-black sky. And then they all brace themselves for the loud splash of contact, for the spray of displaced water that will rise and spread outward in so many long, perfect arcs.

# FIFTH

There were no glaciers in Arizona, save for the tips of a few tall peaks, ball caps you'd barely notice above the bulk of the rest of them. Nothing like the thick kind of ice that showed up in Washington; at one point the Mariners, the whole team, the stadium and the fans and all of Puget Sound, were under three thousand feet. Picture five Space Needles standing tip to toe, frozen into one big ice cube, and then imagine that kind of glacier suddenly sluicing. That'll change your outlook for the game, your prospects for the weekend series.

But fourteen thousand years ago, North America's glaciers began dissolving in earnest. When the half-mile-deep daub of cool vanilla cream melted from its perch on the Colorado Plateau, it sent water south by southwest, a great gusher that must've looked like the rush onto the field that happens when you give the rookie squad the green light to warm up.

These profound floods meant added vegetation in the region—ferns and bogs and big, leafy trees took root in Arizona—and all of a sudden the landscape was verdant. The land was covered in bushes with base-size waxy emerald leaves, was blanketed with soft-palmed ferns as big around as the pitching mound. That kind of green seems unlikely now, about as probable as a National League pitcher hitting an inside-the-park home run. But it happened, a brief spell of lush life that arrived with a big, splashing wall of water.

The Lions ride their own wall of water, and surge forward through the spring. The fielders who went butterfingered over the winter regain their touch; the bats, under Coach Mike's grouchy supervision, grow as strong and thick as banyan trees. The pitchers find their arms, their heat and precision fed by the newly fertile soil that is a team coming together. And the team *is* aligning, starting to look like a cohesive unit, like a contender for the division—the bullish among us suggest the pennant.

"Among us"—how easy it is to insert myself back into the booth, to recall the smells of burned coffee and comped hot dogs and that neon-green relish, the anticipation of getting your stat sheet from some zitty media ops intern. How natural to put myself back in the postgame press conferences, Dorsey Paine bloviating in his charming way, Jimmy Cardozo cracking jokes, Jason, with his normal reticence, refusing to talk about anything but on-the-field action. He won't talk about the Townsend trade or how he feels about that old-timer Monterrey starting again in center field. Won't talk about the divorce or rumors that Nike is making him a shoe or anything at all about Frank Lloyd Wright. If I'd been granted access, if I'd been in the room, I'd've asked: *Is it true you lost half a million on Thursday night after Dorsey dropped you off at the stadium to "get your car"? And another $500K on Friday, not even caring if people were watching you getting mopped?* Sara's not the only one to see him scuttling back across the bridge between the casino and the field, late for his 7:00 a.m. date; I've seen it, too. A guy who works security at Talking Stick, he tells me that Jason Goodyear is in and out twice a day, pregame and post, if not another time in the middle (and how, I wonder, does he manage that?). And it's not like he's sleeping there; only baby Goslin and his helicopter mom have sprung for the six-week suite. If given the opportunity at the presser, I'd've asked: *What the hell are you doing?*

There's an obvious answer: poker, blackjack, occasionally craps. Just like there's an obvious answer for the jack of diamonds tattooed on his chest: this guy's an addict, hooked on poker like he was—hopefully still is—hooked on sport. Is it because one thing—baseball—became too easy that he had to hop to another table? Because now he's seeking competition of any stripe, of all stripes. Hitting balls, throwing rocks, getting women—even mature ladies like Tami—to wobble over him. When you start seeing everything as sport, life as something to win, the thrills start piling up, or at least the possibility of them. That's probably the straw that fucked the camel, to borrow a phrase from Herb, between Jason and Liana. She'd waited patient through the season, was looking forward to a quiet, a regular, a calm off-season with her still-new husband. Instead he went on a surge of his own, manic and brusque and only really focused on working out and then getting back to a poker table and staying there. The whole month of November, he was never once home for dinner. Liana didn't tell me that detail, but her housekeeper was happy enough to share it in exchange for a hundred-dollar bill. The worst of it was when he said he was going to L.A. for a few days, only to drive across town, binge for two nights and a day on the floor, stopping just for food and the john. He played something like two hundred rounds, most of them lost. At the end of that epic session, he was down most of a million.

I wish I could say everyone loves the surge, the newly fertile soil that sends sprouts growing an inch a week, that puts the Lions at the top of the spring standings. Silly, boastful ledes: *The Lions are going to maul the division. These Lions are ready to pounce on the competition.* The surge is good, yes, but of course good is bad for some. Some plants drown in the too-deep water. Others get overshadowed by their neighbors' broad leaves and wither without enough light. Some plants get ripped from the ground by passing water, their roots not strong enough, and are carried so far from where they started they don't even recognize the land where their wave stops. Is that what happens to Jason, when he walks into the casino after dinner and comes out squinting into the morning sun with a game—a real game, a baseball game—to play? Does he recognize that morning, does he know that night?

Some dead stalks stay put in their shriveled state, reminding the rest of their hardships. But more often those unsuccesses are erased entirely, washed away or ground back to dust by wind and cleats. Those poor plants, the ones who will become rootless and overshadowed and incidental to all but a few best friends and lonely fans, in the churn of spring training are treated like they've already been pulverized into the soil even when they're still coming out of the ground. Like Greg Carver: he was cut before he ever had a chance, considered so expendable that Jason Goodyear let him see everything. What's a witness when you know he'll disappear? No sort of witness at all.

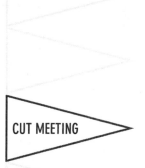

CUT MEETING

A bright afternoon: blue sky, a sharp diamond of sun. Greg
Carver is standing on the rubber and a man—the catcher—is
jogging out to the mound. He knows this guy, this fireplug of
a ballplayer with the long scar on his cheek, the flat nose of a
boxer, a nickel gap between his front teeth. He knows him and
his name is . . . the pitcher tries As and then Bs, running down
the alphabet, *Casey, Dave, Elliot,* as the man approaches, lum-
bering under his gear. *J. Jimmy.*

Jimmy's wearing a Lions uniform, as is Greg—white with
black pinstripes, gold LOS ANGELES across the chest. This is sur-
prising. The last time they played together they were both Stallions. Black and gold, too, but a different creature, with hooves. A
different place, Salt Lake, no red mountains rimming the horizon.

"What's up, Jimmy?" Greg glances over his shoulder, to the
left-field scoreboard. It says that the Lions are winning over the
Padres, 5–2. It says it's the sixth, that they have one out. He sees

a runner on second, the man's hands on his hips. Greg turns back to Jimmy, who's staring at him.

"You okay, Carve?" Jimmy asks. His gold catcher's mask is pushed high on his forehead, a halo.

"Why wouldn't I be okay?" Greg rubs the ball hard with his thumb, trying to ignore the sensation in his elbow. It's coming back quickly, the pain a drumbeat that keeps hurrying up.

"You seem a little . . . spacey."

"I'm fine."

"What did Coach Stu say?"

Greg has no recollection of a visit from Coach Stu, no idea who that is or what he said.

"Nothing much."

"The wing?" Jimmy glances at the cut, the pale skin and red seam, the scarred-over eyelets of the stitches. Twenty-six. *One for every year*, the doctor had said, like it was a good thing to be reminded of his station, that he'd be twenty-seven before he threw again. All winter Greg had worn his sleeves long to keep from seeing it, but this afternoon is too hot for anything more than the jersey.

"It's fine." He flaps his elbow to indicate as much. The pain had been small, rounded soft and smooshed to fit into the palm of his hand, but that up and down sends it spinning into a larger shape, all sharp angles.

The catcher's eyes jump to the arm and back. In Greg's mind, the scar is glowing. The scar is leering. The scar is six-foot-two, brown haired and blue eyed, a minor league pitcher trying to make the team. "Think you can finish out the inning?"

"I'm getting them over the plate, aren't I?" The scar talks, the scar listens. The scar answers to the name of Greg.

The catcher studies the pitcher's face. What did he see from behind the plate? What does he see from a foot away? The sweat dripping down Greg's face? He wipes at it with his shoulder.

"Mostly, yeah."

"It's been six innings?"

"Well, five and a third, but yeah."

"So."

"So—" Jimmy's face bursts into a wide, crooked smile. That gap again. "You got this." He smacks Greg on the butt, trots a few paces, and turns back. "Oh," he says, putting the web of his glove over his mouth, "this guy hit thirty homers last year, so keep it in."

As Jimmy returns to the plate, Greg Carver looks around: the sunny afternoon, the impressive, unfamiliar stadium. The seats of the lower deck are mostly filled with gold-shirted fans. The red mountains he recognizes from Arizona springs past. This is Lions spring training. He's pitching.

Jimmy squats, flashes a signal between his legs. Greg nods, not that he remembers what the signal means but because he knows to nod back. Jimmy spreads his feet, settling into his ankles to receive the impact of the pitch. That he recognizes, his best friend's posture when he's expecting a breaking curve. Greg looks at the ball in his hand, adjusts his fingers. He takes a deep breath and readies himself for a rocket of pain. And with it, the ball goes flying.

◇

Jimmy and Greg were drafted together, came up through the farm system together, fought like fiends to keep climbing— together. Until September 2009. End of the Salt Lake Stallions' minor league season, Jimmy got bumped up to the Lions' expanded forty-man roster. That was the season when Coach Mike finally taught him when *not* to swing, no excuses, and Jimmy's batting average jumped twenty points, from atrocious to all right. Over the moon, they were. Greg? He'd been 5-1 the second half of the Triple-A season, his ERA hovering around 2.8 in August. He and Jimmy were certain he'd get a call, too.

But when Greg's call came, it was orders to meet the team doctor in Irvine. The physician had "heard" Greg's elbow was bothering him. *Sure but*—Greg stammered. His elbow ached some, but it was manageable, and he'd not said a word, not to anyone but Jimmy. He couldn't figure out how they knew, what he'd done to give himself away. *Don't be worried*, the doctor said, trying to sound kind but coming off more like a snake-oil salesman. He had him stick his throwing arm in a contraption the size of a camper. *It's no big deal, just a quick scan. Rat-a-tat* for thirty minutes; it sounded like a nail gun going off next to his head. Then he had to "wait for the imaging" to determine if his life was ruined.

The GM called. This was the second time they'd ever talked; Woody Botter had called Greg to congratulate him after the draft. Greg'd been twenty-one at the time, still so stunned at what, by major league standards, was an extremely modest signing bonus, that over the course of their brief conversation he could only blubber out every variation of *thank you*.

This time Botter told Greg he was getting Tommy John. *Another option?* Greg'd wanted to know. *Retirement*, Botter said with a laugh. Greg could stay in Triple or maybe slide back down to Double-A Kansas, but his arm was nearly shot. *Maybe it's not hurting bad now, but it will*, he had said. *Your whole elbow is hanging on by a thread.*

Greg had heard about high schoolers and college boys getting their arms done before they were drafted, before eligibility even, in order to avoid this exact situation. And the vets who go under the knife, the John Smoltz or Billy Wagner types, already had a guaranteed spot on their clubs' rosters. The young guys, the old ones, *they* could afford to take the year out of their career. Greg Carver could not—2010 was going to be the season when he finally made the team.

*You're twenty-five, right?*

*But I won't be back until I'm twenty-seven.*

Botter harrumphed. *That's a fine age.* Greg disagreed, but swallowed it down, tried to steady his voice and not sound like he was terrified. Which he was; dizzy and queasy and on the verge of tears. *All goes well we'll get you back for the 2011 camp. Then we'll see,* the GM said in a way that made it clear there would be no more discussion.

*We'll see.* Greg tried to tell himself there was hope in those words, a waver of it under the monotone. But the alternative, that backslide from three As to two, a career with the Kansas Oilmen, making a home in Lawrence, fifteen grand a season. That wasn't any life.

So he agreed. Within an hour of Botter's goodbye some woman called and scheduled him into surgery for the first week of October. Greg watched Jimmy and the Lions from his hospital bed: they were the wild card team that October, won the divisional round in a three-game sweep but then got swept themselves in the ALCS.

◇

"How'd you sleep, Carve?" Jimmy plops down in the grass next to Greg, throws a thick leg out in front of him, and tries to wrap a finger around his cleat. He gets as far as his ankle and surrenders, pulling at his sock like that's what he'd meant to do. While Carver was going under the knife, Jimmy spent the 2009 postseason playing backup catcher for the Lions. Even with his shitty bat he managed a couple of clutch hits that, along with his goofball grin, made Angelenos love him right out of the gates.

"Fine." Greg and Jimmy had always bunked up, in spring training and during the Stallions' season, an efficient two-bedroom in Salt Lake and double-queen hotel rooms on the road. But this year, with his starting role, Jimmy elected for a single room, his own California king; Greg, feeling as shaky about money as ever, asked the clubhouse coordinator for a new roommate. He got some kid bullpen catcher who snored like a chain saw—Greg has yet to sleep through an Arizona night.

"That hotel they've got us in is kinda ghetto, yeah?" Jimmy says, switching legs. They've been there four weeks, two weeks just of pitchers and catchers, and now two weeks of the season. "Found a gnarly bug in the bathroom this morning." He struggles for his right foot. "Looked like a damn alien."

Back in 2009 Greg could've told the Lions Jimmy would be their starting catcher, but who would've listened? No, Jimmy had to prove his worth in Los Angeles, and did: the least number of passed balls in the league through the first half of the season. American *and* National League, Jimmy would correct if he was trying to impress someone, usually a lady. Made pitchers look good, catching everything they threw. And all of a sudden every Lion liked to toss to the backup catcher. Even Stan Rogers, the team's ace, asked for Jimmy rather than their old starter. Herb Allison signed him on, the other catcher went packing, and during this last off-season Jimmy renewed his contract for eight times as much as his last. When Greg heard that—Greg, living with his parents, struggling through four-a-week PT appointments at some dingy complex full of geriatrics and high school athletes, just starting to throw again, and without any sort of strength or control—his ears roared with a jealousy that came on so fast and strong it frightened him. Jimmy had been *his* catcher, before the team's even.

"I hadn't noticed." Greg reaches for his ankle and feels a sharp pain in his elbow. He winces but tries to lose the face before Jimmy spots it.

"You okay?"

"It's nothing." He waves. "Postgame stiffness. I'll ice it today, good as new."

"All right, brother." Jimmy pushes himself up and flashes Greg a smile. "Gotta go warm up the kid." The kid is Vásquez, a big guy from the Dominican Republic, so thick he's nearly fat. He signed with the Lions the moment he turned sixteen and has been working his way through the farm system fast.

Jimmy looks down at Greg, adjusts his belt a notch tighter. No one's told Greg outright, but he knows that he and Vásquez are both vying for the four spot. Any other team there'd be five starting pitchers, but Woody Botter is set on a four-man rotation and a deep bullpen so they can get Rogers on the mound as often as possible. That leaves one spot, two right-handers. Greg's not a reliever, not since his freshman year—of high school.

"Don't worry," Jimmy says. "He's a big kid, but doesn't have near the control of you."

"That's a relief," Greg says, but he's thinking Jimmy's the one to find Vásquez's control, to steer and aim and cajole his young arm into shape. He's thinking Jimmy might be loyal as Lassie, but that won't keep him from catching another guy, and catching well. "Have a good game, buddy," Greg says, but Jimmy's already jogging off.

◇

As the stadium starts to fill, Greg runs out of the complex, up the arroyo, and through the municipal golf course. In the year after surgery, conditioning was all he had: six months of long runs, stairs, and squats before he could even *pick up* a five-pound weight with his right hand. March of last year, he could run twenty miles but couldn't open a jar of pasta sauce.

*Eighty-five percent success rate*, the doctor had said, and that's what he keeps telling himself. *Guys return stronger than ever*—the doc had said that, too. He jogs alongside the dry riverbed, the banks of the channel paved in concrete. It hasn't rained since he arrived in Phoenix.

He spots a figure running ahead of him, another nut exercising in the ninety-degree heat. Greg is going faster than the man, and the distance between them shrinks until he's only a few strides away. It's Jason Goodyear, the left fielder breathing hard, covered in a sheen of sweat. His soaked T-shirt is tucked into the waistband of his shorts. Greg slows his stride. To pass the All-Star would be disrespectful.

A few blocks later Jason looks over his shoulder. "You gonna creep back there the whole damn run? Come here."

Greg strides alongside him. "How's it going? I'm Greg."

"I know who you are, Carve. We got you from Notre Dame in oh-five."

"Right." Greg wishes he could do that first line again, better. "Didn't want to assume. A lot of new faces this spring."

The silence stretches, grows. He's been in proximity to the All-Star other springs, taken showers at the same time, caught a few balls he sent back from left. But this is the only time they've spoken. What should he say next? *I'm sorry about your divorce?* Jason probably doesn't want to talk about it—isn't that why he got himself into trouble at Taliesin? "Got the afternoon off?"

"I'm here, aren't I?" Jason spits to the side of the trail. He's meant to be a man of few words, but today the left fielder is so short he's nearly surly. "Dorsey put some kid in left. Wants him to play a game before he's cut."

Cut day. What a different thing it means for Goodyear and Jimmy, assured of their spots on the roster. For them, it just means the locker room's less crowded, they'll know who's going to be hitting before them and cleaning up after. Greg, on the other hand, is staring down the end of his option this spring, and dreads every Friday morning, expecting the worst. If he's cut he'll be released, and no one will sign him, his arm being what it is. Working but not working right. A part of him is amazed he's made it a month without anyone noticing. The team doc has asked for a checkup, but he's so busy with hamstring pulls and back pain he hardly seems to care that Greg keeps rescheduling.

They go another mile. The sun, if possible, is even hotter; both men are sluicing off sweat.

"How far you usually go?" Jason asks, watching Greg's stride out of the corner of his eye.

Greg could answer ten miles, fifteen, twenty, or he could say the truth: however far it takes to be so exhausted that he forgets about his arm for a while. But he senses the left fielder is flagging, even as the man keeps pushing to stay in step. That Greg can best the star in this one thing gives him a small surge of pride, but he pushes it back down. Today's gift is the time with Goodyear. He's known to be a solitary creature, superstitious about routines and rituals. Everyone in the clubhouse knows it's best not to interrupt, not to invade his personal space. Trey Townsend was let inside just a bit; they spent some time one-on-one. But Trey's gone now, already in Florida, settling in with the Braves after a trade absolutely no one saw coming. "I'm cool to turn around whenever."

"Good." The men stop, about-face, begin running again.

A few miles back toward the stadium, Jason points left. "I'm going this way."

Greg says he's happy to follow, thinking he'll do anything to extend their time together—as if proximity will make him a better ballplayer. Jason looks him up and down and nods. Not a yes, but not a no.

With that, Jason turns off the arroyo path and onto an arterial, the sunbaked sidewalk shimmering with heat. Some cars honk as they pass—because they recognize Jason? Or because they are two fit men, shirtless and glistening, running down the midday street? Jimmy, always a few hours away from a conquest, has been telling Greg about the women of Scottsdale, how they are all hungry for spring training and the young men who descend on the retirement town. *Like cougars, they spring*—that's what Jimmy'd said.

Jason's route loops them east, past a sign welcoming them to Pima-Maricopa land. They overshoot the stadium, the hulking casino the only thing between them and the mountains. Instead of turning back toward the field, Goodyear turns toward the casino.

"Where we going, Goody?"

The left fielder nods at the casino. "Five bucks says he's going to go eight innings. You in any rush to get back?"

Greg can't bear to think about what's happening back at Salt River, how well Vásquez is likely pitching. He is in no hurry to see that. "Lead the way."

At the casino's entryway, Jason tugs his soaked shirt from his waistband and pulls it over his head. Greg does the same, though the cut-up T-shirt hardly seems appropriate. "If anybody asks, we weren't here," Jason says as the automatic doors whoosh open.

The afternoon crowd's mostly blue-hairs at the penny slots, a few retirees playing hands of poker, one guy shooting at the craps table. Jason scoots between the felt tables and rows of chirping slots—it's all Greg can do to trail him—and bellies up to the count room window. He speaks to the teller and comes back with ten chips in his palm, a shit-eating grin on his face.

"What do you think?" he asks Greg, his voice buoyant. "I'm thinking blackjack."

Greg isn't thinking anything about what card table to pick. He's thinking those chips are thousand-dollar ones. Where did all that cash come from? Does Goody keep ten grand in his sock? He's got a good contract, one of the best in the league, but—

Jason steps up to a table and lays down two chips. "Two hands, buddy." The dealer nods, reaches for a chip of his own.

"Oh, I don't play." Greg is close at Jason's shoulder, worried that if he blinks he might lose the left fielder in the sea of tables and tourists, the scantily clad cocktail waitresses and the spinning roulette wheels.

"Who said you did? These are for me." Jason rolls his shoulders inward, toward the cards. He looks at his hands, says something to the dealer. He busts on one hand; the house beats the other. Jason lays down another pair of chips. "Let's try that again."

$$\diamond$$

After Jason burns through his initial ten he gets ten more. He wins a hand, finally. A pretty cocktail waitress, her bangs teased two inches, asks them what they're drinking. "Gatorade?" Greg says.

That gets a laugh from the table, a back slap from Jason. She brings him a club soda with lime. Greg's still sweating but feeling frozen in the AC, disoriented by the fact they went from a bright afternoon to this dim and clattering room, where it could be 2:00 p.m. or 2:00 a.m.

When Jason is up to thirty, they wander from blackjack to poker. The left fielder quickly loses all he's gained on a hand of Hold'em with a gray-haired cowboy (his two-pound belt buckle and a ten-gallon hat making Greg, his sweaty clothes now stiff with salt, feel underdressed all over again). At that, the outfielder stands up and says, "Good game, sir. Carve, should we head back to the stadium?" Greg nods, though he hardly understands why Jason is so damn chipper. Thirty thousand is what Greg earns for a whole season in Salt Lake.

They jog through the parking lot, over a short bridge that spans a drainage canal, and onto the Salt River lot. Goodyear picks up his pace, nearly sprinting between practice fields. A few fans taking smoke breaks squeal when they see Jason Goodyear approach the players' entrance, his pumping arms and perfect form, his skin glistening. No one calls out for Greg, thundering down the sidewalk a few steps behind. Inside, the clubhouse TV says it's the ninth inning and Vásquez is still on the mound. Goodyear raises his eyebrows and Greg curses under his breath.

Jason turns and says, "Looks like I owe you a five spot. And remember, we just went for a run." He slaps Greg's back again, but closer to his shoulder, and it sends shots of pain down his arm. He'd nearly forgotten about his surgery, had not thought of his arm since that first whoosh of cold casino air.

Vásquez finishes the game while Greg's rinsing off; he can hear hooting and hollering over the sound of water splashing on tile. When he comes out the locker room's abuzz: complete game shutout. Dorsey never keeps a starter in for the whole game in spring training, but today he did, just to see. The players are whooping, hooting for Vásquez, who is quiet but smiling in front of his locker. Jimmy throws a towel around Vásquez's hips, shimmies it around his ass like he's polishing a bowling ball. Greg gets dressed as fast as he can and speeds back to the hotel, swallowing a pill just as soon as he steps into his room.

◇

The doctor gave him Vicodin, with the standard warning of moderation. *As needed.* But when Greg was supposed to taper— when the *pain* was supposed to taper and it didn't, just kept on pulsing from his fingertips to his neck—he continued with the pills, doubling doses as often as he could without raising suspicions. It's not Greg's fault the doc left his script pads around the office like they were Post-its, that his 30s could become 90s pretty damn easy, that the lady pharmacist thought Greg was some sort of famous coming in to the Walgreens with his team scripts.

He blacked out on the pills. Or grayed out, maybe—it was hard to describe the sensation. Lost time, in any case, three hours or four per pill, though the blank spots hardly seemed to matter through that endless recovery. There was always another physical therapy appointment, always more stretches to do in his parents' basement. The same sitcoms on TV in the living room, the same restless nights.

From the outside, things looked fine. After that first year of conditioning, he was finally able to throw again. Started with easy, slow tosses. So many pitches thrown at a rubber bull's-eye, counting the strikes. Strength came back, velocity, accuracy. Even Coach Stu thought he'd healed up well. *Looking good, kid*—that's what he'd said at the end of the first day of pitchers' and catchers' practice. Like he'd finally done something right.

Greg is scared to bring it up with his doctors, but he's done enough trawling through WebMD to have an educated guess of what happened. Something went sideways on the first surgery, a clipped nerve or scar tissue. Something. If Greg mentions it now, explains that it feels like he's sticking his elbow in an electrical socket every time he pitches, the doctors would want to take a look. And not just look: they'd have to go back in, root around, snip and tuck and hope they fix it right. If they made another mistake, even a tiny one, the Internet says he could lose all feeling in his arm—fingers, too. Something about how the nerves are bundled. How is he supposed to pitch if he can't feel his thumb? At least now he can throw, even if it hurts like a mother.

A second surgery, recovery time, would be another four months. Practically the whole damn season on the bench, and *then* his rehab assignment. Fuck that. Greg took two pills before his last start and couldn't remember a pitch of it, but Jimmy said he's throwing faster than ever.

◇

A bright, buzzing liquor store. Greg's at the counter with a basket full of cheap champagne. The man with a scar on his cheek brings his basket up to the front—light beer with mountains on it—and pays for both of their lots with a credit card that says JAMES CARDOZO.

Greg picks up and palms a muddy, familiar ball. *Jimmy.* He knows Jimmy. Jimmy is his best friend. Jimmy is the catcher for the Salt Lake Stallions. No, the Los Angeles Lions. Jimmy is wearing a ball cap that says as much. "I got it." Jimmy gives the cashier a credit card, signs a slip. "Thanks for picking up the tab at that last place."

Greg has no recollection of the last place, but he realizes that along with the fuzz of the vikings, he's wobbly with booze. He straightens up, tries to ignore the swimming corners of his vision. "No problem."

There is a beat-up convertible in the lot, two women waiting in it. They wave at Greg and Jimmy; the one with brown hair blows a kiss. Jimmy blows one back. "Who are those women?" Greg says under his breath. They look familiar, but he's not sure if it's because he's seen them before or because they look like every dolled-up divorcée in this town.

"Dibs on the brunette," Jimmy says. "Joanne, right?"

"Hell if I know." According to Jimmy, the trophy wives want trophies, too—though these women look too rough around the edges to be anyone's stay-at-home. Pretty, though.

They follow the convertible through the nighttime streets, Jimmy driving, Greg hanging out the window, hoping the fresh air will blow away his fog. And it does, somewhat: Joanne and Tami, those are their names. They'd been sitting on a bench near the players' lot, Joanne saying something sharp and flirty, Jimmy snapping right back with a humdinger. Jimmy: unless he's due on the field, he's always down to meet a lady. They'd gone for drinks at the casino, some lounge with a happy hour fit for a minor leaguer. The whole time there, swilling their vodka sodas, Greg had been convinced he'd run into Jason, and he looked for the left fielder's broad shoulders leaning over every card table. But they saw only Goslin, the wayward rookie, scurrying across the hotel lobby, pretending like he didn't know anyone. Oh, how Jimmy'd heckled, turned the rookie beet red. Jimmy also bought the kid beer, he said, kept him in six-packs, so there was no bad blood, not really.

The palms zip by like so many columns holding up the night. Did he tell the women about their long-distance run, Goody's midgame gamble? Greg had sworn up and down he'd say nothing, but now he can't remember if he'd kept his promise or not. As for the women, the blond one, Tami, knew everything about the team, and a damn lot about him, his surgery and his stats for the spring. Sorta creepy, but flattering, too, particularly after the year at home, feeling like the opposite of a professional ballplayer. Jimmy had so much to brag on, the one-hitter with Stan Rogers and Vásquez's complete game shutout being the most recent; it felt good to have Tami focused on him. He was wearing a long-sleeved shirt tonight, but the way she'd put her hand on his arm, gentle-like, a fingertip tracing the seam under the fabric, it's like she knew everything.

They trail the taillights past a stone sign that says SANDIA HILLS. The car stops just inside the gate, an imposing white-stucco pile.

The women unfold from the car. "This your place?" Jimmy asks them.

"I'm watching it for a friend," Tami says with a serious expression.

"But it's basically Tami's," Joanne adds. She's still making eyes at Jimmy as Tami unlocks the front door. The four step into a double-height foyer, cool terrazzo floors and a glittering, too-bright chandelier.

"Let's go in here." Tami leads them into the great room, soaring ceilings and a stone fireplace, no furniture except for a semicircle of camping chairs.

"Sorry about the furniture," Tami says. "I've just been waiting to find the *perfect* couch." She fishes a champagne out of Greg's bag, unwraps the foil, and pops the cork. It ricochets off the ceiling, just missing another gaudy light fixture. "But please, make yourselves at home."

Jimmy plops down in a chair and scoots it over to Joanne's side. "This is fine with me."

"Oh, sorry," Tami says when she realizes there are only three chairs, four of them. She looks at Greg. "I could've sworn I had another. I can—the patio?" She points toward the back of the house.

"Floor's fine," Greg says and eases himself onto the dusty hardwood. He winces.

"Have you ladies been watching Carve this spring? He threw a great game the other day." What game is he talking about? Greg wracks his brain. The Mariners? He threw five innings, maybe six. Did they win?

"Oh, yes," Tami says as she pours champagne into cups. The bubbles make Greg's head spin. Back when they were both Stallions, Jimmy and Greg did more than a bit of womanizing together, prowling bars in road towns, finding pretty women and following them home—anywhere was an improvement on the team hotel. They found their way into plenty of strange situations, too. But this all-but-empty house, these two women, fifteen, twenty years older than them—this takes some sort of cake.

"How did you get your scar?" Joanne breaks the silence. Greg is ready to answer, but she is looking at Jimmy, at the faint lightning bolt down his cheek.

"Everyone assumes I got a bat to the face. Catcher's prerogative, right?" The women nod, and Jimmy shakes his head. "Mom's boyfriend had a Doberman. I hated that guy from the start.

"But mine's nothing," Jimmy continues. "Wanna see something cool?" He leans out of his chair and grabs Greg's wrist, lifting it like a prizefighter's. A sharp pain pops to the surface. Jimmy doesn't notice Greg's shudder, but Tami does, and she raises an eyebrow at him as Jimmy pushes down the sleeve. "Check out *that* battle scar." Jimmy smiles.

Both women lean in to peer at the six-inch incision along the inside of his elbow. Tami's eyes go wide. "I've never seen a Tommy John up close."

"He's good as new," Jimmy continues. "Procedure's no big deal, tons of pitchers have it nowadays."

Greg wiggles out of Jimmy's grip. "Slow recovery, though," Jimmy says. "This fuck's been coming back for a year. Over a year. Pretty shitty, huh?"

Neither woman replies, but Greg can see something on their faces, like they know what a year can mean. He excuses himself, finds the bathroom, and swallows another pill.

◇

Jimmy wakes him with a shake and a whisper, the catcher's breath warm and sharp near his cheek. He is in jeans and socks, his shirt still balled up in one fist and his shoes hanging by their laces in the other. "Carve, we gotta go. Say bye to the bird."

Greg looks at Tami, her forehead smooth with sleep. He can't remember what they talked about last night, but he has the sense he fell asleep reassured—and not just from the release of sex. He does remember that, at least snaps of it: her naked body, the tan skin of her legs gone a bit loose with age. Her breasts, still round, the nipples big and hard as leather. Had she said her ex was a pitcher? That she knew someone who came back from surgery? He can't remember. Greg steps into his jeans, grabs his wadded-up clothes, and follows Jimmy out of the house, both men dressing as they go.

"Damn," Jimmy says, hustling to his car. "I sure hope we're not late for pregame. Gotta get you warmed up. You ready to start?"

The only thing Greg is ready to do is curl up into the fetal position, but he smiles wanly.

"Atta boy."

◇

Every throw hurts. It starts before the throw even, screaming when he lifts his arm up and back for the motion.

Jimmy holds up his palm, gets out of his crouch, and jogs over to the rubber. "You okay, Carve?"

"Just sore."

Jimmy gives the pitcher a hangdog look. "I am, too! Joanne kept me up half the night. How'd you make out, champ?"

"Fun time." Fun, if that's what it's called to burst into tears after sex, soaking some stranger's pillow. He remembers now— he'd actually said it, out loud: *My elbow's wrecked.* Tami, she'd just put her hand on his chest, right over his breastbone, and pressed. Hard but soft. That opened the floodgates.

"It's good to have you back." Jimmy grins. "Last season was no fun at all." Greg smiles, sort of, then says he's gonna take five.

Tomás Monterrey is in the clubhouse bathroom, standing at a urinal. He busted his wrist against the outfield wall two summers ago, and Greg is pretty certain he's got something. Might not be the same, but that hardly matters—he can't start the game feeling the way he feels, pain so sharp he might puke. And he can't tell Dorsey he's hurt, that'd be curtains—tomorrow's cut day, and as it is he's hanging on by a thread. "Tomás, hi," Greg says. He offers a hand, and then sees Tomas's hand is around his dick. Greg crosses his arms. "I'm Greg Carver, a pitcher with the Stallions? I mean, hopefully the Lions, but last time I—"

"I know who you are." Since they traded Townsend, Monterrey's been starting in center. Not exeptionally good at it, but not fucking up, either.

"Oh, good. Right. I wasn't sure, since I've been out—"

"What you want, Carver?" Monterrey looks annoyed and finishes pissing with an exasperated little shake.

"See, I'm starting today, and I'm out of, well—I'm looking for some vikings. I've got plenty more back at the hotel, but I'm starting in thirty. I'll get you back, plus some. Or cash. Whatever you need."

Monterrey zips himself up and disappears with a scowl. Greg hears a locker open, the rattle of pills in a bottle, the locker closing. Monterrey returns with two tiny white pellets in his palm. "You know what you're doing with these, man?"

"Yeah. Thanks. You're a lifesaver."

"Fifty bucks tomorrow," he says, glancing at Greg's scar. "And tomorrow's cut day, so make sure you get me my money before you go."

Greg wants to punch him, but someone else walks into the bathroom, clomping in his cleats. Jason Goodyear, unzipping as he walks. "Tomás, Carve," he nods to both, giving Greg a quick look like he knows everything, Greg's loose lips and the old broad and the half-abandoned house, the nerve damage that'll end his career, the pills clutched in his fist. Greg might know about the gambling, but the scales are impossibly tipped. Greg throws the pills into his mouth, swallows hard. "Absolutely, Tomás. Of course."

◇

Sinking into the pill while pitching is a strange sensation. In the first inning the pain dulls. A guy gets on base but no damage is done. In the second the ache in his arm slips away and he begins to float above himself, like he's a fan in the grandstand, watching the action on the field. Someone hits a ball to deep left, but Goodyear is there, waiting under it. He hardly has to step. And he throws back to the mound, a rocket. Greg feels that, the heat of the throw through the leather of his glove.

Two men out, a runner on first. The stadium is loud and the afternoon bright, but to Greg it's all muffled sound and hazy gray. He nods at the signal, pulls his arm back and snaps it forward, letting the ball fly. That release, and, a half second later, the slap of the ball in Jimmy's mitt: with that, Greg Carver is gone.

## SIXTH

And with the end of that brief, green promise came people. Players from Asia traveled across the Bering Strait, whole teams came charging down the West Coast, wearing fur-coat uniforms and carrying honking-big spears. What they found alongside the McDowell Mountains: mammoths in marshes, competition that proved to be as easy as a slow runner with a too-big lead off of first. Watch them dance, and then . . . *blam*. Sometimes, when I'm feeling sorry for myself, I think us old-timers must've looked not unlike those mammoths to the Internet-savvy newcomers, the guys who bought out the papers and speared all the union guys before anyone could turn their creaky old heads. Not that feeling sorry for yourself is any sort of productive, but the metaphor seems apt.

But the new team couldn't get too comfortable with that 1-0 advantage. Change was upon them, not fast but disconcertingly steady. It was in the warming air and the drying up of the new lakes—these in turn sent the megafauna packing north and farther north, past the Rockies and the Pacific Coast League, steady north till Aloysius Snuffleupagus and his kind ambled right off the edge of the world. Suddenly, the prehistoric humans couldn't find anybody to play them. Is that how Jason felt when he started plunking down $100,000 bets and the game went quiet? When he was the last one at the table, forty-eight mind-melting hours into a tournament? Poor Liana, her hair could've been on fire, and her husband wouldn't have looked up from the draw.

So he pulled a few hands of blackjack in the middle of the afternoon, what's the harm in that? He and Carver didn't have anything better to do. Sure, his competitive drive made him the best left fielder since Ted Williams, made him stick with Greg Carver on that run even when he was certain he was going to puke, made him the lead-by-example player the Lions needed in their clubhouse. But competitiveness isn't something you can turn on and off like a light switch. Hell, it doesn't even have a dimmer. And that same competitive drive that got him the Triple Crown in 2009 has taken him to the table more times than anyone can count. One source at the casino says he usually stays longer than they do, and they're holding down nine-hour shifts.

No one will go on the record yet, jittery as they are about their jobs, about staying in the good graces of one of the country's most famous men. Did you know that one of Jason's million-dollar nights could net a dealer a $100K tip? Fuck, I'd keep quiet, too. Folks I've spoken with can't say exactly how high he's gone (or how deep he's sunk), but they all remember seven-figure outings—*outings*, plural—Jason winning some of them but losing more often than not. One of the gals in the count room told me that two nights after he and Carver came in for their afternoon dalliance, the casino cut off his credit—nothing left in the linked accounts, less than nothing, the kind of overdraw that could get them in trouble with the gambling commission. Goody was mad for all of a day, huffing and puffing at the count girls and cursing out their boss, but he came back the next night with a pocket full of thousand-dollar chips. It's straight out of Dostoevsky, his doggedness.

No one has ever even seen him in the casino's sports book, and I can't find any record of him in an online fantasy league or any college hoops bracket. That's a relief. Things have changed since the time Mickey Mantle was suspended for "association with known gamblers"— A-Rod and his escorts, everything Jose Canseco ever did, the continuing tumble of Lenny Dykstra—but Rule 21, betting on baseball, will still lock you out of Cooperstown quick as a Stan Rogers fastball. In the commissioner's head, it's a slippery slope from gambling to cheating to self-destruction and the Black Sox, which will, in turn, lead to the all-out implosion of America's pastime. Suddenly, that mum's-the-word divorce is making a lot more sense. Liana might be mad as hell that Jason's picked poker over her, but she still doesn't want word of it getting back to league officials—that'd screw her alimony.

For now, let's stick with history and that ancient, adaptable team, because I know how *that* part goes: What do you do when the competition disappears? You find a new table; you play a new game. That ancient team, missing their mammoths, did the same: they sharpened their tools, aimed with better precision at new and smaller foes. The deer and rabbits proved to be worthy rivals, not much power but light on their feet, the kinds of guys you have to watch on the base path. It's still a living, playing the small game. Look at Pete Rose, for chrissake. He became the Hit King, all out of bloops and sprints and so many singles. Though bringing up Rose anywhere near Goodyear and gambling makes me squirm. Charlie Hustle knows plenty about Rule 21.

Look, I did it again. I'm trying to tell you about the ancient team, the men and women who would become the Hohokam, and I go off to left field. Okay, here's history: A bunch of drafts and vets and trades and called-up Triple-As stand on a field and examine their new configuration. (Their wives and girlfriends, sitting in the stands, do the same.) They've been playing for years, but never with these teammates, never with these game calls and strategies. Eventually, with the day in and day out of it, with the mistakes and corrections, they find a new type of cohesion, a coming together that feels good enough to be true. It happens to the Lions every spring, and as much could be said of the Lions' wives, that sisterhood forced and finessed until they become a unit, ready for the long season.

The ancient dwellers banded into clusters of floodwater farmers, roving at first but then setting up more permanent camps. They built houses on poles, clapped adobe around the buildings' sides like they were tarring their bats. Made pottery to hold their sunflower seeds and chew, etched seashells they brought home from the long road trips to Baja. Tied the shells on hide strings and hung them round their necks, tucked under their uniforms like a pitcher's lucky charm. Did they know the same shells were buried right below their feet? That this used to be an ocean?

Of course not. How could they? They were progressing just like the rest of us: one foot in front of the other. Or one pitch after another, in the case of the Lions. Or one party after another, in the case of the Lions' wives.

And they weren't calling themselves the Hohokam yet; that came later. After all, do you know what *Hohokam* means? *Those who have gone.*

But I'm getting ahead of myself again.

THE OUTFIELD

The baseball wives know you don't want to be the first to show up in Scottsdale, but surely you don't want to be the last to arrive at the party. And it *is* a party: luncheons and spa days, cocktails and color consultations, mornings at the furrier's and afternoons with the jeweler. There is a great deal of time between the rare preseason moments when they have their husbands' attention, their calls to duty. Those calls: To cheer him from the family section of the ballpark, loud enough that he might just look over. To get him steak on Sunday nights, to rub his feet on Wednesdays, to dangle—and deliver—a blowjob at the end of the week as reward for all his hard work. There are many ways to earn one's keep.

Spring is a sensitive time for the ballplayers, who are working out the kinks of their winters, proving themselves into pitching rotations or fighting to keep themselves in starting lineups, competing against younger knees, quicker bats, unmarried men.

They need their support network, the rooting of their *numero uno* cheerleader. The baseball wives know to stay out from underfoot, to not complain when pitchers and catchers report to camp on Valentine's Day (again), to not ask about where their husbands go until four in the morning on the nights before cut days, to not complain when they aren't taken out to brunch even *once* in the month of March. It's a sacrifice, what the wives do, uprooting their lives from the Southern California desert to the central Arizona one, leaving the kids with their mothers-in-law or the well-vetted help for a few days, a few weeks, a month or two. And in this sacrifice they need one another, and so they make their own support network of domestic partners to these improbable, impressive men. Now, their lives are improbable and impressive, too. Imagine, getting plucked out of a crowded bar or chosen through a professional sports matchmaking service, being picked up on the beach in Puerto Rico or selected from the Los Angeles Lakers' Laker Girls lineup. Imagine, some handsome—or at least talented—man saying, *Now, here, this is your new life.* It is strange, indeed, and theirs is a necessary sorority.

Those who don't come to Arizona at all—not even for ten days, a few long weekends, maybe a three-day stint in February and another in March—those who *can't possibly manage* to get over from L.A., who miss the whole damn party: highly suspect. Jane Rogers, for instance, the Lions' ace's wife, was absent last year, and her appearance this year is looking doubtful. The baseball wives can't imagine it, how a woman could manage the six-month season without the preseason legwork. It's like going to the beach without tanning beforehand. A bed, spray-on, that bronzing cream. *Something.* Make some sort of effort. If you don't, you'll stick out like a sore thumb—and you'll get burned, red as a lobster. The wives are already striking Jane from their Memorial Day and July Fourth barbecue lists, uninviting her

fifteen-year-old daughter from the yet-to-be-planned pool parties. Melissa Moyers, who has been doing this the longest—her
husband, Hal, has pitched in the majors for nineteen years,
twelve of those with the Lions, and is, if not the best on the
squad, then at least, and most definitely, the oldest—once put it
well: *Play nice or we'll throw you out of the park.*

◇

The baseball wives know it's best if you call ahead, tell the people who take care of things you are coming. Give them a week.
They have services for this, not just for the baseball wives but
for all the wealthy part-time residents of Scottsdale, Arizona.
There are crews with Windex and Lysol and rubber gloves and
an endless supply of garbage bags, because it doesn't matter
how clean the wives left things, their homes will be dirty. The
autumn sandstorms, those funny-sounding haboobs, get grit
everywhere, even under the lips of the rubber-sealed, triple-
pane, energy-efficient windows. So over the phone the baseball
wives explain where their hide-a-keys are (of course they have
one—for the pool guy, for the maid, for the florist—hidden very
discreetly, no one would *ever* guess to look under the potted
Christmas cactus to the right of the door), tell them to let themselves in. No reason the year's first impression of Arizona should
be a dead mouse on the kitchen floor. No reason their husbands'
white-shirted elbows should get gunked up from resting on the
kitchen counter, the counter covered in dust the exact same
color as the imported stone. *How was I supposed to see that?*
is not a good excuse. There is no acceptable excuse, in fact, for
anything less than immaculate.

　　The cleaners throw away the shriveled cacti the wives forgot to put on the back patio for the yard men; after several
months without water, none at all, the plants look like a line

of sad-old-man penises, spikes sunk in on themselves. The top companies will replace the cacti, returning them to bright green sheaths, erect and pointing and so similar-looking to the originals that no one—not the wives, not their oblivious husbands—knows a thing of their suffering.

Someone will need to run the water, flush the toilets, start the cars—things husbands might do under other circumstances, but the baseball wives know not to ask, not in spring. There will be hiccups in these systems: coughing pipes, murky tanks, engines sputtering as they try to draw from hibernating batteries. Ideally, the advance crew can handle these jobs, too. *More legs, less legwork*, the wives like to say. Last year, feeling independent, Eliza Summers tried to jump her car herself and got second-degree burns on both palms. Better her than her husband, Melissa Moyers pointed out. He's the best the Lions have in middle relief.

◇

The baseball wives, even hapless Lisa Putney, know not to let their husbands manage real-estate acquisition; a ballplayer would pick a house with two bedrooms, half a kitchen, and an entertainment room the size of an elementary school auditorium. That would be the first place they'd furnish, too, chockfull of leather recliners, arranged in a semicircle around a TV screen the size of a California king bedsheet. Men, it seems, are happy to eat off paper plates while standing at the kitchen counter, don't see the point of headboards, and think they're doing well if their clothes are in *folded* piles. Some of these men would be fine to stay in hotels or short-term rentals, the way they did when they were just coming up, when they didn't think anything was wrong with hotels or short-term rentals or being single. But the wives insist they *must* own; what would people think if they were the only ones still renting? And so they buy, $1 million homes, $5 million villas, Southwest estates in the low eight figures.

A lesson to them all came at Jane Rogers's expense: she let Stan pick out their Arizona place, and he bought a man cave with two and a half bathrooms attached. His was a quick trade from Pittsburgh, and the family was scrambling to set up two new homes and sell two others. *I have my hands full with L.A.,* she'd rationalized when Melissa Moyers called to introduce herself and offer help, *and Stan refuses to stay at a hotel unless he's on the road. I told him to get whatever.* Jane was overwhelmed by finding a year-round home, getting her kids, then six and thirteen, into the right schools during the awkward, midyear move. *It'd be easier if I could just give someone a big envelope of unmarked bills*, she'd said, her Nashville accent turning some words short, stretching others long. *Ease-yer, on-vell-ope, bee-yalls.* How peculiar, Melissa had thought but did not say. She had also thought: You can. Her kids had done fine, switching into L.A.'s top prep school the week after Hal was traded. *Donation*, that's what they call the grease on the wheels. *Charitable contribution.*

It's not like they'd had roots in Pennsylvania, Jane had continued; they hated the place, nearly everything except for those neat Carnegie museums—her little boy loved the dinos. If it were up to her, they'd be back in Tennessee somewhere—she was from Franklin, she and Stan had been sweethearts at Vandy—but the closest major league teams were St. Louis and Cincinnati, and who wanted to live there? Melissa clucked in agreement but wondered how much longer this woman would ramble. Jane was lonely, Melissa impatient, and the difference in the two women's frequencies set the line humming and popping.

Later that first spring, Jane visited Arizona long enough to order the kids' beds and a dining room set. She also acquiesced to an afternoon out with the wives: a strained lunch and then a game her husband started, Jane clapping politely after every single strike. Melissa treated Jane to the meal and cheered when Stan Rogers made his outs, even as she resented each one. The team has room for only one ace, and the Lions' had been Hal, with his beguiling curve, his impossible stamina, his conveyor-belt consistency. What he lacked in speed, Hal Moyers made up for in wiles. ("The Trickster," players called him in the dugout; "my trickster," Melissa called him in bed.) Melissa knew the team would still play well behind her husband, but there's a special oomph the team makes for the number one in the rotation. Because every team wants a guy with twenty wins and an ERA under three. Jane was unconscious of the conflict, all the way through air kisses at the airport. Then, not even a thank-you note. Save for a couple of home-game starts, Melissa has hardly seen her since.

The rest of the baseball wives, those who took more care with their real-estate acquisitions, they *love* their Arizona houses. Melissa Moyers has twenty thousand square feet. Lisa Putney sprang for the Italianate countertops in the kitchen but also in each of her five bathrooms. For some, if they're being honest, Scottsdale is their first-choice residence. Sure, there's the cache of Malibu, the glint of Hollywood celebrity, but they prefer the clear desert sky to the gritty sunsets of Los Angeles. In L.A., they have to compete with basketball and hockey wives, the Dodgers *and* the Angels, Hollywood execs and Japanese tourists just to make a reservation for dinner. The pro-Arizona subset comes to visit for a week or two in October, maybe the month of November. Just for the change of pace. If there are no kids or if the kids are away (in Melissa's case, one's already in college, a fact she doesn't like to admit because it makes her feel *o-l-d*; the other two are so programmed in their extra-curriculars she's lucky to get two meals with them all week), the trip's an easy midweek jet or a leisurely drive through the desert. Sure, Phoenix is sprawling, but compared with L.A., Scottsdale is a dense nugget of goodness. The wives are perched close to the edge of civilization—five minutes from the south entrance to the preserve—but downtown Scottsdale (everything from the dry cleaner to the gym to Terrazzo, the poolside dance club that is *good enough*, now that they're married and just flirting) is fifteen via their preferred livery. They love their Arizona cars, champagne-colored Lexus SUVs and shiny black Bimmers, but there's no reason to look for parking downtown, to risk driving drunk (Melissa got caught once, in 2005, eighteen months' probation, and it was a cautionary tale to them all), when their sometimes drivers are a text message away. They can even pick their preference: Lincoln Town Cars, Cadillac Escalades, stretch Hummers. Their usual Friday night driver, Anton, a chatty transplant from Venezuela, said the service had had a traditional limousine, but they'd put it out to pasture—sold it to a funeral home in Mesa—because no one ever asked for it.

◇

For another subset of women, Scottsdale is their *only* residence, the second home they got in the divorce. And here is a tricky thing for baseball wives: ex–baseball wives. They are still baseball wives, having endured minor league ball and the onerous winters with husbands underfoot like overgrown teenagers. The exes are still friends to the current baseball wives, having listened to their gripes, having griped themselves. Together, these women have bought vibrators to keep them company when their husbands were on the road and sexy lingerie to entice their husbands upon return. These women know too much *not* to be friends. And the baseball wives—as much as they'd like to deny it—have some niggling, just a teensy hint of fear, that at any point, they, too, could become ex–baseball wives. Melissa almost lost Hal once, during their last season in Boston, to a kinesthesiology intern from Harvard; she caught him fooling around again, a few springs ago, with some sun-stroked harpy named Tamara. More than one of the current wives have broken up perfectly healthy marriages, severing a ballplayer's ties to his high school sweetheart or the patient woman who slogged through the farm system. *That bitch*, the baseball wives mutter when a cleat chaser usurps a friend's position. *It's the circle of life*, the baseball wives explain when a woman they like more replaces one they like less. This uncertainty, the either-way of it— the baseball wives know it also means, *It could happen to me*.

◇

Liana Goodyear, the former wife of Jason Goodyear, is a perfect example of this treacherous territory—not of the cheating and stealing, but of the problem associated with the divorce. Jason, handsome enough to contend for Sexiest Man in America, clean-cut enough to be, rumor had it, in development talks with Disney, had two American League MVP awards and nary a smear on his rap sheet when he plucked this elementary school teacher out of thin air. Whirlwind courtship, a family-only wedding in an undisclosed location. And just like that, one of the country's most eligible bachelors was off the market. Liana quit working and did her best at all the baseball wife duties: attending games, keeping house, befriending the other baseball wives.

They were married for a scant two seasons. Official word was *mutual consent*, the split called *amicable*, but to most baseball wives, it seemed too clean a break. Was he having an affair? Trouble in bed? The media pushed hypotheses—this was one of *People*'s sexiest people of 2009, after all, of course there would be gossip—but the ex-couple stayed mum. The baseball wives were stuck in the same dark room as the *Enquirer*. The wives knew Jason moved out and that Liana had kept the Arizona house; Maggie'd run into Liana at the shopping center and gleaned as much. Liana told Maggie she didn't know where Jason was staying for the spring. *Don't care*, she added with a toss of her blond hair, like that line could hold any water at all. And for some inexplicable reason, she'd gone back to work. *First grade*, she said, smiling as if she *liked* all those snot-nosed kids and their germs climbing on her five days a week. And public school! When Maggie told Melissa that, the older woman gasped.

*She took him to the cleaners*, the women whisper, and he gladly consented to be scrubbed, soaped, and tumble-dried, conceding much more than their prenup had outlined. By the second week of spring rumor had it he was *broke*, as impossible as that seems. Where could all of that money have gone? None of the wives can get any more information out of their husbands; if they broach the subject the men get stern-faced and say, *Leave him be*. It's like they all caught the outfielder's stiff-lippedness, his reticence.

Over weekday mimosas (without children around, the wives enjoy day drinking), they continue to weigh the possibilities: that he is gay, that she is gay, that they realized they are distant cousins. It is complicated by the fact that no one *really* knows Goodyear. On the field, in the dugout, he's the strong, silent type, more desperado than amigo, his entire game day replete with routine and superstitious traditions that no one dare interrupt. And he'd never once been out with Liana, never had them to his home. Being private is one thing, but the baseball wives—they're practically family. Is he too good for them? Lisa mentions the wives' reputation for opulence, for having wild nights; maybe, she gingerly suggests, he is trying to stay away from compromising situations. There are commercials to consider. Shoe deals. "I heard he just signed with Nike."

Melissa glares across the table. "There's more than one reason a man will keep his nose clean," she says. "Sponsorship opportunities, sure." Her husband, surly on the mound and haggard-looking even after a good night's rest, has done very few corporate promotions over the years, while Jason's face is plastered everywhere. If she's being honest with herself, Melissa will admit it is brilliant brand-building—Herb Allison has always been good at that. For now she holds up a pinkie. "But maybe he has a *little* something to hide? That'd explain his holier-than-thou behavior—and the divorce."

The women cackle at that.

◇

After Christmas break, in a classroom across town, Liana—she kept Goodyear, of course, what baseball wife wouldn't take and keep her husband's famous name?—drilled her students on subtraction and looked forward to the spring arrivals, promising herself she would try doubly hard to reconnect, to preserve all those meaningful friendships she'd built with cheerleaders and waitresses and art historians, women who have nothing in common except for their men.

Jason had preferred she socialize *out* of the house, so an appropriate fuck-you was to throw a welcome-back cocktail party the first Saturday of the spring season in their home. Her home. And the baseball wives came in droves, the Lions' but some other teams', too, even a few other exes, a pair of retirees (skinnier than ever, their faces stiff with Botox), and, somehow, two women who both claimed to be Jimmy Cardozo's recently exed girlfriend. Hillary Oliveira worried there would be a catfight between them, but Melissa sized up the two women, watching how they watched each other, and shook her head. *Nah, they'll be fine.*

It was a stellar party—Liana'd invited a midlevel celebrity chef to make the finger foods, a locally revered mixologist to man the bar—and everyone was excited to catch up. The wives doted on Liana. *How* are *you doing?* She was fine, she said with the tone of an aggrieved and regal widow. She was getting by. If anything, Melissa noticed, Liana was more beautiful than when she'd first appeared in the family section, her blond ponytail pulled through the back of one of those snap-back ball caps; more beautiful than when she and Jason were married in a secret ceremony in Hawaii. (Melissa bought *Star* that week and examined the grainy clandestine photos in her bathtub.)

*Are you dating again?* Hillary asked.

Liana shrugged, bare shoulders as wide and polished as a wooden coatrack. She'd played beach volleyball for Arizona State; apparently got as far as the Olympic trials for 2004. *Oh, you know.*

Melissa, overhearing this conversation from the charcuterie station, did *not* know, but she clutched her drink tighter, letting it slosh around the rim. She would never admit it, not to anyone (the *Star* went into the recycling before the tub had emptied), but Liana's casual laugh, her shrug: it scared her. She knew she should feel sorry for this woman, but she saw only a threat. Melissa drained her Cosmo and went in search of another.

The next day, the wives were at Pilates, inverted and scheming a lingerie party. *Should we invite Liana?* Hillary asked, her head between her knees, her ass wrapped in hot-pink spandex.

Melissa has a formula, a computation for how often the still-pretty exes should be invited to things with the active baseball wives. She did the math in her head, then reached for her toes. This was before she'd seen the news, his picture plastered on the local paper—*Bad night for Goodyear*. Her phone was on silent; she hooked her fingers around her toes. *Mmm, let's not.*

◇

The current wives sit together in the family section, behind the Lions dugout. Week one they all observed the men, swinging in the on-deck circle, thinking about how much weight the athletes had gained, how much time it might take to work it off. They remarked on the bachelors, the untaken ones, guessing at who would be the next to go. They examined their own husbands, wondered if they still appeared hunky in those stirruped pants. And, surreptitiously, they watched one another, to see who had puffed up or slimmed down, who had surgery or dye jobs or gotten prominent new jewelry. Hillary Oliveira's boobs kept getting bigger, and Maggie Monterrey was wearing diamond earrings, each bauble the size of a baby's fist. Melissa Moyers's forehead was stiff, the telltale sign of a recent injection.

Week two all anyone could talk about was Jason Goodyear. Not the divorce, though everyone had thoughts on Liana and her show-off party. No, the wives were abuzz about Jason's arrest, the cleat chaser who nearly got him thrown in jail, her harebrained scheme to break into Taliesin West. What was he thinking? It just sounded *too* crazy. The wives watched the other men play, of course, but whenever a ball sailed into the outfield, whenever Jason was on deck or on base or even watching play over the lip of the dugout, they were observing him, scanning for cracks or mars, tics or troubles. Did they spot anything? Hard to say: He dropped a fly ball on the warning track—not the sort of mistake he made—but it was an impossibly hot afternoon game, the angle of the sun all wrong. He struck out swinging twice—also unlike him—but maybe he was just rusty. He threw a rocket from deep left to second, and instead of reaching Putney standing on base, it beaned the runner, who cursed so loud it could be heard on the radio broadcast. Each mistake was, on its own, tiny—not necessarily even an error—but did it add up to something more?

Week three there is a new girl, the young Dominican pitcher's wife, sitting in the row behind them. *Vásquez*, that's his name. *Victor Vásquez.* She has the smooth face of a teenager, and beautiful amber eyes, giant like a kewpie's. A small child sits on her lap—presumably the pitcher's son—and his round face makes their mouths water and coo. They all love babies, the fat little limbs and gurgling lips, the peach-fuzz hair and plum-dust skin. But Melissa Moyers does not coo. Instead her eyes go back to the woman—the *girl*; she looks younger than Melissa's oldest, and may well be. Her small body is somehow tight and curvy all at once; it is hard to imagine this butterball emerging from her belly just eight or nine months ago. The only point Melissa sees to the contrary: the girl's milk-swollen breasts are huge, bigger than Hillary's, bigger than Melissa's and Lisa's combined. Her chest might topple her were she to forget her continued effort at uprightness, her determination to keep her shoulders up and back. Melissa gives her a tight-lipped smile.

When the baseball wives are not looking, the squirming baby reaches down for the bright chains around the women's necks, for strands of their shiny hair, for their smooth shoulders.

"Hijo, no." The girl pulls her child's hand back. "No toques." The fatness of the baby, versus the slightness, the wide-eyed naïveté of the girl in her artfully distressed jeans and bright sneakers and brand-new Lions T-shirt: the two seem evenly matched, like the baby might even win.

Who brings their children out? the baseball wives wonder, whisper among themselves when the girl excuses herself to go feed the fussy child. The baseball wives miss their children, but they know better than to bring them here. The baby's mewling is a distraction, unnecessary, and they think of the girl in the dingy stadium restroom, swaying with her child at her breast. How hard it would be to attend to their husbands' needs—never mind going out with the other wives—if they had children on their hips. Doesn't she know about nannies? Mothers-in-law?

Vásquez, the team's young prospect, has thrown four innings with two hits, two walks, and seven strikeouts. Another batter swings through three. The young woman, back from wherever she went, claps the baby's hands within her own, and the baby squeals. "Mira, tu padre," she says into the child's ear.

Really, Melissa thinks. She has borne three children, had them each weaned by nine months and in a nanny's arms at nine months and a day. The oldest is away at college, the younger two, a boy and a girl, each have a driver to get them to and from their many activities. Baseball for the boy, of course; Japanese lessons, too, in case he's not good enough to make it in the majors (it was the boy's idea to be so pragmatic). Soccer and violin for the girl, a quiet child who doesn't seem to like Melissa very much. *We're too old for nannies*, they'd complained when they started middle school, and she'd agreed, at least to such an extent that she hired male nannies who didn't mind wearing a driver's coat and hat. The boy is now old enough to drive himself but says he prefers their current arrangement.

◇

The wives are gathered on the patio of the place they eat lunch on Wednesdays in spring, a nouveau Italian joint in Old Town, when one of the wives, Eliza Summers—wife of Nick, middle relief—encourages them to "do something." They do plenty, they say, swirling their white wines. Their calendars are full, they add, thumbing through their annotated phones as proof. Charity luncheons. Museum fundraisers. The PTA (even if they miss a few meetings). They join their husbands at charity events, go to others in their husbands' steads, have philanthropic causes of their own. Not in Arizona, mind. This is a break, a whole state free of benefit committees and donation envelopes.

But Eliza, a former staffer for Los Angeles mayor Antonio Villaraigosa (she met her husband at a golf fund-raiser), has brochures, has mailing lists, has buttons with the tiny, laminated face of Candice "Candy" Hill, a candidate for Phoenix mayor. Eliza fans literature over the white tablecloth, plunks down a button by each woman's spoon. I WANT CANDY! the buttons proclaim. The wives frown, the wives scrunch their noses.

"Really?" Melissa arches her eyebrows up (the Botox has loosened).

"She's for women," Eliza explains. "And the incumbent is a real—"

"But we don't even vote in Arizona," Maggie points out. "We don't live here, remember?"

Eliza doesn't care. "California is as blue as the Dodgers, and Antonio has our interests in mind. He doesn't need our help. Arizona does. Candy does."

She says each woman can contribute up to $2,500.

"Twenty-five!" Maggie squawks, sloshing her sauvignon. "That's a fur coat." All year, the women look forward to visiting Evans Furs & Leathers. Better stock, more colors and cuts, lower prices than anywhere in L.A.

Melissa fumes. It is an unwritten rule: this place is off-limits to the shilling they are so accustomed to in the rest of their lives, the wives swapping thousand-dollar-a-head dinner tickets like so many trading cards. She spends what feels like sixty weeks a year doing philanthropic work in Los Angeles: underprivileged boys, at-risk girls, public education, and landscape preservation. She can't, she *won't*, break the seal on this, an untainted place, a place where money is still hers to spend as she pleases. She stabs at her lettuce. She will *not* get involved.

"It's eighty degrees," Eliza says. "Ethical considerations aside, once global warming kicks in we won't need furs. We'll need rights, as women. We need the right to choose, to decent child care, to reproductive health, to—"

"It gets cold at night," Melissa counters, thinking about how Eliza's husband pitches middle relief, how he's not even that good. "You have to be prepared for that, too."

"Just take the brochure, okay?"

The baseball wives slip the brochures and buttons into their handbags and finish their meal in strained silence. At the end of the lunch, everyone takes one bite of the shared tiramisu and then they drive, all in a row, toward the stadium. Their husbands are playing at 1:35, and they'll be fashionably late.

◇

It's part of the life: baseball wives get traded away, to seasons in Baltimore or Chicago, to springs in the Grapefruit League, Sarasota or Clearwater or Vero Beach. These women are like friends from summer camp—rambunctious, beautiful girls who were briefly the most important people in the world but are now remembered in dull colors and with vague edges. With some cajoling, two come to visit—one wife now with the Phillies, one a Devil Ray. The women hitch a ride from Tampa in a chartered jet, and the Sky Harbor reunion is a swirl of squealing, the excited tap-tap of stiletto sandals, and the whoosh of billowy fabrics going in for bear hugs. The visitors will stay with Melissa; her house is the biggest by a long shot.

The Floridians have scant interest in the Thursday-night interleague matchup, so the baseball wives skip their husbands' game and go to Old Town. A nice sushi dinner, plenty of sake, and then they sway over to Bloom. The wives stay out until three, flirting with the handsome strangers who slide in and out of their expansive booth. The ladies, in their ad hoc batting order—and with plenty of champagne to fuel their night—swing in turn. Maggie gets the number of a heart surgeon, Melissa lectures a recent grad on his career prospects in the field of physical therapy (she is an expert, as her husband underwent shoulder surgery two winters ago and has made a complete recovery), and Hillary puts her hand on a stranger's thigh. When they are done, the bill for the champagne is approximately $2,000. Feeling generous after a washroom encounter with a retired point guard from the Phoenix Suns, the visiting, soon-to-be-ex-wife of the Rays' third baseman picks up the check, leaving, with gratuity, $2,400.

Elsewhere, Cecilia Vásquez watches her husband throw against the Giants. Her baby, swaddled in blankets and more blankets against the desert evening's chill, sleeps soundly in his carrier, occupying a seat just below her. That row, usually reserved for the more senior baseball wives, a line of skinny white women with too much makeup and fake-looking hair, is empty.

"C'mon, Jimmy!" Another girl moves down from somewhere higher in the stadium to occupy one of these empty seats. She seems to be clapping for the catcher, who, with no one on base, is lazily returning the ball to the mound with a loose, arcing lob. The girl eyes the baby. "Cute kid," she says and glances back at Cecilia. "Is it yours?"

◇

Even though the lingerie party was Melissa's idea, Maggie will host it—she is eager to show off her new twelve-person sectional. They pick March 19, the Saturday of the weekend the team is down in Tucson. *Don't bother coming*, the wives know their husbands would say. *Long drive for nothing much.* The wives also know that part: it's a town where you're lucky to find a Starbucks, much less a decent kale Caesar. But it's near enough to the end of the spring season—twelve more days—that the wives stand a fair chance of seeing their husbands relatively soon, and the lingerie could be useful. Even if it's just for an hour or two between the end of spring training and the start of the regular season: they want to be prepared.

Melissa and Maggie talk to the buyer from Neiman's and arrange for teddies and push-up bras and panties in bright silks. A trunk show, of sorts.

"Sizes?" the buyer asks.

Maggie and Melissa consider the question. "On the top, we've got everything from As to double Ds." They are thinking about voluptuous Hillary. What comes next . . . F? G?

The buyer makes a note. "And what about teddies?"

"Small, definitely," says Melissa. Like a cheerleader at the start of her season—gain 5 pounds or lose 5 pounds, you're on probation—she has stayed 107 since 1998, when her last child was born. "Some medium." Then she remembers Brenda

George, the third baseman's wife, who must've gained 20 pounds since September, not that she was skinny then. "A few larges, too."

A subset of the wives decide to get their hair done. Not that it's necessary—they'll be pulling tops on and off all night—but because a blowout is fun. One of Jimmy Cardozo's "girlfriends" is there, getting her hair reddened to the color the stylist calls cinnamon, and she squeals, foil wrappers shaking, when the group comes in. They vaguely remember meeting her at Liana's party, but the girl, Cynthia, has their names down pat. The way the hellos go, the hugs and leading questions and wide, expectant smiles: Melissa has no choice but to invite her along. Cleat chaser, Melissa thinks, even as she says, "See you later, Cynth."

◇

Maggie's house has an open floor plan, the kitchen's marble island opening into the cathedral-ceilinged great room. That chef Liana used was not available, so Maggie offered the cute cheese guy at Whole Foods $300 to set up some finger food. He's done well: the dining room table is decked out with a vertiginous cheese tower, a platter covered with an elaborate pattern of sushi, and a tray of jigsawed crudités.

Turns out Chad, that's his name, is in design school. "Graduate degree in textiles, ma'am." Maggie does not like being called *ma'am* under any circumstance, and a grimace floats over her face before passing back into a smile.

Chad has brought a friend, Eric—"painter, good at mixing things"—to man the bar, which is set with magnums of moscato, prosecco, and sauvignon, three oversize Grey Goose bottles lined up like so many members of the cavalry. When Maggie comes into the kitchen in her dress and heels, he is ready, and raises a tumbler in salute. "Miss Maggie"—slightly better than *ma'am*—"try this."

He's holding a caramel-colored cocktail, something that she can smell from four feet. "What is it?"

"I call it the Desert Sun. Similar to a sidecar, but with whiskey."

Maggie accepts the glass and draws it to her lips, eyebrows going up at the sound of the doorbell. "Mmm. Thank you, Eric," she says before clacking away. She swings through the living room on the way to the front, waving at Chantelle, Neiman's underwear girl, who is laying out silk robes in emerald and sapphire and cabernet. "We good here?"

The woman smiles and nods, "Oh, yes."

"Love that purple one," Maggie says, pointing at the latest deposit on the footstool. "And try one of his deserted cocktails." She raises the tumbler. "It's delicious." The doorbell peals again.

"I let myself in," Melissa says from the foyer, just as Maggie reaches the front hall. Melissa is taking advantage of the night's chill to wear a half-length mink; below it flashes the sequins and beads of a short, tight dress.

"Oh, you look fabulous," Maggie says. "Let me take your coat." Melissa is loath to part with it, but she reluctantly does. "It'll be right over here," Maggie assures before disappearing into a room-size hall closet. "Who did that?" she asks, her finger sticking out of the closet, wagging.

"Cavalli. You like?" Melissa does a subdued sashay and runs a hand over her beaded thigh. "You're looking sexy as well. You send a selfie to Tomás?" Part of being a baseball wife: just enough distraction.

"Not yet." Maggie pops out of the closet as a knock comes at the door. "Can you get that, Mel? I've got to check on something."

Cynthia and Cecilia smile widely on the front stoop. "Hi!" Cynthia says. Her new red is garish, as is her dress, a low and short tube of sparkly fabric. She hugs Melissa. "It was great to see you this afternoon. Thank you *so much* for inviting me. Us."

Like I had a choice, says the voice in Melissa's head.

"Do you know Cecilia Vásquez? She's Victor Vásquez's wife. Have you seen him pitch? He's a-maze-ing."

"Isn't that nice," Melissa says, flipping through the games, trying to remember any that Hal did not start. She turns to Cecilia, small and pretty and impossibly young to be a colleague. "We haven't been formally introduced." Melissa reaches out. "Pleased to meet you."

"Hello." In order to shake hands, Cecilia shifts her load from her right hand to her left, and only then does Melissa see: she has brought the child. Melissa cannot hide her surprise at the bundle in the carrier.

"He's asleep, no problem," Cecilia says, her accent making itself apparent. "If he gets up I'll—" she nods to her swollen breast.

"Sure. Well. Come in, come in."

Melissa shows them through the foyer, eyes scanning desperately for Maggie. Who brings a *baby* to a *lingerie* party? The girl is herself too young to understand, of course; perhaps something has been lost in cultural translation. But still.

They step into the living room. "Maybe over there, in that corner?"

"Perfect." The baby is beautiful, Melissa has to admit, an entirely round face, lips pushed together in a pout. Were her children ever so flawless? They must've been. Something about the silky smooth skin seems impossible here in Maggie's cheese-tower house, even more exotic than Chantelle's leopard-print thongs.

"Now," Maggie appears from somewhere, clapping her hands together. "Who wants drinks?"

The noise stirs the baby, not into a cry but a wet gurgle. "Oh my," Maggie says, approaching the carrier, a long, acrylic nail pointed toward the baby's face. "Who do we have here?"

◇

The women have moved from robes to rompers and are now into teddies, have drained two glasses or three. The baby has interrupted them only once, and only because he'd spit out his pacifier, more surprised than upset, and Cecilia calmed him easily. But Cecilia and baby Pedro are not the night's only unexpected guests: half an hour ago Liana arrived, with another ex, a tall blonde from the Angels organization. While Liana has kept a decidedly low profile since her divorce, word is that this other woman, Tonya, was a Cinderella at Disney and is already trying to reenter baseball's koi pond–size dating pool, with eyes on Ray Putney. "Bitch better stay away from my guy," Lisa now says under her breath, holding her wineglass so tight her knuckles go white. Across the room, Tonya chats politely with Hillary about the traffic in Santa Monica.

Liana's arrival also puts the kibosh on the wives' latest gossip about her ex. Cynthia said she'd heard from a friend of a friend who worked at the casino that Jason'd frittered away all his money playing poker. *Gambling!* The women don't believe it, or its source, this woman with Tabasco-red hair. "My friend says he has a debt collector out after him." Cynthia looks like she's enjoying this, but the women are incredulous—what Cynthia is describing is lurid, tawdry, the stuff of crime procedurals. "What do you think he was doing up at Taliesin? Sightseeing?"

"Ladies, look at what we have here." Chantelle waves an elaborate red corset through the air, flicking her wrists like a matador. "Wouldn't this do wonders in the bedroom?" The baseball wives snap back to attention, ask about other colors. Melissa *knew* this Cynthia was not to be trusted.

"Or maybe this?" Chantelle reveals another one-piece, pewter this time, ass-less save for the string of a thong. The wives tingle at the thought of wearing *that* when their husbands return from a two-week road trip. "Great support, push-up bra built right in." Chantelle cups her own small but perky breasts. "He won't be able to resist."

A throaty mewl startles the wives, the wet gurgle giving voice to how more than a few of them feel. "Oh!" Cecilia says and pops up from the couch. "Lo siento. I mean, sorry." She hurries to retrieve the child.

Quieting the boy, Cecilia settles into an armchair in the room's far corner. Chantelle continues with the corsets, demonstrating snaps and clips and reversible ribbons.

"Oh my god!" Cynthia cries. She is not watching Chantelle's rainbow of silks or still gossiping about Jason but staring at Cecilia in the corner, the girl's shirtdress unbuttoned, her milk-swollen breast uncovered. Cynthia's eyes are like dinner plates, her mouth a wide-open grin. "They're huge!"

The whole room turns to look at Cecilia, her baby cradled in her arms. Her exposed breast *is* giant, taut with milk, a latte color with a rose-pink areola. Instantly, the hearsay about Goodyear is forgotten, Liana's vulnerability ignored, Tonya's roving eye forgiven. In fact, for a moment, their interest in men slides right off the edge of their planet: this is something else, something better.

With their eyes on Cecilia, the wives know that nothing in Chantelle's trunk will improve the young mother. She is, at this moment, perfect. The baseball wives feel awe at this, but also, and mostly, regret: for having zoomed by this chapter, for having avoided it completely, for having surgically replicated it in a way that will never feel quite right. There are different kinds of beauty, and this—

"What?" Melissa's hiss interrupts the group reverie. Her words, dulled by three Desert Suns, are less crisp, less clipped than usual. "You've never seen a woman breastfeed before?" She has, and has forgotten it, the urgency and beauty of the act buried under everything else that has since come her way. She turns to Chantelle. "Chantelle, please continue."

As the clerk drapes a rainbow of thongs across her forearm, the doorbell rings. "Another friend," Melissa says, raising her eyebrows at Maggie. "Wonderful."

Maggie shuffles into the front hall, returning with Eliza Summers and another woman. While the baseball wives are all wearing strappy dresses, ruffles and ribbons, this woman is in a plain pink suit coat and matching skirt. Melissa thinks she looks familiar but cannot place her.

"This is my friend," Eliza says. "Candice."

They sit down with the group. More thongs have appeared on Chantelle's arm, the bright laces now stretching nearly up to her shoulder. "Candice, what do you do?" Maggie asks.

Melissa watches her carefully, hunting for a clue. Where is this woman from?

"I work in government."

And with that, the pieces click into place: *I want Candy!*

Melissa stands, tells Chantelle to order her two of the thongs in cranberry, and asks Eliza to help her get some wine for their new friend. In the far corner of the room, kitchen sink running to cover their whispers, the inquiry begins: "You brought *her* here?"

"Why not? She wants to see the offerings."

"She wants to hit us up for money. Arizona is *off-limits*." The whiskey makes her tongue thick.

"This is not a campaign stop. I swear." Eliza raises her right hand. The scar from last year's car-battery burn is a pink shadow across her palm. "She wants to buy something for her girlfriend."

"What! She's gay? Oh, you're despicable."

"Marriage equality is important. It's a big part of her platform."

"She can marry a duck as far as I am concerned. But we're talking about *intimates* here. It's like inviting a rooster into the henhouse. Allowing the volleyball team's towel boy into the girls' locker room . . . letting a little boy make cupcakes."

"That doesn't even make any sense." Eliza frowns.

"*Of course* there will be trouble."

"Lesbians wear teddies, too, Melissa. Lighten up."

Instead, Melissa slams off the water and pivots to the bar. "Eric, I'll have another—"

But Eric has left his post—Maggie made him and Chad vacate once the lingerie came out—so Melissa pours herself the best approximation of a Desert Sun she can manage: whiskey over rocks, a splash of lemon juice, sugar cube plunking to the bottom of her tumbler.

Gripping two wines, Eliza returns to the circle of women. Melissa has a sudden, pressing need for fresh air, and steps with her cocktail out onto the back patio. The yard is quiet, save for the gurgle of the hot tub. Steam spills off of it in thin, gauzy sheets. It's chilly, and she wishes she had her beautiful coat.

Through the windows, Melissa can see the women admiring a slinky bra. Eliza is cajoling Candy to take off her jacket; below she is wearing a cream-colored camisole. Chantelle holds the bra up to the woman's chest, and the baseball wives smile.

In another window, Cecilia sits in an armchair, her child on her lap, the chair's reading light casting her in a warm glow. She looks like a Madonna, like a child herself, a doll. Was Melissa ever that young? That certain of herself, that unafraid of what the world might think? She wants to be Cecilia, to start again with a young husband, a new baby. How much she'd do differently.

Across the patio, the blue light of a giant television spills into the yard, the two-headed silhouette of Eric and Chad against the den's six-foot TV. They are watching basketball, the Suns versus the Bulls. The Suns are ahead; she can read the score from here.

Melissa drinks the rest of her glass in a gulp. Now she does not need her jacket; the whiskey warms her from the inside.

"Hal wants to get a divorce," she says to the potted aloe. There, she's finally said it. But nothing happens, not a rustle in the pointy leaves, not a lightning strike, not anything. Just the steady gurgle of the hot tub, the hum and tick of the desert night. "He's going to leave me."

She's not a crier, but she feels her eyes getting hot and heavy with liquid.

Candy says something funny and the baseball wives all burst into a laughter so loud it carries through the triple-pane glass and out onto the well-swept patio. The woman has charisma, Melissa will give her that. Inside, Candy holds up another bra, shimmies her shoulders. Another wave of laughter.

Melissa decides in that moment: they can all stay. The beautiful baby and the cleat chaser and the randy politician, all those women she hated and those she thought were her friends. Instead, she will go. She will slink back through the yard and up the hillside and through the desert mountains. She will go into the night, and no one, but no one, will notice she is gone.

The Hohokam wanted more control than *Flood* or *No Flood*, and so developed technology to build canals. And not ditches or divots, the kind of grooves a focused batter can dig out with his cleat. Channels, fifty feet wide, twenty feet deep, gravity pulling water along for nearly twenty miles. That's some sort of relay play, as good a 6–4–3 as the Lions' own horn could ever hope to string together.

"Masters of the Desert," that was another name for them—later. Then, they were just farmers, guys playing well—if not an undefeated season, then one where they sat comfortably at the top of the standings. Maize, beans, squash, and cotton grew where the bluegrass thrives today. They ate like sluggers at the midnight buffet, then traded away what they didn't need for more of everything else. It was the kind of surplus that would make any owner lick his chops, thinking about all the players and coaches and real estate he could buy. The sort of excess that'd get a star's agent on the phone, talking opportunities, talking five-year deals, talking championship rings.

The Hohokam weren't just king-of-the-hill farmers and master en-gineers, they were ballplayers, too. The men and women both played sport—how's that for Title IX? For the guys it was a game not un-like basketball, with a hoop and ball; the ladies had one with sticks, something more akin to field hockey. Ball fields popped up every three miles, up and down Salt River, built as regular as bus stops on the Scottsdale–Tempe–ASU line. And these were not just meadows with trampled deer grass and a couple of half-sunk tree limbs marking fair and foul. No, a Hohokam field was a dug-out oval coated in caliche, stretching anywhere from eighty to two hundred feet. That's like the stretch from the plate to shallow center, nothing small about it. They even constructed sloped, rising sides round the field, so a crowd could gather, sit down, and watch. Not a lot different from Salt River's own outfield lawn, the patchwork of beach blankets and picnic baskets that fans spread out today.

The Hohokam may have had a winning streak, but for Jason, the bright afternoons are getting darker and darker. What's the opposite of a trading surplus? He's liquidated all he can (the Cadillacs, the mem-orabilia, the fancy furniture and kitchen gadgets) to cover his losses. Apparently his Pacific Palisades house was on the market in February, stripped clean of everything but the staging furniture. But its sale carried him only a few weeks; quickly, again, his bank account sloped into a sorry state. Sara, who has become an ally (like Liana's house-keeper, she responds well to hundred-dollar bills), passes me details while she smokes in the players' parking lot between innings. It's Sara who confirms that he's sleeping on a cot in the stadium's supply shed; there's no way Joe Templeton could say no to the MVP. She also tells me Jason asked Herb for money, but Herb, still pissed about Nike and his lost commission, thought Jason was joking. He told him to go fuck himself, in any case. It's true, sometimes these athletes need tough love, but Sara, in telling me about Jason's pitiful plea—how the three of them went to Herb's favorite restaurant and Jason, mustering up the courage or humility to ask for help, looked like he was near about to cry—just shakes her head.

As the spring season sprints toward its close, as Jason's debts continue to tumble down the mountain, the threats against him increase: of physical injury, of insurmountable indignity. Jason knows that if his lender goes public, all his endorsement contracts, present and future, will go the way of his Nike shoe. When was the last time anyone saw John Daly selling any damn thing? Maybe he's more likely to get a suspension and a dozen league-mandated appointments with a shrink (though Liana's already tried that, so much therapy, solo and couples' and even hypnotism) than what happened to Charlie Hustle, but still— what would happen if Twitter got a hold of this? His money guy wasn't exactly a check-cashing operation. These kind of associations, this kind of tomfoolery? They'd tear him limb from limb, and then, no one'd touch him. Why should the Lions be loyal to him when he's fraternizing with scumballs, making poor decisions, acting highly irrational? When he's sleepwalking in left field and skipping out on games for a round or three of blackjack? Even with his tank on empty he's better than most players, but then he makes one error, and another; he's swinging and missing more and more. *Herb's about to blow a gasket*, Sara tells me one morning, and she looks like she's running a bit ragged herself.

*Just give me a few days*, Jason begs the man on the other end of the phone. After all these decades of hard work, of being the best player in T-ball and in Little League and in high school and in college, after leading the major leagues and then leading them again, his future in the sport has boiled down to a few days' scramble, to coming up with half a million in cash. The hole is actually much bigger than that, but that's what he needs to produce now. The man makes an unhappy noise on the other end of the phone.

*Just give me a few days*, Jason begs again. For the longest time it was just playing cards after the game, a few hands of Hold'em to blow off some steam before bed. For years it was seven-card to pass the time between home stands, two-day tourneys to get his kicks when nothing else short of the season starting up again would deliver that thrill. He was playing with Monopoly money; between salary and endorsements he was bringing in more than he could ever imagine spending. It was just about the competition, the adrenaline that came with putting it all on the line. *All in.* But then the thrill, his forever rabbit around the greyhound track, is suddenly gone from his view. Is it too far ahead? Behind him somewhere? Or chomped and lifeless on the dirt? Jason senses it out there, but doesn't remember last seeing it, doesn't know how to find it, doesn't have the time to search for it, not now. Now that man on the other end of the line has the capacity to break his hand or shatter his career. Ruin him, one way or another.

*A few more days*, Jason asks again. *Please.*

And, remarkably, the man agrees. *Friday*, he grumbles before hanging up.

## THE CYCLE

There has never been an E-flat in "Take Me Out to the Ball Game," at least not when it's played in its standard key of C. Lester Morrow knows this, but he hits the note anyway. The song lurches; the crowd stutters in their stretch. The Mariners' shortstop, tossing warm-up with the third baseman, drops the ball into the dirt.

Nothing to do but keep on keeping on, so Lester plays out the line, half humming, half muttering to himself the familiar refrain: "One, two, three strikes you're out at the ooooold baaaaall gaaaaaame!" He runs his fingers over the keyboard in an upward arpeggio, two hands racing at once. Like a flourish at the end will save him. With the last note he winces at the creak in his left hand, but he keeps the keys pressed down for a full two measures. One, two, three; one, two, three—and release. Outside his open window, the organ reverberates through the ballpark and loosens into the spring air.

As the song ends, the crowd settles back into their seats. The Mariners, dressed in gray, toss their practice balls toward the dugout and take their positions, doing what they can to preserve their energy in the Arizona heat. Lester twists to watch the action, resting his left elbow on the ledge of the keyboard and cupping his chin in his palm. William Goslin, Los Angeles's top draft pick and great-grand-something of Goose, leads off the bottom of the seventh for the Lions. He takes a few last triple-bat whiffs in the on-deck circle, then drops two of the sticks, taps his spikes, and steps up to the plate. In the next booth over, Lester's colleague announces, "Number nineteen, William Goslin, first base." The sound carries from the mic to the stadium's PA and back to Lester's booth on a flutter of wind.

Lester scrutinizes the rookie. The team has high hopes—Goslin was their first rounder, eighth overall, in last June's amateur draft—but he's had a tough spring, batting all of .185. He'll be going down to Double-A, if he's lucky. From Lester's vantage, it's unclear if, in keeping him around into the third week of March, management is giving him good experience or letting him writhe a bit. Fair response, either way.

The boy points the tip of his bat to first, second, and third base, then settles into his knock-kneed stance. The pitcher rolls his shoulders and cracks his neck; the second basemen arranges the dirt in front of him with a pointed toe. All of a sudden a sharp, chromatic bleat tumbles out of Lester's machine. The batter and the pitcher both look instinctively to the sky. A flock of amplified geese?

"Christ," Lester mumbles. He reaches for the power button, a tiny red beacon on the machine's upper left corner. On the way, his finger traces over the Marimba, Xylophone, and Tuba options, but also Pack of Dogs–Large, Pack of Dogs–Small, and Elephant. He'll never get the hang of this newfangled thing.

Give him a couple of woodblocks and an air horn any day. He depresses the red button. Off. "Phew."

The kid is down in the count, having watched one trail outside and then taken two bad-miss swings, when Joe Templeton bursts into the booth. "Lester, what the fuck?"

"Hi, Joe." Lester glances toward the open window, worried the profanity will drift into the crowd. "Sorry, Joe."

"Sorry my ass! You playing with your toes or something?"

Lester shakes his head no.

Joe Templeton, director of stadium operations for Salt River Fields, starts pacing, heaving his short frame across the small booth in three strides, pivoting, heaving back. Since the season's gotten under way, the man's year-round tan has deepened to a strange, dark reddish-orange, almost the color of a tawny port. "Just don't fuck up again, okay? Nowadays they got computers to do what you do. Just one touch and . . ." Joe shoulders up to the keyboard, forcing Lester toward the higher octaves. He checks that the machine is off, then concentrates on the many buttons and keys and decides to press a big white one: C, an octave below middle. He holds it down with a fat finger. Lester notices his boss's cuticles are a mess. "Dun-nuh-nuh-na, duh-na!" Joe sings and lifts his index. "One button."

"Charge," Lester says, sounding deflated. Below, the kid hits a soft groundball to second. It's an easy out.

"Exactly." Joe crosses the room and reaches for the doorknob. "I know you've done this since the Jurassic, Lester, but you're in *my* stadium now, and I want it to be *right*. I'm watching you."

A quick one-two, the door slamming shut and the ball cracking against a bat, and Lester whips his head back to the field. Jimmy Cardozo has made a solid connection with his first pitch. The ball sails over the shortstop's head, drops shallow of the left fielder, and starts a slow roll across the diamond-cut grass. The catcher accelerates around first and slides into second, just under the baseman's tag.

Lester rushes for the On button and places his hands on the keys. He plays fanfare, the rising chords familiar under his fingers. "Dun-nuh-nuh-na, duh-na!" he sings along. Only as the last chord resonates over the field does he realize that the song was performed by a chorus of cats.

$\diamond$

"Nice work today, Goose." Tomás Monterrey pulls his damp towel taut and flicks the rookie in the ass. William Goslin, already bent over to untie his cleats, bites his lip but continues to loosen the laces.

Jason Goodyear, a few lockers down, turns to the pair. "Hey, Tomás. Don't call him that, he doesn't like it."

Monterrey scowls at the left fielder. With Townsend gone, Monterrey is now starting in center—something neither man is used to, nor particularly likes. Corey Matthews, the second-round draftee who looks like he might actually make the team without the way station of the minors, does his best to hide in his locker.

Monterrey continues. "What do I care if he fucking likes it or not? I care if he hits the ball and drives in runs. I care if he covers first like he knows what the fuck he's doing. Giving his grandpa a bad name playing like that. Mierda."

"Calm down, dude." Goodyear unbuttons his dirt-stained jersey and drops it on the bench, then peels off a damp T-shirt. William glances over to the left fielder, almost expecting to see a big red *S* on his chest. *Superman!* Not a lot of East Coast kids follow West Coast teams—half the time the games don't start until ten—but William has always loved Jason Goodyear, from his first cover shoot with *Sports Illustrated for Kids*. He'd never admit it here, but he still has a Goodyear poster hanging in his bedroom. The left fielder's chest is just sporting a strange tattoo of a playing card over his heart, sweat, and a couple of damp hairs in the cleft between his chiseled pecs. "Come on. You remember being a rookie."

"Yeah, but I wasn't no first rounder. I had to fucking claw my way up from fucking Kansas." William didn't even know they had a team in Kansas—he thought it was Oklahoma, maybe Nebraska. Somewhere with corn. "Did you hear about Tampa's first rounder?"

"That kid who hit for the cycle?" Jimmy Cardozo comes out of the shower, still dripping, a too-small towel wrapped around his thick waist. "Tough break, fuckface," he says in William's ear, and his tone sounds almost sincere. Jimmy isn't exactly a friend, but sometimes he buys William beer and he offered him a lift to the last split-squad game. The catcher drops his towel in front of his locker. He's got a tattoo of a catcher's mitt cupping his left butt cheek.

"Yeah, that one," Monterrey says. "I'll tell you what he's doing: running fucking circles around his teammates, like a first rounder *should*. Do you see any circles here?" The outfielder spins his finger around a tight, invisible ball. "I mean, besides your big fucking *goose* eggs."

A few lockers down, Goodyear steps out of his shorts, shaking his head. William, still in his sweat-stained undershirt and boxers, peeks, as discreetly as he can. He'd been hitting the gym every day, eating more calories than Michael Phelps, and he has only eight pounds to show for it. Eight! Now, in a room with fortyish half-naked men, trunk-legged power hitters and pitchers with shoulders like sawhorses, he feels, rightfully, like a pipsqueak. Glancing at Goodyear's package doesn't bring any relief. He'd heard Goody's small dick was why his wife left him, but he looks pretty well hung to William. If *that* is small—he glances over again, and back—where does it leave William? His penis shrinks just thinking about it.

"And Seattle got that pitcher, man. He already threw a shutout. And us? Do you know how much we paid for this kid's signing bonus? Sometimes I think the bossmen are fucking loco." Monterrey throws his towel down in disgust.

"Great-great-uncle," William says, so quiet it's barely audible over the hiss of showers and clank of lockers.

"What's that? You finally got something to say for yourself, chico?" Monterrey turns, his eyes narrowed into slits.

"Goose Goslin was my great-great-uncle. And they called him Goose because of the way he flapped his arms when he was catching a ball, not because of the Goslin part."

"Well, I guess you'd have to flap-flap-*catch* some balls for us to call you Goose then, hmm?" The outfielder steps out of his pants, his legs darkly hairy in the span between his briefs and sanitary socks. "Thank you for the history lesson, chico."

"Give it a rest, Tom," someone says from the next row over. A damp hand towel flies over the lockers and lands on Monterrey's head.

"What fucking gives?" He holds out his hands, palms up. "I'm not the one with sixteen errors!"

Just then, Paine blows out of his office and into the locker room, announcing his presence with two sonorous claps. Striding forward, he assesses the bodies in various stages of undress, so many dogs at a kennel show. The players shift uncomfortably; he's been known to pinch when the spirit moves him. "Good game, everyone! Well"—he glances at William and his face drops slightly—"mostly everyone." That gets some chuckles, but he's already across the room, and he does an about-face at the media room door. "I think we just about got ourselves a ball club!" he shouts. "And you know what they say, gentlemen: a team that showers together, stays together. So have a good scrub and I'll see you jackals in the morning."

He strides out, only to pop his head back in. "Don't forget, tomorrow is payday!" The team hoots with excitement.

"Or cut day," Monterrey says into William's ear as he passes.

◇

Lester played organ for the Phoenix Firebirds—the San Francisco Giants' Triple-A team—for thirty-two years, nearly the whole history of the franchise. Now *that* was a good organ, a customized Hammond B-3, electric but still with knobs and stoppers enough to make things interesting. He was a one-man effects studio: he had half a dozen whistles, a cowbell for home runs, woodblocks for clapping cheers . . . even a foot-wide spring to boing for foul balls. When the expansion team came to Phoenix—the Diamondbacks showed up in 1998—they scooted the Firebirds down to Tucson. Tucson'd offered him a job similar to what he'd had at Phoenix Municipal, but he'd declined. Not an awful city, but it was ninety minutes away, and if he keeps his hands on the steering wheel that long, the knuckles of his left were liable to start aching worse than normal, which is to say, hurting bad. And there's no chance he'd've moved to Tucson, not without his Steinway. He can't remember exactly how they'd gotten the grand piano into his third-floor walkup—they'd removed a banister and mashed the tread of three stairs, he recalls that much—and there was no way short of demolition to get it back out. He was stuck on the old side of Old Town Scottsdale until the wrecking ball or the undertaker came—whoever rang first.

The new Diamondbacks stadium had all the late-nineties flashiness you'd expect from a boomtown in the middle of going boom. A retractable roof, air-conditioning, a swimming pool *and* hot tub, right in the stadium! They could've built a primo organist's booth, they had the money, but instead they bought some big computer loaded with all sorts of sounds and prerecorded crap. Lester heard they hired some "computers" major from ASU to press keys at the appropriate times, typing up fanfares and "Take Me Out to the Ball Game" like a secretary at her Underwood. Where's the music in that? They didn't even play the national anthem, just cued up a recording. *A recording.* Lester'd refused to set foot in the stadium when he heard that.

So Lester squeaked by on weddings and funerals, filling in for Cactus League games when somebody got sick. They all knew one another, the church-on-Sunday, ball-games-through-the-spring, we-also-do-bar-mitzvahs keyboardists around town, though most of them had families to keep them occupied when they weren't at the keys. Lester's closest remaining relative was a second cousin in Omaha, and he'd been unlucky in love for decades now. He was left with the *Arizona Republic* delivered to his doorstep, his daily trip to the diner, his Steinway, and his Stoli.

Even though social security kicked in a couple of years back, without the Firebirds gig, things were lean, the measly Lutheran church checks spent in a day's time. When the casino opened last year he landed a gig playing in the cocktail lounge. Not the busy nights—and not because of his hand (no one around here had an ear sophisticated enough to pick out the augmented ninths he couldn't hit, the half-diminished chords he occasionally flubbed), but because he wasn't as nice on the eyes as he used to be. He knew that to be true and didn't mind; the girl they had playing Fridays and Saturdays was real cute and could even sort of sing. The Sunday-to-Thursday pay was decent, plus he got a comped dinner and a couple of big pours from Eric.

Lester saw the new sports complex going up next door, watched it coming together week after week. When they started hiring, boy, did he jump. For the money, but also because following in the paper, listening on the radio, isn't like being there. He missed it.

The Salt River Fields folks were interested—how could they not be, with his résumé of Newport Jazz, the Copacabana, all the places he'd played before he was even twenty-one, to say nothing of his thirty-plus years with the Firebirds. But when he tried to negotiate a fee per game, Joe, the tightfisted midget, insisted it was a flat fee for the season or *nada*. So Lester, with some gripes, took the three grand and a parking pass.

◇

William leaves the stadium in a funk. He'd known it would be weird, being the youngest guy on the team, the rookie straight out of high school. Objectively, he knew he'd get cut, too—it was unheard of for a recruit, even a spectacular one, to jump straight to the majors—but through those months of psyching himself up for his big fucking debut, he'd hoped that he would be the exception. Look at Matthews, he thinks now—two home runs last week! There is talk of him staying with the club, not even stopping at Salt Lake. Meanwhile, William has been batting like shit—even after two hundred hours with that cranky geezer batting coach—and can hardly hang on to the ball at first. Every Thursday this spring has felt like his head is in a guillotine, waiting for the Friday cut he knows is coming. Instead, Paine calls him in and gives him his envelope of meal money—with hardly more than a nod and the line, "Don't spend it all in one place."

The parking lot is emptying out, a few TV trucks packing up in the press section. William weaves through a pair of rented

Mustangs and goes past Jason Goodyear's beat-up Jeep. He recognizes Stephen Smith, one of the owners of the team, as his Audi A8 glides by, and lifts a hand to wave. The man at the wheel does not acknowledge him. He's probably feeling pretty bad about his investment right now. William sidles up to a 2011 Porsche, custom-painted Lions gold with black pinstripes. His baby, borne of his signing bonus. His parents sat William down months before the draft to talk to him about financial planning and long-term savings but they had allowed him this, and how he loves it. He drove it the twenty-four hundred miles from Bay Head, New Jersey, to Scottsdale, Arizona—an act of rebellion that had made Sheila Goslin, a hoverer even among helicopter parents, crazy—but he was only a couple of speeding tickets worse for wear. And even a week's worth of road food (the wrappers wadded up in the foot well of the passenger seat) hadn't gained him any weight.

An ancient Olds that must belong to a janitor or something is parked alongside his Porsche. Whoever parked there clearly can't read: a sign posted above the cars says PLAYERS ONLY.

William's car starts up with a satisfying purr. He looks over his shoulder for traffic, sets the car in reverse, and *crunch*. He sees the end of the Olds through his rearview mirror.

Muttering to himself, he pulls forward, parks, and gets out to inspect the damage. The car's an ugly thing, a rusty Cutlass Supreme in a taupe that might've once been white. And it's angled fifteen degrees off parallel, not really between the lines at all. It's a wonder it didn't hit his Porsche on its way in, he thinks. William glances inside the dusty window: the back seat's covered with sheet music and unopened mail, a few days' worth of *Arizona Republic*s, and, tucked underneath some papers, the plastic top of a cheap bottle of booze.

He crouches down next to the Olds's long back flank to inspect the damage. A fleck of gold paint from his bumper is pressed onto the metal, and the point of contact on each car is slightly indented. He tries to rub the metallic stamp off with his thumb, then licks the finger and tries again.

He looks around the lot to see if anyone has noticed him. His stomach churns. Could he just go?

"Where'd ya get me?" The man who asks is lean to the point of skinny, tan and creased like worn leather. His hair, a fluffy white rim that rounds a sizable bald spot, is a little long and very mussed, and his eyes are wide and watery behind large, out-of-date frames.

William stammers. "I—I—I just—"

The old man stoops to study the mark. He's so close William can smell him—vodka, plus an aftershave that reminds him of his grandfather. His scalp is dotted with sunspots.

"I am so sorry, sir. If there's anything I can do, I mean, repairs or whatever."

The old man beams a mouthful of graying teeth. "To this car? I reckon it's older than you!"

"Well, still. I feel awful."

"Right." The old man squints. "You're that Willy Goslin kid, aren't you?"

"Yes, sir." He feels his face flush.

"Having a go of it, huh? First time out is always sorta—"

A modified golf cart zips around the corner, a wobbly stack of sod flapping on its flatbed. "Hey!" the driver calls. "Hey, hey!" The machine whirs over a curb cut, totters momentarily, and then speeds toward the men, swerving and stopping just behind William's rear bumper. The driver, a tan man in a polo and too-short shorts, purses his lips and flares his nose.

"Mr. Goslin, is Lester bothering you?" The monogram on

his chest has the Salt River Fields logo and under it an embroidered title: DIRECTOR OF STADIUM OPS.

"No, I just was—" William wonders how best to explain the situation. Would they call the cops for something like this? He thinks of the overdue tickets in his glove compartment. That's the last thing he needs. Sheila would have a conniption.

Before he can come up with a plan, Templeton says, "*He's* not supposed to be here. Staff parking's past third base." He's glaring at the old man as he indicates a farther lot.

"It says 'players.' I play." The old man wiggles his fingers in the air and flashes a crooked grin.

"Keyboards don't count!" Templeton barks and points more vigorously. "Over there, Lester."

"Okay, okay." The old man shows his palms in surrender. "I'll get going."

"And you won't do it again." The short man turns his gaze and makes a concerned face. "Mr. Goslin, I'm very sorry for the inconvenience."

"It's—it's okay?" William's confused more than anything else, but before he can ask what just happened, the golf cart has zoomed off, leaving with a poof of exhaust.

"We all get our knocks, huh, kid?" With that, the old man raps the trunk of his car twice, gets in, and drives away. On his way out of the lot he honks, sticks a hand out the car window, and waves. "Good game, Goody!"

William hadn't noticed, but Jason Goodyear is standing at the edge of the lot. Did he see the whole debacle? William raises a hand, hello, and the left fielder nods before walking away.

◇

It's said that desert air is good for preserving pianos, and Lester's Hamburg Steinway, a 1927 model taking up a quarter of his apartment, is just getting better as the years tick by. That hot, dry air is supposed to be good for bones, too, though in Lester's experience it doesn't make things *better*—it just keeps them from getting too much worse.

That's why all the blue hairs come to Arizona, to keep the slide from happening too quick. Lester also moved here because he was trying to slow a slide, but not into old age. What happened, or at least where it started, was that Scott LaFaro crashed himself into a tree in upstate New York. Lester and Scott, a mean double bassist, had been buddies in Manhattan. Lester was just eighteen, scrawny as a scarecrow, and pie-in-the-sky about jazz piano. Scott had been about the same but with a bass, and they started a nice little trio with a drummer named Kimball Morton. Played a club in the Village every Friday night of 1958, right up until Scott started gigging with Bill Evans. Lester didn't blame Scott for saying yes to a good opportunity, but the trio losing its low end meant things slowed down for Lester and Kimbo. And then, on that one awful night, they just flat stopped.

July 1961, Lester and Scott were driving back from Newport (where Scott played, Lester listened) by way of Scott's hometown. They were late getting started but Scott was eager to get home, as he had a big-eyed girl from New Bedford with him. Lester offered the girl the front seat so she and Scotty could talk. She died, too, when they wrapped around that tree.

Lester was the lucky one; he walked away from the crash with a lump on his head and a smashed-up hand. Nearly every bone in his southpaw was cracked or crunched. A string of operations got him to the point where all the fingers went up and down, in and out. After another six months of therapy he could make a fist and play a major triad. Adding the seventh, flatting the third: those things made him wince. And hitting the ninth, getting his mangled thumb to stretch that far? Forget about it.

He also forgot about making it in New York. He'd bought Scott and Bill's Village Vanguard album—the one they recorded just before Newport and the crash—as soon as it came out. Sort of spooky, listening to a dead guy play, but Lester was glad to hear his old friend again. On the record Lester also heard what he already knew: he wouldn't be able to touch Evans with a ten-foot pole, not before, but especially not now. A legit piano player with one bum paw? Might as well put a golden retriever at second and expect him to start turning double plays.

Without jazz there was nothing much left for him in New York—a couple of ex-girlfriends he'd rather not see and a cramped apartment that started costing too much. And besides, he wasn't sure his southpaw could handle the cold of another New York winter—the snow felt like a vise clamping across his palm, a vise that would then fill with tiny stilletoed dancers doing the cha-cha until Lester found a bottle of something. So he decided to try the desert. He had an uncle, Artie, dealing Oldsmobiles in Phoenix.

Lester started playing at a church and then with the Firebirds. His left hand came back slowly, until he was hitting ninths more often than not. And in 1971 he found the Steinway almost by accident—he was chasing an out-of-town skirt he'd met while working her cousin's wedding. The date didn't go well— she left him at the hotel bar with the bill and a friendly pat on the arm—but on his way out Lester spotted the Steinway under a big Indian blanket, boxed up and dusty and not doing anyone any good. He gave the hotel every dollar he had and promised every penny he made from the Firebirds that season and half of the next. It was worth it, even if it meant he ate toast and beans for most of a year.

◇

William *could* walk back to the hotel—the parking lot for the casino starts just past the end of the stadium's east lot, a dried-out drainage canal with a footbridge in between—but he drives the long way around, gunning his car up to sixty for the short, clear straightaway. Of course he drives: he's muscle-sore from the morning's lifting and dehydrated from the afternoon sun. Besides, he's got to blow off his steam somehow, and he's *not* doing it by running the base paths. He revs the engine and enjoys the satisfying hum climbing up his leg. He got on base twice today, a walk and a sad excuse for a single, but never got closer to second than a lead-off. He hasn't been on second since last Thursday, hasn't visited third for a week and a half.

When William refused his mother's offer to chaperone his spring season, she suggested the extended-stay option at the Talking Stick Resort and Casino. It was convenient to the stadium, it was safe (twenty-four-hour concierge and security), there was laundry service and a buffet. Her son had to keep up with his six thousand calories a day—they were going to get him to break 175, hook, crook, or cream pie. And while they didn't want him to be spendthrift with his signing bonus—his parents had a three-track financial plan for him, minor major leaguer, middle major leaguer, All-Star—he *could* afford a few weeks of comfort, particularly as this was his first extended excursion from New Jersey.

Sheila's hovering has some legitimacy. William graduated last May and is still technically a teenager through September. Up until Arizona, his mother did his laundry and cooked his meals,

William capable of only frozen pizza, tuna salad, macaroni and cheese. And while he's had sex—his high school girlfriend finally put out last summer (convenient how their coupling coincided with her hearing, like everyone else across ESPN's viewing area, that he was a sudden millionaire)—he performed the task with the sloppy, desperate determination of a hungry boy uncertain of where he'd find his next meal. He had found several with her, but then she left for UVA. He could have gone to college, too, had signed a commitment letter to Louisiana State, but he'd been so surprised and flattered by the first-round pick (never mind the scores of scouts who'd showed up for his games that senior-year spring, the clump of stopwatches and radar guns that came out every time he stepped up to the plate), of course he signed. He stayed in New Jersey as his classmates packed off for college. The girlfriend, now ex, was home for Christmas break, but they did not rekindle their relationship. William heard she was dating a Virginia lacrosse player who had eighty pounds on him.

Once back in his room, William orders room service, a triple-stacked club sandwich and a plate of sweet potato fries. He gets one of Jimmy's beers out of the minifridge. The catcher is one of a very few guys who have been nice, forgiving him his stumbles, telling him to keep his chin up. That man can handle anything, William thinks—a wild pitch to the groin, a foul tip to the face—and keep smiling.

He's missed a call from his mother—she rang right about when he was getting popped by Monterrey in the clubhouse. With Monterrey, it doesn't feel like hazing—it feels like hatred. It's not his fault expectations are inflated. Sure, he put up fifty home runs and a .400 batting average last year, was the best player in the state. Of course there was hype. But that was against *high schoolers*. In *New Jersey*. It's not like he could say, *You really shouldn't pick me until the third round,* or, *Sorry, guys, my reputation is overblown. We can't all be A-Rod.* How did they expect him to jump up to major league pitching? William'd tried to get himself into one of those fall developmental leagues, so he could get a running start, but his agent told him not to hazard the injury. *You'll be fine,* he'd said. *Enjoy your signing bonus.* William hadn't pressed the point, but now he's wondering if he should've insisted on some D-league action.

William returns Sheila's call. First, as always, he reports on the game: runs and hits, walks and strikeouts. Not like she needed the rundown: the Goslins watch first pitch to final out on some three-digit cable sports network.

"Your father says that really was a bad hop," she says of his error. "Anyone'd have played it the same." It was his dad's father's father's brother who made the family name a household one. Uncle Goose never had any kids of his own, just distributed among the members of his extended family his bats and gloves and knickknacks, whatever Cooperstown didn't want. A young Howard came home from Thanksgiving one year with a disintegrating glove and an autographed 1928 ball. That mythology, the signed baseball sitting on the mantel, the glove boxed in glass like it was some sort of rare specimen, planted the seed in young William's mind. He started T-ball at four and never looked back.

For most of William's childhood, Howard Goslin, a locally known architect, didn't care two sniffs about the sport—he was too busy building his reputation and acting like he made a lot more money than he actually did. He couldn't be bothered to attend games, and saw no more than half a dozen throughout William's amateur career—and that included the three-game playoff for the state championship. But after the draft, with its $2 million signing bonus, Howard suddenly took a pointed interest in his son's sporting life. William couldn't believe the about-face; Howard was delusional if he believed he'd be any help. Did he think they'd play fucking catch in the backyard? More than once this winter, William wanted to drop a dumbbell on the guy's foot.

"Should we come out this weekend? Your father would like to see you play. He thought we could take you to Taliesin while we're at it."

"What? No."

"It's one of the wonders of modern architecture, William. I wouldn't be so quick to dismiss—"

William interrupts. "I mean, sorry, no, not this weekend. Tomorrow's cut day and I don't even fucking know if I'll be playing again. Ever."

"Please don't swear," his mother says, and then the line is quiet. He knows she is worrying on the other end. "Are you sleeping okay?" she says. "I'm concerned you're staying up too late with those video games." He'd become all but nocturnal this fall, with his friends away at college. Wake at noon, work out until dinner, Xbox until three or four. The console offered a much-needed outlet for his competitive streak. Offers it still— he'd carried the gaming system in the back seat of his car and hooked it up in his hotel room. Most nights, he spends an hour or two shooting enemies, slam-dunking on the opposition. If he loses here, he just presses Restart.

"I'm not, Mom."

"Have you talked to Herb lately? He's in Arizona this month and would be happy to—"

"Of course I have." In truth, William has been avoiding his agent's calls. Once, Herb and his too-pretty assistant took him out for dinner; William spent the whole meal staring at the woman's breasts and wondering how Herb had found *her.* "I'm fine.

Eating good and everything." As if on cue, there's a rap at the door, a muffled *Room service*. "That's dinner, Ma. I gotta go." Once he collects his sandwich, he checks his e-mail. OkCupid pings three new messages. According to his profile he's a graduating senior at ASU, studying architecture. YoungFLW is his handle. He lies about his age so he can suggest drinks; he lies about baseball to cut down on the gold diggers. And because, well, "professional athlete" doesn't quite feel true, not yet. Architecture seemed a viable route; he'd absorbed enough jargon from his dad to be convincing for a few drinks.

The first potential paramour, a stern-looking Slavic chick, seems like she's fishing for a green card. The second candidate is too old, a divorcée with kids; William can see the wrinkles even in her thumbnail-size profile picture. The third, a brunette calling herself Emillionaire, seems intriguing. Midtwenties, writer/artsy type, nice smile. *Up for fun.* He pings her back: *How was ur day?*

He chomps into his sandwich, waiting for a reply. This has worked once so far, in the form of a sloppy hookup with a bottle-blond sorority girl from Tempe. Drinks at the hotel bar, lots of laughing and whiskey, then back up to his room. She seemed to buy the architecture bit, and chose to believe his uncle was an investor in the casino and so he could stay over whenever it got "too late to drive." She didn't ask about, or didn't notice, the bats in the corner, the duffel bag spilling with gold-and-black gear. She had noticed the circuitry of video game consoles he'd jury-rigged around the flat screen. *You play a lot?* she'd asked, inspecting his thin frame and farmer's tan in a way that made him want to hide under the covers. She'd slipped out during the night. It sent a quick pang through his chest when he discovered she was gone—not that he'd seriously liked her or expected to see her again. But he'd liked *it*, touching another body, the motion of sex feeling as natural as scooping up a ball and stepping on the bag—the dip, pressure, and release of a well-executed play. He fell back asleep and when he awoke again, hours later, he called down to the kitchen for pancakes.

Halfway through his sandwich, his computer chirps. A new message from Emillionaire. *Dinner with the rents. 2 late after?*

He types: *No, l8r is perf. Drinks at the casino? I like the balcony lounge.* William's fake ID is laughable, the kind of bad Greenwich Village counterfeit that Jersey teens have been getting for decades. It and his baby face wouldn't get him within twenty feet of most bars, but Eric, the bartender of the casino's upstairs cocktail lounge, is a Lions fan. William can drink whatever he wants—everything shows up on his room's tab as a hamburger or a milkshake, just in case Sheila asks for a spot check—and if either guy sees anything suspicious, William makes a quick move for the elevator.

William opens another beer and turns on *SportsCenter*, watching the ticker tape for the Nets score. They lost to the Bulls, 97–84. "Shit," he says under his breath.

A text comes in from his mother: *Heading to bed. We love you. XO. —Your biggest fans.*

◇

Lester pulls into the casino lot, takes an appetizer hit from the bottle in the glove compartment, and shimmies out of his car. His ride's nothing to look at, a '91 he bought new (the dealer's discount price, may his uncle rest in peace), but he loves it for its longevity and relative reliability, and because it reminds him of Uncle Artie. He inspects the scratch again, a divot of gold. Stupid kid, he thinks and shakes his head, but worse could've happened. It's drivable; no need for the insurance folks to go counting DUIs over a ding.

He steps inside the casino and shuffles onto the gaming floor. Waitresses in metallic vests carry trays through the rows of perms, serving watered-down drinks to ladies mesmerized by the digital chime of the slots. He passes a grid of green felt tables and their black-coated dealers. A mix of sunburned tourists and deeply tanned old-timers crowd around the five-dollar tables; the twenty-dollar bettors are scant. The high-stakes room, tucked behind a frosted-glass wall but with enough of a view to be alluring, holds a few Japanese businessmen and Jason Goodyear. The left fielder, or someone who looks a hell of a lot like him, always in a blank red ball cap, has been in there just about every time Lester's passed by this spring. Everyone's got their vices, Lester figures; at least Goodyear can afford his. He cranes his neck once more—they're playing Texas Hold'em—before grabbing an escalator up to the cocktail lounge.

The lounge is made to look old, the bar laminated with antique-seeming hardwood and its chairs upholstered in dark faux leather. At least the piano is real—not a Steinway, but a peppy Baldwin baby grand that's fun to play. He makes a wave at Eric, who dims the house music to nothing, and then Lester opens the piano's lid.

Lester tries stretching across a seventh chord, C-E-G-B, and lands it without a hint of pain. "Now that's what I'm talking about," he chuckles to himself. He flats the B—C7—and shifts his left hand down a fifth. F major reverberates against his fingertips. Lester feels a warmth spreading through his chest as he flats the E and his fingers start an easy loop around the circle of fifths, one chord leading to the next to the next. That's what he likes about the progression—it's not *up* or *down*, but *around*. Tension and release, tension and release: it never gets old. When he gets back to C Lester smiles and starts into the same melody he opens with every night: "I Let a Song Go out of My Heart."

◇

Lester hits the last chord of "When Sonny Gets Blue" and looks to the bar. Who does he see but the bad-driving rookie, his face turned toward a basketball game on TV? He's seen this kid here before, but tonight's the first time he puts two and two together. Lester's about due for a set break, so he stands up from the bench and shuffles to the bar. Clippers and the Trailblazers, playing in L.A. "Guess you're gonna have to become a Clippers fan now."

The kid does a double take. "How'd you find me? Is it your car?"

"The car's fine. As for *me* finding *you*, I work here. Piano man." Lester thumbs toward the piano. "Now, who's stalking who?"

"Oh."

"Hey, Eric!" The bartender comes over, cocktail shaker aloft. "You know how old this kid is?"

The boy goes ashen, begins to stammer. Lester holds up a hand, points from William to the shaker. "Kidding. Jeez. His next is on me."

"You got it, boss."

Lester leans against the bar, waiting for a whiskey sour. One of the Clippers makes a defensive block and tosses the ball far ahead, to a teammate at midcourt. The player catches it out of the air, dribbles quickly into the key, leaps, and makes a smooth layup.

"Good play." Lester nods in approval.

"Yeah." They watch the replay.

"Bet he screwed it up plenty of times before he got it right."

"What's that supposed to mean?"

Lester stares at the screen, a little smile on his face. An ad for some big, shiny truck. The kid'll figure it out.

"Frank?" A young woman suddenly appears alongside them. Lester squints at her. "Who are you? This here's Willy—"

"Emily?" The boy leaps up from his seat, getting between the girl and Lester.

"Yes. Hi."

"Nice to meet you." The boy hugs her awkwardly.

"Sorry I'm late," she starts. "I just saw Jason Goodyear, the baseball player, downstairs. I got his autograph!" She waves a cocktail napkin in the air.

"Goody?" Lester says. "No surprise. He gambles like I drink, by which I mean, within reason." The girl looks confused. "Oh, where are my manners?" He sticks his hand over the boy's shoulder, and the girl shakes it cautiously. "I'm Lester. Emily, you said? Beautiful song by that name. A waltz." Lester starts humming, enjoying the melody. "You know it?"

Her eyebrows go up and she slips out of his grip. "Uh, no." William looks stricken, but Lester keeps smiling.

"Look it up."

◇

"So who was that guy?" Emily says when they're settled into their seats, Lester safely back at the piano.

"Oh, nobody," William says, watching her eyes flick from him to the piano and back. She's pretty, wearing a sleek black top, a skirt, and pumps. The kind of outfit that's trying to make a good impression. He regrets his faded New Jersey Nets T-shirt.

"Obviously he's somebody. Seems like he knew you."

"I hit his car."

Her eyes go wide.

"Not hard or anything." Mercifully, her wine appears, and William takes the opportunity to swallow a big gulp of his whiskey. "How was dinner?"

"The same." She rolls her eyes. "You know, parents. Always worried about *something*. It drives me crazy! They won't quit getting in my business and—"

"—asking a thousand questions. I know it." He nods sympathetically.

"Yes! About the new job, about what I'm eating—"

"—if I'm sleeping enough, if I'm dating . . ." Their eyes lock.

"Exactly. Though I can tell you one thing: there are exactly zero eligible dudes in my life right now. I'm living at home. To save my savings, you know?" She looks nervous, revealing the fact, but William shrugs. He lives in a hotel. "Every single man in the neighborhood is over fifty or under five. That's why I'm here. I mean, why I went online. Which is I guess why I'm here. Oh, you know."

"I do."

She puts down her wineglass and squints at him. "It's crazy, but I keep thinking you look just like this baseball player. My dad's from L.A., so he's a big Lions fan, and they've got this rookie . . . fuck. I can't remember his name."

"Huh. Is he any good?"

Emily drains her glass. "He sorta sucks."

◇

Lester looks over to the chatting couple. "Cute girl," he says to himself. Not going to win any pageants, but handsome in a quirky way, bright eyes and wavy hair and an interesting profile. *Big nose*, that's another way to say it. She reminds him of the bohemian chicks he went with in the Village, way back when. Birds chirping about women's liberation, too busy to shave their pits (but not their legs, thank goodness). He did well for himself, for a while there. He could talk just about any woman, fourteen to forty, into his bed. Emily cracks up across the room, her laugh like a trill.

Young love. A lot of good songs about it, too. "There Will Never Be Another You." "You're My Everything." "All of Me." Those kinds of feelings seem a long way off now, but at least he knows what they're singing about.

Lester takes a long draw off his whiskey sour and starts into "Emily," nice and easy. The stretch of the piece is in the right-hand melody, low then high, and Lester has no problem with that. E-B-G, E-B-G, E-B-G. Wow, he loves this song. His left hand spreads into a G7, pain-free. E-A-A, E-A-A, E-A-A. It was written for some bad movie, but Lester first heard it performed by Bill Evans, back when Scott was playing with him in the Village. After that, Lester couldn't put on an Evans record without hearing another version: he plays it on *Conversations with Myself*, on *Live in Paris*. He recorded it in San Francisco, too, just a few days before he died.

When Lester finishes, a few light flourishes in the right hand over the low rumble of C-sus, he looks up. The girl is gone, and Jason Goodyear is sitting in her place.

$$\diamond$$

Emillionaire was a bust—their conversation went well enough, but she seemed more interested in the free wine than getting to know "Frank," and when he invited her up for a nightcap in his room, she let a quiet laugh slip out before saying no, she had to be heading home. So William is left alone to watch the muted *Late Late Show* monologue—Craig Ferguson gesticulating like a marionette—and listen to that weird old piano man. It is while he is sitting at the bar, feeling supremely sorry for himself, that Jason Goodyear sidles into the seat next to him. "This one free?"

Eric is so startled at the player's appearance that he forgets a tap, the beer foam spreading over the lip of a pint glass and down his arm before he snaps to attention. Jason waits patiently for him to wipe up the mess, then orders a beer of his own. "You need anything?" he asks William, then nods at his near-empty glass. "He'll have another of whatever that is."

"So, how's the spring going?" Jason asks once both men have their drinks.

"Great." William's heart is in his throat. Sure, Goodyear has said a few things to him in passing, stuck up for him when Monterrey was giving him grief. But the idea that they'd sit together and share a drink—he can't believe it. "It's such a dream to be here."

"You can be honest." Jason takes a draw of his beer, and sets down the glass carefully on his coaster. He's in no rush.

"I really suck."

The older man laughs. "Everyone who makes it—and most of the guys who don't—were *the best* somewhere. A lot of places. The best on his Little League team, the best in his youth league, the best in his high school division. The first time you realize you're not the best anymore . . . it's no bed of roses."

William knows he means the petals, but he thinks of the thorns. Has Jason ever faced that day, faced any sort of failure?

They watch the TV, Ferguson silently talking with some forgettable celebrity. When a commercial rolls, William tries to get the conversation flowing again. "How, uh, is your spring going?"

"Shitty." Of course. The divorce, the trespassing kerfuffle. William is so wrapped up in his own crap spring, he completely forgot about Jason's troubles.

"Sorry, stupid question."

"It's okay." Jason takes another sip of beer, side-eyes the rookie. What was that look? William wonders. Was it *I need to talk to someone*, or *Fuck you, rook*? William can't tell, but Jason *did* sit down and start a conversation . . . "Do you want to talk about it?" William thinks he sounds like a therapist—or a girl—asking that.

Jason drops forty dollars on the bar and rises. "Not here." And then, to William's amazement: "Come with me."

◇

They walk out of the casino and into the parking lot. Jason continues through the rows of cars, weaving between shiny Bimmers and rusted-out Mercurys and past William's own Porsche. "Where did you park?" William asks as the cars start to thin.

"I didn't," Jason says. Ahead, there's a footbridge between the casino and the stadium complex, one William has never taken—he always drives the short distance. They cross it, walk across another lot, and start down a path between dark practice fields. Everything's clean, in its place, ready for the morning sessions that will begin—William looks at his watch—in six hours. How did it get so late?

Jason leads them to a small cinder-block building, takes out a set of keys, and opens the door. Inside it's a simple arrangement: a hot plate and half-size fridge in one corner, a single cot in another, covered in a cowboy blanket. Cactus League pennants on the walls, a small shelf of books. A television, snaking the stadium's cable, and a ratty secondhand loveseat. A laptop open on a card table with two folding chairs. Under the table a bucket of batting-practice balls.

"You live here?"

Goodyear shrugs. "Easy commute." He points his finger toward the stadium, to the casino, and back. "You want a beer?"

William is well on his way to drunk, but he nods. Anything to keep this going.

"I'm sure you heard the wife kicked me out."

"I hadn't." Of course he had, but this doesn't seem like the time to mention it.

"I know what the guys are saying." He passes William a beer and opens one for himself. "It's not because I have a small prick. And she's not into chicks. Any of that would've been easier." He takes a long pull of beer.

William takes a sip, too.

"You know, Willie Mays was suspended for gambling."

William didn't know that.

"Mickey Mantle, too. 'Associating with known gamblers.' But it's bullshit. Spring training in Florida, the Grapefruit League, just about everyone ends up at the horse track. You ever bet on horses?" William shakes his head no. His gambling starts and ends with March Madness.

"I remember when Pete Rose was going through all his trouble. I was just a kid, but I kept thinking, How could he be so fucking dumb? Why doesn't he just quit already? Let me tell you: it's easy."

William feels suddenly queasy. He's signed his life over to the Lions, at least the next four years of it. What would they do if their star is booted? The team would collapse, William's prospects along with it. "Did you . . . bet on baseball?"

"Fuck no. But I got myself . . . into a pretty bad hole. That's the *real* reason Liana jumped ship. 'Thrill-seeking behavior,' whatever the fuck that means. I know I just like to win, and she was sick of it."

William stares at the floor, recognizing himself in Jason's confession. He likes to win, too. "How much did you lose?"

"Tonight, I came out with about the same amount I came in with. Maybe down a hundred grand."

"Sounds fine," he says, though it sounds impossible. That's a Porsche, what he lost.

Jason laughs, it coming out more like a bark. "That's *to-*

*night.* I didn't tell you about this morning." Both men are quiet. Jason takes another pull from his beer. "How much was that signing bonus?"

"Two."

"You spend it yet?"

"Just the car."

"That's good, that's real good." Jason puts his can down and presses his hands together. "In that case, I have a big favor to ask."

◇

William falls asleep on Goodyear's loveseat, legs dangling off the end, and wakes only when the left fielder throws a glove at his belly, telling him to borrow it for the day; they are late. They do what they need to on the bank's website, then Jason rushes off somewhere in his Jeep. Out on the sidewalk, William squints at the too-bright morning and walks slowly to the stadium.

There's a note on his locker, and Paine is waiting for him in his office. "You weren't answering your phone," he says.

"Outta juice," William says, not making eye contact. He hopes he doesn't smell like beer.

"Anyway, here." Paine hands over an envelope. William eyes the contents, a stack of twenties. Paine says, "That's a week, kid. But today's your last game. You report to Single-A Carolina on Tuesday."

"Yes, sir."

"Work on those breaking balls. And when you are fielding, I've noticed you have a little stutter-step to the right. Try to cut that out by next spring."

"Yes, sir."

"I know this spring was disappointing, but I look forward to seeing you next year."

"Yes, sir." William walks out of the office, drops the envelope in his locker, and heads for the showers. He turns the water to scalding, hoping to feel the heat—nothing else seems to be registering at the moment. Not getting cut, not moving back to the East Coast, not being handed another chance next spring. His skin pinks; the room steams until it's nearly white.

He's the only one in the locker room—that's never been the case, not all spring. After his shower he walks up one row, down the next. The lockers for the starters have their names spelled out on laminate nameplates, the rest of them are written on masking tape. There are plenty of empty lockers now—the residue of tape where names have been, guys he can hardly remember, even just two weeks gone. He stands in front of his own locker. A nameplate, GOSLIN. Someone made that decision, too. He can hear sports radio coming from Paine's office. He slips the plastic out of its rails and puts it in the envelope with his meal money. Next year.

He suits up and steps onto the field. Putney is already at home with a bucket of balls, waiting to practice fungoes with him. The shortstop has been doing this twice a week all month, not complaining, just trying to get him better. Maybe there are a few decent guys here. "You ready, Goose?"

William jogs toward first base, steps on the bag, and settles into position. "Ready."

Above him, the stadium organ comes to life, a creaking progression from one chord to the next. Dissonance, resolution, dissonance, resolution. The notes get louder, more confident, all the way around the loop.

No team ever stays on top of the standings—nothing is static, remember—and right around 1400 the Hohokam had a rough go of it. No one's sure what happened: maybe it was a drought, a flood, or some asshole GM making bad trades, breaking up all the best parts of the team. But whatever caused it, the whole civilization collapsed. The Lions have their own five-game skid the last week of March, but as catastrophic as it feels to Woody Botter and Stephen Smith and everyone else who has a hand in cutting and trimming the Lions to their final iteration (down from eighty to thirty-six by March 25, one more round of paring to go, the last of the probable cuts walking around with targets on their backs), it is a blip in the grand scheme of things.

No, the Hohokam's fall was more than just a sloppy wipeout, a dust-yourself-off-and-get-some-stitches sort of spill: they went poof, just disappeared. Closed their lockers one day, walked out of the stadium, and never came back. Left their ball courts, left their pole houses, left their pottery and spearheads and so many other bits scattered about their desert compounds. With time and mud, all of it got buried, just like the shark teeth, the rhinoceros footprints and fern fossils and whatever else's been sunk below the sod. Given that vanishing act, now their name makes sense, right? *Hohokam*: those who have gone.

The Pima people took up the Hohokam mantle, settling along the Salt River. They managed the wave of Spanish explorers, sent them on to New Mexico and the Grand Canyon. They welcomed the westward-moving Americans, made friends enough that they became scouts for settlers, proving themselves to be useful allies. Another team, the Maricopa, came calling in the middle of the nineteenth century. Mergers are hard, but the Maricopa seemed a good partner against the Apache (the bench-clearing brawls were getting more frequent). It's not unlike the dynamic of these men gathering every spring; strangers until they're not, competing until they're teammates.

And as for the team, as the spring season nears its end, the Lions head toward their own clubhouse détente. The starting pitchers are set—that game Greg Carver threw, right after his night with Tami, that would be his last—and the outfield looks like it will settle into Goodyear-Monterrey-Matthews. They cut all the bullpen catchers and auxiliary infielders, the young guys who were wearing down the starters with their overeager smiles and underwhelming play. In the clubhouse the men can move around again. This feels sustainable, they think, this configuration and scale.

No doubt the Pima and Maricopa heard about Jack Swilling's arrival in East Phoenix, how he set up his namesake mill along the river. Were they nervous? Did they know about the Indian Removal Act, the Appropriation Act, the Trail of Tears? Did they hear tell of the great battles on the Plains, the burned pioneer wagons and night raids? In any case, as the Sioux War raged farther east, the Pimas and the settlers reached a much less bloody solution: to the northeast of Phoenix, just over fifty-two thousand acres were set aside for the tribes. A contraction, yes; an affront, agreed. But no one was walking to Kansas, they kept their good farmland, and Red Mountain still sat like a perfect, rose-colored cone along the eastern border.

The Pima were glad for their legal claim because, in 1888, the U.S. Army chaplain Winfield Scott bought the adjacent 640 acres. It took Scott's new town six years to call itself Scottsdale, another twenty to top one thousand inhabitants. A school, a blacksmith, a general store . . . Then, like a rookie gunning, improbably, for the single-season home-run record, Scottsdale leapt ahead in the standings. The first luxury resort opened in 1910. Fashion models and movie stars followed, showing up for nose jobs and mud masks. Frank Lloyd Wright pitched a tent on a side of McDowell Peak in 1937. Baseball landed in 1955, the Orioles right downtown.

But baseball was just the tip of the iceberg: the area boom-boom-boomed, growing faster than nearly anywhere. Construction spread to the steep edges of the mountains and then seeped around their contours, up to the edge of the reservation. The historic downtown—Old Man Scott's haunts and that first little red schoolhouse—got wrapped in luxury shops, open-air malls, and high-end condos. Growth stuttered in 2008, but nothing could keep Scottsdale down for long. Across the street, on Pima-Maricopa land, there was a casino to be built, and a stadium, too.

That brings us up to just about the present, the 2011 spring season and this shiny new stadium, which, after four weeks of sun-bake and heavy use, has lost only an ounce of its luster. That new grit and grime are imperceptible in the eyes of a six-year-old, one moony, baseball-loving Alex S. For him, the place just about glows with wonder, and there're no imperfections or scuffs.

I wonder what he'd say if I told him his hero-among-heroes, Jason Goodyear, was in trouble. Would Alex believe that the left fielder was as broke as his family? That the athlete was homeless and squatting, too? My guess is that the kid would just giggle at me, shake his head, and say, *Rawr*. That's what he says to most strangers these days, the kids at his new school and his momma's friends, the ones who come over for parties that start after he's already meant to be in bed, gatherings that he watches from the shadows at the top of the stairs. The social worker at school said she's worried about this little man's roaring, but his momma waved it off. *He's just going through a phase.*

*Coping,* his sister told me as we drove to school. I'd picked them up at the bus stop, Michelle knowing better than to get into a stranger's car, but also knowing they'd missed the bus again, and she didn't want to be late for her first-period exam. *It's what he does when he feels scared,* she said. *And what do you do?* I'd asked, but she just chewed her lip. I gave her a hundred-dollar bill, too. Not like I'm made of money, and not like she demanded it, but after Sara and Liana's housekeeper I got accustomed to keeping a few bills handy, and Michelle, maybe more than anybody else I've met down here—she and her brother needed it. It seems whatever her mother was earning went right up her nose, and those kids were making do with next to nothing.

*Rawr,* Alex said when he jumped out of the car. *Thanks,* Michelle said, taking the bill as she exited. Thinking more about it, I believe Alex is on to something. It's not a half-bad idea, figuring out some phrase that could make us think fondly of our grandpas and our heroes and convince us, even briefly, that we're big and bold and fierce. We've all been in situations where we could use a bit more courage.

Like Jason, this morning, as he shook that sleeping rookie awake. He was hoping that today, at last, something would go right.

# HOMERS

"If the teacher asks where we live, say, 'I forgot.'" That's what Momma tells Alex to say. It's breakfast and they are eating Corn Pops. He is—his momma just has coffee in the morning.

Momma fills her mug again, sloshing some coffee onto the rough wood counter. She doesn't wipe it up.

"Say, 'I forgot.' I mean, you can say you live here in Scottsdale, that's good, and that you and your momma and your sister have a real nice house near Sandia and you even have your own bedroom, and that I love you more than plenty. But if she wants to know your address, like street name and number, just say that you forgot it and that she should call me. You got that?"

"What about Randy?" Alex asks. Randy is Momma's boyfriend. They met at the Oregon Country Fair, and it wasn't too long after that that Momma moved them all to Arizona. She said Randy was a handsome man and a kind one, and that Arizona would be a good opportunity.

"What about him," she says.

"You said we moved down here to live with him." When Michelle protested the move—she wanted to finish high school in Eugene, with her friends—Momma said she couldn't do this alone anymore, and Alex had said that she wasn't alone, and that made her lips go wobbly and her eyes get wet. "So do I say he lives with us, too?"

His momma frowns. "No, he has his own apartment. We live *near* him, and sometimes he stays with us. And he helps, too, getting us settled." They had been staying with Randy in his tiny apartment for a week when he gave them keys to the Grandpa House. Then, when they'd had to leave there in a hurry, he brought them to Sandia Hills. "I don't miss Oregon, not one bit. Do you?" She stirs some sweet, milky stuff into her coffee and Alex wants some but knows she'll say he can't have any, that he has to drink regular milk until he's a big boy or else all his teeth will fall out, and not just the baby ones.

"No," Alex says, though he did like the duck that was on all the posters and sweatshirts and he did like seeing his grandpa all the time. Momma and Michelle had lived with Momma's parents, but then Grandma died and Grandpa didn't like Alex's dad and so they moved out. Momma doesn't like Alex's dad, either, not anymore, but they can't move back in. They had to move to Arizona instead.

"Don't make him lie for you, Mom. We're fucking squatters." Alex's half sister, Michelle, is sitting across the table, reading her math book and eating her third Pop-Tart of the morning. She has a cup of coffee, too, because Momma says it'll help her lose weight and wake up, but Michelle makes a frowny face every time she takes a sip.

Momma's face is like something smells. "Don't swear in front of your brother. And Alex," she says, "put on your shirt."

"I don't have none."

"It's *any*—you don't have—I mean, here. You have plenty." She tugs a shirt out of the laundry bag. They went to the Washateria last week, the one with washers so big Alex could fit inside, but Momma still hasn't folded their clean clothes, and Michelle will only fold her own clothes, that's what she said and that's what she did, so Alex's Jason Goodyear T-shirt, which Momma brought home from the stadium, is clean but all wrinkly. They left most of their laundry at the Grandpa House and couldn't go back and get it because one day when Michelle and Alex were coming home from the store there was a police car parked in the driveway and the grandpa and grandma from the pictures were standing on the lawn and the grandpa was waving his arms and shouting something. Alex saw them first and said, *Michelle, look*, and she stopped the car real fast and turned around in the neighbor's driveway and they drove away. When they were around the corner Alex said, *Michelle, why can't we go home?* She said, *Just be quiet now, sweetie. I have to call Mom.* Turns out Michelle was the only one who kept everything in her car like Momma said they should and so she still has almost everything. Alex didn't and now he doesn't have his coloring books or his Spider-Man shirt or most of his underwear.

Momma shakes out the shirt and pulls it over his head, hard, which tugs at his ears. "Owww," he says.

She waits for him to put his arms in the armholes. "Any day now, Alex." Momma musses up his hair and winces. "Jesus, when was the last time you washed your hair? You're as greasy as a pepperoni pizza."

"He hasn't all week," Michelle says. She is calm like a turtle, slow and round. "How can he, when we're out of shampoo?" Michelle goes back to her math, which looks like another language,

Egyptian or Greek or Chinese. Michelle has a test soon about whether or not she can go to college.

"Jeez, Miche. How am I supposed to know you kids are out of damn soap?" Their new house has three bathrooms: one for Momma—it has a bathtub with a Jacuzzi and it's just for grown-ups—one for kids, which has a bathtub but no walls, and one downstairs for guests. That one just has a pipe where the toilet is supposed to be. Alex is old enough now that he takes baths by himself, which he likes, but sometimes they're too hot and sometimes he misses Momma helping and telling stories about when she was little and swimming in the ocean. She had good stories about swimming in the ocean. "I'm never in there. Trying to give you your pri-va-cy."

"I told you Saturday. And again on Monday," Michelle says. Alex wiggles his arms into his sleeves and drains his bowl, swallowing the last Corn Pop whole. He wants to get on the school bus before his sister and his momma start fighting again. They are almost always about to start fighting again.

"It's Thursday. Christ. Can you pick some up at lunch? I'm at the stadium all day." Momma got a job at the stadium near their house, Salt River Fields at Talking Stick. It was like her job in Oregon: she sold hot dogs and popcorn and soda pop to the green-and-gold Ducks fans, now she sells hot dogs and popcorn and soda pop to the black-and-gold Lions fans, but it's baseball not football and sunnier here. *I get to watch the Lions every day.* When she told Alex that, the boy thought Momma was the luckiest lady in the world. The Lions are his favorite team because they are his grandpa's favorite team because before his grandpa moved to Oregon to marry his grandma, he lived in California and worked on an almond farm and cheered for the Lions, who were baby Lions back then, brand-new. Grandpa is the one who taught Alex to go *rawr.*

"We're not supposed to go off campus." Michelle goes to Chaparral High, but only the seniors can go off campus at lunch and she's in eleventh grade. "It's against the rules," Michelle adds, and takes another big bite of Pop-Tart.

"The store's right across the street." Smoke looks ready to come out of Momma's ears. She says she's trying to fight with Michelle less, but right now it looks like she wants to fight more. "After school then?"

"I'll miss the bus, and *somebody* took my car." The Grandpa House had a two-car garage with two cars in it, a fancy black one and a not-fancy light-blue one, so Momma used the nice one and Michelle used the other, which wasn't nice and didn't always have AC but was fine for driving to school and back. But then, a few weeks ago, Momma came back from a date with Randy and the fancy car looked like a giant had smooshed it up in his fist: the windows were all spiderwebs and cracks and it had lots of dents all over. The next morning it was gone and Momma's eyes were all red and puffy and she kept saying they almost got caught, what if they'd gotten caught, and Randy, who'd slept over and was eating Corn Pops with them, said, *But remember we didn't. We're fine.*

"I need that car more than you do, and we both know it." After the fancy car disappeared, Momma took back the old blue car from Michelle.

"You *had* another car and you sold it or wrecked it or I don't know what." The family came to Arizona in a Buick that was older than Michelle, but when Momma got the black Cadillac the Buick disappeared and nobody's seen it since.

"That car was on its last legs." Momma keeps her voice even, like nothing's wrong, like they're not about to throw mugs. "I know, why don't you walk? The exercise'll do you good." Momma likes to exercise whenever she isn't too busy working or being Randy's girlfriend or doing Momma stuff. Sometimes she walks over at Gateway nature park and sometimes she does jumping jacks in the garage and sometimes she even jumps rope with Alex. She's as thin as Michelle is thick, but Michelle says it's not from exercise.

"It's five miles!" Michelle crumples the Pop-Tart wrapper up in her fist. "And it's going to be what, eighty-five degrees today? Ninety?"

"Fine. Randy will come get you, then." Momma chugs the rest of her coffee and leaves the mug in the sink with the other dishes. They don't have a dishwasher, just a big box-shaped empty space under the counter where it will go. Most days they use paper plates.

"Will you text him? I want to see you text him." Michelle squints like she's trying to see inside Momma's skull.

"Really?" Momma asks, but Michelle doesn't blink. "Jeez. Last I heard kids were supposed to *respect* their parents." Momma picks up her phone and begins to peck at it with her ruby-red nails, narrating as she types. "Work-ing late. Please get M at Walgreens at—"

"Tell him I'll be at the library on Shea. Five p.m."

"At library on Shea at five. T-H-X. Send." She puts down her phone and the noise sounds like a slap. "Happy?"

Michelle swallows the rest of her coffee in one big gulp. She grimaces. "Are you kidding? I haven't been happy in years." She shoves her math book into her bag and stands up. "Alex, c'mon, sweetie, we gotta catch the bus."

◇

Michelle and Alex walk past a bunch of houses that look like theirs but with nobody living in them, then past the one that looks like theirs but has bushes planted in front and a lady named Miss

Tami living inside, then out the front gate that doesn't have any gate on it, just gate hinges and big stone posts and signs that say SANDIA HILLS and LOTS FOR SALE—DISCOUNTED PRICES!!! Randy is friends with somebody who stayed here and he said it would be fine for them to live there for a while, too. Alex likes the neighborhood because Momma says he can play in the street because there are never cars around, so he throws baseballs against the sides of empty houses. Plus, lots of cute cats keep showing up from somewhere, and he says *rawr* at all of them.

As they walk, Alex thinks about what Momma said, turns it over and over like it's a penny but strange. Is it lying to say *I forgot*? He thought lying was something else, like saying you didn't break a window when you did or you don't miss your grandpa when you do. He thinks it's not lying because their neighborhood doesn't even *have* street signs and the houses don't have numbers yet, they're too new. "Momma's not a liar," he says to the back of Michelle.

"What?" She turns around. Walking to the bus the other day Michelle told Alex they were homeless, but he didn't think that's right, either, because first they lived with Randy and then in the Grandpa House and now they live here. That's three homes, not no homes. That night, he asked Momma about it and she asked him why he was asking and he told her what Michelle had said. Momma told him he shouldn't worry about Michelle and what she thinks, that it's hormones and that Alex should be nice to her, but then after that he heard Momma yelling at Michelle about how she's fat and mean and gonna get them in trouble, and Alex thought that that wasn't being very nice.

"Hurry up," she says when he doesn't answer. Michelle is walking fast because she's sure they'll miss the bus. She worries this will happen every day but most days they don't.

Michelle and Alex see other kids standing on the corner.

Those kids live across the big street in Sandia Valley, another neighborhood that looks like Sandia Hills but all the houses are done being built and full of families and kids and puppies. There are big kids waiting and little kids waiting and that means neither of them missed the bus. "Oh, thank gawd," Michelle says as her bus comes around the corner. Then it stops and she kisses Alex on the head the way his momma does and says, "Be good," and gets on the bus and waves at him through the window. Her face is wider than Momma's, but from the side they look just the same.

Alex's bus comes next. He lets the other kids get on first, then he says hello to the driver and sits up front next to a fourth grader who pretends Alex isn't there. That's fine to Alex; he watches the streets go by outside his window and outside the front window and outside the window across the aisle. That seat has two third graders in it, twins named Linus and Neal, and they tell him to stop staring and he says he's not staring at them, but look, it's the baseball stadium. "My momma works there," Alex says and the boys scrunch up their faces. "Girls don't play baseball," one of them says, and Alex explains his momma makes the food for baseball players and the people who like them.

The bus bounces past a mall and then across a big street and then the houses are all really small and look faded, like they've been in the sun too long, and there are more restaurants with tacos than restaurants with hamburgers, and that's where the bus picks up the Mexican kids. Alex's grandpa, who Alex saw all the time when they lived in Oregon, used to say the Mexicans were ruining the country, but Alex thinks they're okay; they're nice most of the time and some of them are really smart. The Mexicans aren't ruining the elementary school.

The school bus rolls into the part of town that is just plain old. There are a lot of apartment buildings that look crowded and sad and remind Alex of the places they lived in Oregon and all the cars in the parking lots look like Momma's old Buick. The bus slows. Alex's friend Sam usually gets on here but he's not there so the bus speeds up again. Sam misses the bus a lot.

Alex's school, the one he's been going to since they arrived in Phoenix, is all one story and all light brown mud-stuff and has a flagpole and fifteen palm trees out front. (There used to be sixteen but one got hit by a school bus and started dying so they had to cut it down.) All the kids get off the bus and have five minutes to get to class, which means four and a half minutes for Alex to run around on the playground and thirty seconds to get to class. He rushes over to the jungle gym and starts climbing to the very top. There's some other kid, a kindergartner, trying to climb, but Alex is bigger and faster than him and he *rawr*s and the littler boy gets out of the way.

He makes it to the top of the jungle gym and looks out on the playground and sees that most everyone is already inside, the fourth graders and the third graders and then Bobby Plotkin disappears, which means the first grade is inside, too. The gym teacher sees Alex and waves his hand and shouts for him to get down from there before he breaks an arm. Alex did that once when he was three and again when he was four, but he hasn't broken his arm for two and a half years, which Momma says must be some kind of record.

He gets down and the gym teacher walks him inside and all the way to Ms. Goodyear's door and watches him go into class like he might just run off otherwise. The kids have assigned seats in the first grade and he is in the second row in the middle section and when he sits down he hears kids behind him snicker and whisper, "Look, he's late" and "What happened to his hair?" Alex likes Ms. Goodyear and sometimes wonders if she knows

Jason Goodyear, but when he asked about it she just said, *We are NOT talking about THAT.* This morning Ms. Goodyear narrows her eyes at Alex and says, "Nice shirt."

Ms. Goodyear says that today class is going to learn about plants and animals and the history of Arizona, which sounds boring to Alex until she tells them that sharks used to live here. Then Alex listens to everything she has to say about the dried-up oceans and woolly mammoths and the beginning of the mountains. She takes two math books and tries to smoosh them together and instead they both push up and she says that's how mountains formed.

Alex gets lunch for free, but it doesn't matter it's free because it's gross, lumpy mashed potatoes and broccoli that's slimy and not salty at all. Sam is at school now because his mom dropped him off and he has cheese crackers and he shares those and gives Alex half of his cupcake and then they run around the playground and climb to the top of the jungle gym and spit on girls down below because they are princes defending their castle from witches.

The first graders have gym next and they're playing baseball today, which is great because Alex loves baseball. He's sure he is going to hit the ball over the fence and break all the windows of all the buses that are waiting for the end of the day, but then he doesn't hit it very far, just to the second baseman, who throws Alex out. Alex plays outfield when the other team is batting and no one hits it that far before it's time to do math. Alex gets all his math problems right, except for four plus six, which he has to do twice before it is ten.

When class is over the kids go outside and find their buses and Alex finds his. Alex's bus goes the same way it came in the morning, but backward. When it gets to his stop he gets off and so do Linus and Neal, and they are whispering and staring at him and then they say, "Hey, Alex!"

He is surprised they even know his name, so he turns around and says, "Yeah?"

"Where do you live?"

Just like Momma said to say, he says, "I forgot," and they start hooting and calling him a dummy and his face feels hot and he pretends to tie his shoe and waits for them to move. Instead they just stand there laughing. Finally they cross the street and go into their neighborhood of houses that are full of people and dishwashers and toilets and toys. Alex straightens and says *rawr* as loud as he can say it, but they don't turn around, so he walks into his neighborhood of houses that are empty. Except for Miss Tami, who is in her front yard in her bikini, tanning on a pool chair. When she sees him go by she sits up and waves hello.

◇

That night they have cold hot dogs for dinner. Alex gives his momma a note that says there is no school on Friday because the teachers are getting trained on how to do new things, and Momma says she needs Michelle to stay home and watch him. Michelle says she can't because she is taking a practice SAT on Friday. Momma is drinking red wine and nearly spits it out. "It's the last weekend of the season. We're going to be slammed," Momma says. "Besides, why do you have to practice if you're so smart?"

Michelle says it's too fuckin' bad about Alex, but he's not *her* kid. Momma starts screaming, "Don't cuss at me," and, "I am your mother," and Michelle starts yelling, "I'm getting out of this shithole," and they yell at each other like that all the way upstairs. Then some doors slam.

When Momma comes back to the kitchen she tells Alex he will go to the stadium with her because there will be no one at home to watch him and he's too little to be by himself in a big house all day. "It's like when you watched the Ducks with me."

Usually Grandpa would watch him when she was working, but when he couldn't or wouldn't because he and Momma were fighting she brought Alex to the stadium and said he was a volunteer from the Cub Scouts. Mostly the ticket people believed her, but one game it didn't work; the ticket person asked to see his ticket, which he didn't have, so Momma left Alex in the car with the car keys and told him to sit there the whole game. She said to hide in the back if anyone came looking because they might try to steal him and the car and then what would they do? *If you're cold turn on the heater*, Momma said, because it was rainy and cold that day. *You remember how to do that?* And Alex nodded because he did. *Good. Be careful*, she said, and kissed him on the top of his head and then watched him lock the doors. Sitting in the car, Alex could tell when Oregon scored because it was so loud the whole stadium shook and the parking lot shook, too, and the hula dancer that Momma stuck to the Buick's dashboard started swaying. Then the game was over and Momma was knocking on the window looking scared until he sat up and let her in. He'd fallen asleep on the floor of the back seat, a space that wasn't big enough for an adult and wasn't even big enough for Michelle but it was plenty big for Alex. *Oh, honey, you scared me*, Momma said, and, *I couldn't see you*, and, *It's cold outside, how'd it get so hot in here?* He'd turned on the heater, he said, just like she told him to.

◇

Now it's Friday and Alex is up early. Alex and Momma give Michelle hugs and wish her good luck on her test and Momma apologizes for what she said at dinner about Michelle being too smart for her own good. Then they drive to the stadium. There are hardly any other cars in the lot so they park close to the entrance in a section marked PLAYERS ONLY. "You ready, sugar?" Momma asks, and Alex nods because he can't wait to go inside to see the field made of a river made of salt. He wants to find the talking stick, too, but Momma tells him it is hidden out past the outfield so good no one can find it. Alex says he bets her a million dollars he can find it and she says, "Deal."

They go to a gate by the left field foul post that says EMPLOY-EES. Momma waves at an old man in a yellow-gold polo and says, "Hey, Troy." He waves back.

"Who's the whippersnapper?" The old man reaches for Alex. His hand is knobby and crooked-looking and he has big white hairs coming out of his nose.

"*Rawr!*" Alex lunges at the man.

"My baby, Alex." She swipes her ID in a machine on the wall that makes a loud beep. She puts a hand on his shoulder.

"I'm not a baby!" Alex wiggles out of her grip.

"How old are you, young man?"

"Seven." The machine beeps again and a light on it turns green.

"Almost," Momma says. "He's six till next month."

"Definitely *not* a baby." Troy nods, and smiles at Alex with yellow teeth. "You working one twenty-two again?"

Momma shakes her head. "They have me over at section one thirteen today. You're gonna have to walk farther for those free hot dogs, Troy."

"And you'll have to go farther for your lemonade." He winks.

"Lemonade?" Alex spots a small cooler behind Troy. "I want some!"

Momma tugs at Alex's shoulder. "It's for grown-ups, sweet pea. Come on, I'll get you a soda pop."

They pass a concession stand and she waves and says, "Hi, Dot," to a lady putting on her apron, and they walk by a guy driving around a small tractor with a big cube of Cracker Jack wrapped up in Saran Wrap.

When they get to her stand Momma starts popping the popcorn and thawing hot dogs and getting out the salt so she can salt the pretzels. By accident Alex spills a can of popcorn butter on the floor and then he slips in it and gets butter on his butt. She makes him clean up the mess with wadded paper towels and when he can't do it very well she sighs and says, "Just forget about it, Alex," and takes him by the hand and walks him up the aisle and into the empty stadium and tells him to sit down. She says that he can't leave the seat until the person who owns that seat shows up, and when that happens he has to come *right back* to the hot dog stand and sit in the corner and not touch anything, definitely not any more popcorn butter.

"Don't move a muscle, Alex," she says again before going back to the stand, glaring and looking meaner than a wet cat. Last week Michelle told Alex that Momma's on drugs again and that's why she's mad and mean and skinny, and Alex thinks maybe that's true but maybe Michelle is jealous that Momma is skinny and Michelle isn't. When Momma got a nosebleed Tuesday night Michelle whispered, *See, I told you,* and Alex was confused because he thought you got nosebleeds from being in the nosebleed seats at the football stadium, not from doing drugs or working on the ground floor. Michelle says Randy sells drugs and that's why Momma likes him so much, but Alex thought Momma liked him because he had pretty eyeballs.

There are only two people on the field, a guy at home plate with a baseball bat and a big bucket of balls and a guy at first base swinging his arms around like he's a windmill. Alex recognizes the batter as Lions shortstop Ray Putney, but he doesn't know who's on first. He looks young, like he's maybe the same age as Michelle. When Putney hits a ball bouncing up toward first base the guy bends down to scoop it up and Alex can see the name on his back: GOSLIN.

It is so quiet in the stadium he can hear the players talking. "Don't insult me, Putt." That's the fielder saying that.

"Just getting warmed up, Willy. Don't you worry." Putney tosses another ball up in the air then swings around and hits it, harder this time. It zooms so fast Goslin has to put up his glove to protect his face and then the ball is in his glove, *whap*. "That's it, Goose. Nice catch."

The first baseman throws the ball back toward home and it hits the bucket of balls and makes them rattle and they almost tip over but they don't. "I told you, never call me Goose, got it?"

"Okay, okay. Gos-lin. Got it." Putney pulls another ball out of the bucket. "Pop up?"

"Sure." Goslin punches the leather of his glove and looks up at the sky. But the ball leaves the bat charging along the ground in fast, mean bounces and it goes right by him into the right field. Alex laughs.

"Fuck you, Putt!"

Putney smiles. "You got another left-handed batter willing to practice this JV shit with you?"

Goslin is quiet and gets back into his crouch, his glove on his knee. "Gimme another."

"That's what I thought."

The two players go through the whole bucket of balls and then collect them and go back into the dugout and there is no one on the field. Alex counts the number of times he sees the word *Lions* around the stadium and is up to twenty-two when some other players come out, and an old guy that looks like the grandpa from the Grandpa House. Someone else wheels out a big machine that looks like a vacuum on stilts. The old man stands behind a metal screen and feeds balls into the machine and they get spit out and fly at the batter. The first guy misses five balls and then goes to the back of the line. The second guy hits three, misses two. The third guy hits the first one up real high, straight up, and it comes falling back into the seats with a loud clatter. It's just a few rows away! Momma says that Alex is not supposed to leave this seat no matter what, but he can see the ball rolling around and he figures it'll be fine if he goes and gets it.

Turns out the players hit foul balls all the time, because after Alex finds the first ball, it is only a few swings before he hears the *bang, bang, bang* of another ball bouncing against the seats, clattering like those big coins that fall through the maze when his grandpa watched *The Price Is Right*. He finds that ball, too, and then a third foul ball nearly hits him on the head and then one lands out in the left field seats, but he finds it. He carries his treasure in his shirt like a kangaroo. When he looks up from finding one by the visiting team's dugout, he sees the old man is dragging the ball-spitting machine off the field and somebody else is pulling the screen back to the hole in the outfield wall and all the players have gotten rid of their bats and now have gloves and are throwing balls back and forth between first and second, first and third, shortstop and first, around and around like pinball. There are more people in the stadium now, fathers and sons and some old-people couples in black-and-gold T-shirts, stadium attendants in bright yellow helping people find their seats. Alex surveys the crowd. It looks like somebody is sitting in his seat now, and anyway, he wants to find Momma and show her all his balls.

But when he goes out to the concourse and looks for the sign that says HOT DOGS PRETZELS PEANUTS it's not Momma but some lady he doesn't recognize lining up hot dogs in the hot dog–spinning machine. There's another place that looks just like the first, but Momma's not there, either—it's that lady she called Dot. The woman doesn't pay attention to Alex even after he says, "Excuse me, ma'am? Excuse me!" It's like he's invisible even when he's loud and polite. He goes the whole way up and the whole way back and he sees six HOT DOGS PRETZELS PEANUTS signs but he doesn't see Momma anywhere.

"Hey, kid!" It's Momma's friend Troy. He has his scary hand on Alex's shoulder again and Alex doesn't like it, but he likes seeing someone he's met before. "Whatcha got there?"

"I caught these." Alex shows him his balls.

"My word, you've scooped up more than Willy Goslin."

"Huh?"

"Never mind." His breath smells bad, sweet and stuffy and stinky all at one time. "Your momma was looking for you."

"You've seen my momma?"

"She and that Randy fellow had to run out for just a minute. 'An errand.'" The old man scratches his nose. "Here." He hands Alex Momma's car key. "She told me to tell you to wait in the car. And to put on the air because—"

Before Troy can say anything else or touch him with that gross hand again, Alex has snapped up the key and is running back to the car, fast but not too fast because he doesn't want the balls bouncing out of his shirt and rolling away into a gutter or under a car, especially a car that's still moving.

The key only works on the front door, so Alex opens that one and then opens the back door from the inside and then goes in the back seat and locks both doors and stuffs the key in the seam between the seats so he won't lose it. He lets the balls out of his shirt and they roll around on the back seat and then he lines them all up in a row. Nine balls! He picks out his favorite, which is the newest, brightest one, and he wipes it off with his T-shirt and some spit. There are a lot of people coming by now, tall boys in shirts that say ASU with pretty girls in tank tops and lots of grandmas and grandpas and some other kids and their dads, too. A girl sees Alex in the window and waves and he waves back, but then he wiggles into the space between the front and back seats. He doesn't want people to see him, because then they'll ask what he's doing by himself and where's his ticket and where's his momma and where does he live and he'll have to tell them *I don't know*. He's a kind of scared but also happy, because he has his new favorite baseball and he's almost totally invisible. He lies there in the dimness, rubbing the ball's leather, hoping Momma won't be too mad at him for leaving his seat. Alex counts the red stitches under his thumb but then he loses count and starts again, ticking them off like they were seconds on a clock.

He can see the tops of the people's heads walking by. Then the stream slows and he can hear the national anthem sounding tinny, like it's being played on a kazoo. After that only a few people pass, someone talking on their phone, a man whistling, a couple who are quiet. And then it's just the bright blue sky out the window. It's getting warm, so Alex scrambles to the front seat and puts the key in the ignition and starts the AC. Hot air blows on his face and he waits for it to cool off. Alex knows sometimes it takes a long time. It's still blowing hot and not getting colder so he turns off the car. He'll try again in a little bit; that's what Michelle did when the blue car was her car and sometimes the air would blow cold the second time. Sometimes the third.

Something good happens because the crowd cheers and the car's windows rattle. There's a new hula girl on the blue car's dashboard, which looks like the old hula girl on the old car's dashboard, and she shakes her hips. Alex watches her sway for a minute and tries the air-conditioning again. Still hot. He climbs back into the space between the seats, reaches for his favorite ball, and starts counting its stitches again. He wonders some more about where Momma went, but he knows she'll be back soon.

Many things are improbable. Geology—all of it. Sharks, their general existence, but especially that they were once in Arizona. That woolly mammoths were, too. That Arizona was a sea, a swamp, anything at all other than this stark brown desert. That oceans dry up, that oceans surge, that mountains climb into mountains and then they start to shrink.

It's improbable that once, millennia ago, men built coliseums and called them such; it's also unlikely that centuries later men again arrived at coliseums and called them something else. The fierceness and ferocity of competition—but the growing industry and indifference of sport, too—these things are improbable. It's improbable that even in the age of ESPN and digital ticker tape, of satellite TV and baseball apps, that after the death of the sportswriter, there is still room in this world for the story of the long game, that we've made time to tell it the meandering way around, to pull all the strings together. I'm thankful for that. Four home runs in a single game—only fifteen men in the history of the league have done that. Unassisted triple plays: I've seen only one. Bases loaded, and Goodyear was playing shallow left, close to the shortstop. Caught a quick-sinking fly—that's one. Tagged second—that's two. And touched the runner on his dash from first to second (so certain that Jason would drop it, he was already past the baseman). Three. That was something. Jason was a rookie that year, if my memory stands, and I believe that's when I first really started to take notice of the man in left. The Lions weren't even my beat back then—I had the Dodgers. But I watched him grow into his stride like a big-footed puppy, grow into his swing like the lumberjack he's now known to be. And it was a joy. Later, I had seniority enough to write the weekly sports column, half human interest, half old-man opining, and I got to do more Lions coverage. I was the one to write about it when his first contract expired and ten teams were hoping to nab him, how Stephen Smith went near to the ends of the earth to come up with the cash to keep him in Culver City. I was the one on a soapbox when he was robbed of the MVP in 2006, and I was tossing confetti across the sports page when he won his first, then his second, trophy. Those columns were the kind of writing I thought (wrongly, apparently) a big-market paper needed, and that it had needed, right up until the axman cometh. Anyway, I kept watching. Wife dead too soon, kid grown and working back east—it's not like I have anything better to do.

But this isn't a story about my career trajectory or how much I miss my wife. This isn't about the downfall of newspapers or why my son won't go ahead and make me a granddad already. It's about Jason, all the improbable things that got him—us—to this very instant, to right now.

This spring? It was improbable that Salt River Fields would open on time; they were still installing toilets the day before opening, much to Joe Templeton's chagrin. Improbable that the Lions center fielder would get traded away because he bruised a very important ego, but that happened, too. Improbable they'd let William Goslin play so many games, Dorsey already knowing the kid needed two years and twenty pounds before he'd be ready for the big time, and then only maybe. And it's improbable that Liana and Jason will ever get back together— though she does come to the hospital when he calls—but wait, now. I'm getting ahead of myself.

## TRIPLE PLAY

Jason's mother didn't know a lick about sports, but saw in her young son an interest in baseball, an outsize eagerness to play with the bigger boys as they drove by the sandlot games and high school practices of their small Iowa town. So she signed him up for Little League, and, according to his coach, that enthusiasm quickly became a natural gift, which grew into real and profound promise. *He could go pro*—more than one coach told her that. The best they'd ever seen, they were saying even before his voice changed and his lanky frame filled out. She didn't know what those sorts of compliments meant, just that she wanted a route out of Iowa for her boy. By the time Jason was fifteen, she understood she had a prodigy lurking in the basement and did what she could to facilitate his rise—which more often meant staying out of his way, working extra shifts to afford the travel-team dues, paying for that elaborate cable package (broadcasting East Coast starts all the way through the

West Coast ninth innings), and buying him a gently used Jeep so he could get himself to early-morning sessions at the cages, to afternoon practice and home.

There was no baseball on TV all winter, save for the occasional highlight reel, but on those same channels that had been showing the Lions all summer, ESPN2 or 3 or 13, Jason found another world series taking place: poker. It was better than drinking in the cornfields with the other kids—he cared about his body too much for that—and he wouldn't waste his time with girls. Jason was interested in tits and ass like any sixteen-year-old, but set on avoiding a wet-blanket girlfriend who couldn't understand his priorities. His teammates called him a monk way before anyone started in with Goody Two-shoes.

Maybe the other boys were right to rib him, but watching the late-night tournaments was something to do. He gleaned the rules and the strategy, but also, as the camera panned around the table, the poker faces and the personalities, noting the signature hats (ten-gallon cowboy, goofy-looking beret, backward baseball), the wraparound sunglasses that never seemed quite fair, the twitchy tics that might give you away. Jason would play his own hand against the TV, throwing his grandfather's old chips, excavated from a corner of the basement, into a kitty on the shag carpet. He'd go all-in a few times a night, lose everything by increments a few more, and when he was cleaned out just gather the pile right back into his lap.

In high school he played against teammates on the back of the bus, unburdened them of their vending machine money. Same thing happened in college—across a few road trips he made a killing, everyone's beer money and then some—until they decided it wasn't much fun to lose to him all the time, and they opted to sleep on the long rides back from Evanston and South Bend. So he started going to casinos, right around when he went pro—that and turning twenty-one all syncing up in a convenient way. Long weekends during the off-season, maybe a few hands on the road—off-days only—if he knew of a casino or private game nearby. Nothing serious, even if the bets expanded with his salary to numbers his mother would have thought impossible. A day's work as a physician's assistant spent on one bet. A week's effort in the doctor's office won in a hand; a month's lost in two.

What did he like about it? The adrenaline, of course. Winning a hand gave him the same kind of thrill as connecting with a line drive. Folding felt like watching four balls wobble by before trotting to first; bluffing like digging a double out of a slider. End of a night at the tables, like at the end of the game, he could look back on his performance—two for four, once to second, one run—though recounting a poker session felt better than that, because it wasn't just how he'd helped in the scope of the team's effort. At the table, he and he alone could control the win-loss column. The Lions weren't bad, particularly, but in their current configuration they were hardly their best. Sometimes Jason's efforts felt like pulling a training sled across the outfield, the rest of the team lounging on its armature. When he was playing solo, he could win everything. He would. And if he didn't, well, that was on him, too.

And he met Liana at a casino. They tell everyone they met poolside at a resort—*told* everyone, now that the getting-to-know-you narrative is moot. Yes, the casino's hotel did have a pool, and yes, had they both been poolside, they'd likely have noticed each other. She'd been a collegiate athlete (volleyball, and she might have made the Olympic team if she'd been born two years earlier or two years later), and Jason's toned body was notorious among a certain segment of baseball fans. But their relationship didn't begin at the pool—it started with her hollering, her voice husky after two days at the craps table. He looked over to see her tossing the dice down the felt, kicking her leg out and throwing her arm so far ahead she looked like some sort of six-foot-tall hood ornament. That's what got Jason to fold his pair of nines, to stand up, walk over, and say hello. She had him blowing on dice for a hot run that lasted an hour, worked the whole table and a dozen observers into a frenzy. By the time the streak had faded, when she was back where she started, chips-wise, and deflated like a rag doll, Jason was smitten. By her big smile, her teeth like bright chicklets; by her shoulders, which she knew still looked good five years out of competitive play, and so she kept them bare even in the frigid casino AC. By the way she shouted, halfway to a laugh; there was something infectious about it. Jason wasn't attracted to showboats or the types of drama queens his teammates brought home, whom they bragged on and then rolled their eyes over. But when he sidled up next to her and she put a hand on his arm, when she looked at him, something clicked. That's how it felt, or the best he ever was able to explain it—outside, with everyone else, she could present this ruckus and delight, but between the two of them was a quietude, a calm. It felt telepathic, almost, like Jimmy must feel with his pitchers. They didn't need to talk, didn't even need to signal: they just understood each other, and understood they're better off playing together.

That day (that night—they stayed on the floor until sunrise), after they'd both burned through their chips and then some, they went up to his room and fucked for hours. They changed that part, too, when they told their friends and family, or improved it to include a horseback ride, a picnic. But really they slept in a tangle of sheets through the afternoon, ordered room service hamburgers and champagne, screwed again, and then went back down to the floor. Like before, he started at poker, she at craps, but the second night she burned through her cash fast and wandered into the high-stakes room, watching him play, her fingers twiddling the tiny hairs at his neck. He didn't need her next to him, but having a pretty woman by his side, having her put her hand on his thigh and whisper smut into his ear—everything good can be made better. They were married six weeks later.

◇

She always played low stakes, being an elementary school teacher with bills to pay, but Jason seeded her the same $50K a night that he started with. They took weekend excursions to Vegas, Atlantic City, the tribal casinos up the coast of Oregon. On these off-season trips neither had the expectation of retiring at a reasonable hour, of eating dinner together—any meal, really—but that was fine. If you were hot, you stayed at the table, right through breakfast. No questions asked, no answers needed.

They came to Arizona last January, not long after the wedding. The new couple visited her parents in Surprise. Talking Stick wasn't open yet, but construction was well under way, and when they drove by the future casino, Jason squeezed her thigh and said, *Just you wait.* On that same trip they bought their spring house in a new subdivision of North Scottsdale. Jason didn't think long about the insides, just wanted to make sure the backyard was flat and had room enough for a batting cage. Liana cared more about the interior, but didn't quite know what to look for. Her parents were the original owners of one of those ranch-meets-adobe homes in Phoenix's far-west subdivisions, and since moving out she'd lived in dorm rooms or studios or other unimpressive apartments. When she met Jason she ditched her one-bedroom for his L.A. home, which was some sort of modernist architectural landmark way up in the hills. Yes, four bedrooms would be fine, they told the Scottsdale agent. The open-plan grand room, the stainless kitchen—okay, okay. They paid cash, closing in time for pitchers and catchers.

They had been married maybe six months when one of her credit cards was declined at a boutique on Rodeo. *Isn't that strange? Try this.* She passed the clerk another. Back in the car she texted him about it. He was playing away, probably already at the stadium doing his pregame rituals—one of which was to avoid his phone at all costs—and by the time they connected there were other things to talk about, his stand-up double and something going strange with the house's ancient plumbing. It'd happen every so often through the summer, a card getting declined, Liana blushing and apologetic and reaching for twenties. But by Labor Day all of the cards started falling like so many dominos. How her face burned behind her oversize sunglasses as she promised the sales clerk and the grocery checker and the waiter that she'd be back once she straightened things out with her husband, once she cleared things up with her bank, once she ran to the ATM. But when he came back through L.A. he was too focused on game prep to answer her texts or write back to the notes on the kitchen counter that she set out before heading to bed. Then he left again, for a long ten-game stretch on the East Coast. The Lions were probably not going to make the post-season, but there was a sliver of a chance that they'd get the wild card, and so she let him be. She took a few gowns to the consignment shop, sold some jewelry for cash. Five games into the road trip is when the orange notices started, mail with red stamps so bright they looked like they were bleeding. FINAL NOTICE.

She finally got a hold of their bank accounts—the bank didn't make it easy, even with her being his *wife*. Everything was drained, and there was a new mortgage on the Arizona house, a line of credit against their California home. Whatever was going on, this wasn't a hundred thousand in chips every week or two like in their early days. Those were lavish weekends, first-class tickets and posh hotels, seed money for them both—but well within their means. She never went to the casino without him, but clearly he was going without her. And clearly he was losing, more every day. When, in late October, she and Jason were finally in the same place at the same time and both awake, she asked her husband, point-blank, but he was dismissive. *I'll take care of it.* Would he take care of it by winning big? And how much, exactly, had he lost? He shrugged and she packed up her things and told him to call her when he got his shit together. She drove to Arizona that same night, arriving in Scottsdale just as the sky started to pink.

His solution? Put the Saarinen house up for sale, which was fine by Liana. Jason and Herb were always fawning over historical architecture, but the goddamn house was *crooked*, and its plate-glass windows made the AC run like a vacuum cleaner. He called her in Arizona to tell her the news. But where would they live during the season? She meant to ask that in a reasonable voice, but of course it came out as a yell. *We'll cross that bridge,* he said in a way that sounded like they never would. She gave Jason the option—the ultimatum—of gambling or her. When she'd arrived in Arizona she'd quit casinos cold turkey, chewing through a pack of gum a day and drinking more tequila and grapefruits than she should. He'd hung up at that.

She'd quit Jason cold turkey, too—by January she had her job back and was ignoring voice mails and texts from anyone but her lawyer. She knew that sometime soon Jason would be driving across the desert in his beat-up, beloved Jeep. (He'd gotten two Cadillacs as part of his compensation for the ad campaign, but sent one to his mother and lost the other, he confessed, in a game of Texas Hold'em.) Whatever else was going on in his life he had to get ready for spring and the long season ahead. Where would he stay? She didn't give a rat's ass.

At the time of their wedding the prenup had seemed conservative—an amount that would keep her comfortable but felt small in the context of Jason's $150 million contract—but by early 2011 that number was most of what he had left, and he knew he had to give it to her. Liana was a kind soul but an imperfect one. *She's got a little wild in her eye* is how Herb had put it. And Herb didn't know about the craps, just remembered how once she convinced Marlene to go skinny-dipping in Herb's hot tub; another time she took Melissa Moyers to a pole-dancing class. And without an NDA she might talk, as she had a gift for gab that made everyone, from first graders to baseball wives to recalcitrant Jason, feel at ease. And so their lawyers took care of the paperwork, shuttling back and forth their drafts and revisions, one of which included Jason's request to have access to the new batting cage in the backyard of their Arizona house. He'd built it custom to his specs; construction had just finished in December. She struck that line and wrote in the margin, *No fucking way.*

◇

Jason didn't—still doesn't—know what changed, but something sent him spinning. Was it marrying Liana? Herb getting sick? Was some team dynamic bringing him down? The way his body had begun to creak? None seemed an obvious cause, but for whatever reason last season he started finding more casinos on the road, driving his rental as far as ninety minutes to play. He'd go for several hours before crawling back to the team hotel at sunrise. Sometimes he stuck to fifty a night, but sometimes he edged it up. Doubled it. He pulled out half a million a couple of times, just because he had a good feeling. It felt mostly fine when that kind of night was followed by a 7:00 p.m. start, but then he started hitting the tables with day games right behind. Running on fumes, operating on three hours of sleep, he always played well—but he also recognized that he was sinking.

He knew he was sunk when he started playing *during* a game. Even if it was a practice game against Milwaukee's B squad. Dorsey made it clear that they were a team—you were supposed to be there, suited up—and Jason felt the same, though not the same enough to keep him from making the excuse of a run, of actually running but then also jogging over to the casino. Greg Carver was there, trailing him like a wide-eyed puppy—harmless, or at least inconsequential, by Jason's assessment. He knew Carver would say nothing. At the time it didn't feel awful (afterward, it did). At the time, it was just an itch that had to be scratched.

And it was an impossible itch, never satisfied. He couldn't help it if he pushed past when his ATM stopped spitting out cash, past when his checks were no longer accepted at the cage. One of the guards was watching this, Jason chewing out some square-jawed cashier who kept a stern expression on her face, the woman too old to care about his flirting or his ire. As Jason walked away from the cashier, that guard passed him a slip of paper with a phone number.

He dialed it, of course he did. On his cell, right there in the casino. Gave his real name, too, because as slick as he some-times felt sitting at the big stakes table and being in magazines and standing at the plate, he was still a bighearted midwestern boy at his middle. The guy gave him fifty grand on the spot—not quite on the spot, but within thirty seconds of hanging up, a pretty waitress was pressing five $10,000 chips into his palm. He couldn't figure how they'd found him so quickly, but also didn't ask: there was a good table going in the VIP room.

That night had gone okay, but the next night, and the next—it seemed impossible to get back up. So he called again. The first fifty had been on name recognition, the next was on promise of the signed balls, the 2008 MVP trophy. Another guy, not the loan shark, but "an associate"—a skinny, tall man who looked sunbaked and shifty—collected the bucket of balls from Jason's shed one morning. He crossed paths with Sara making her daily delivery of coffee and a bran muffin, and Jason watched from the door as the two of them brushed shoulders. Sara stonewalled the guy, stared right through him like he wasn't even there, like he wasn't leaning sideways with the weight of the bucket of marked-up balls and grinning at her. Like she recognized him but didn't want to. The skinny guy laughed and said it was funny, their meeting here. Sara waited until he was good and gone before she handed Jason his coffee. *Who was that?* Jason asked.

Sara chewed her lip. *I could ask you the same.*

◇

Then he had a good night at the table, after an ugly loss to the Padres (he'd scored, but they lost 9–2), and that got him a few feet closer to the surface. He didn't have to call the shark again for a week, but then he did, having started an evening with half a million of his own chips, then getting down to nothing. He felt absolutely certain that with another hand or two he could turn it around, get it up to $750K, maybe even a million. He *was* certain. He'd done it before, million-dollar nights. The shark didn't sound too happy to answer Jason's call at midnight, but he also answered on the second ring. A waitress came over with a Jack and soda and a handful of chips.

◇

The spring continued, and his losses mounted. That creepy associate showed up on the floor at odd hours, playing Texas

Hold'em at the next table (and folding every hand after the kitty, watching Jason's table rather than his own game). Jason would see him around the stadium, too, where the autograph seekers and desperate women loitered. Ten-mile stare, or leering like a wacko—the guy had both looks down pat. Sara still delivered the morning coffee but was jumpier now, worried that she'd see him, too. Apparently, she had known him in some past life—she admitted he was a friend of her ex, both of them bad news—but she wouldn't say any more about it.

By mid-March all Jason's accounts were drained, the Saarinen house proceeds long gone. He wasn't about to call Iowa, to repo his mother's Cadillac—she'd worked too long, too hard, for him to pull a stunt like that. He offered to sign another bucket of balls but the shark said the market was "saturated." Fuck if it didn't sting to hear his signature wasn't worth shit.

So, Herb. They got together at the agent's favorite steak house. Sara was there, too, driving that tank-size car and wearing something unnecessarily tight and short. Not that she didn't look nice—she did, and Herb sure wasn't complaining. What did he call her? A nurse? No. Assistant? The way she talked around him, how she acted, it was like he wasn't even sick, and it was clear Herb appreciated that. Deserved it, too. How Marlene took the diagnosis, slumping around the house like the grave'd already been dug, well, that didn't do anyone any good.

They were sawing at their steaks, and Jason decided to take the Band-Aid approach: pull it off quick. He asked for half a million.

"I just don't see why you'd ask the man with a nickel and three pennies when you're holding ninety-two cents of the same damn dollar. Does that make any sense to you, Sara?"

"Cents!" She giggled.

"Thank you, Sara." Herb lifted his wine to his lips. "Unnecessary, but appreciated. Goody, I thought you said the divorce was buttoned up?"

"It is." In fairness, Jason had given Herb a good deal, front-loading his commission to years one through three, rather than spreading the agent's 8 percent evenly across the decade. Another $3 million went to taxes annually. And Liana got the equivalent of three years' income in the house and her payout.

"I'm sure that your accounts look scary after the divorce, but you'll be fine. I have a guy that can help with that kind of stuff. Do you need a guy?" Jason cut into his sirloin, thinking about the guys he already knew; the deep-throated shark and his twitchy errand boy. "And my insurance is covering all the court fees around your recent escapade, you know. For you and your, ahem, friend. That's not an insignificant sum."

"I appreciate that, Herb. But the money, it's not for that, either."

"Do I want to know what this is for?" Herb stared at Jason.

"You don't," Sara said. Her tone had lost its giggle, and Herb set down his knife.

◇

The shark called from unlisted numbers. Left threatening voice mails, sent mean text messages. He promised to call the commissioner, to break Jason's fingers, to go to the press. The tunnel seemed darker, narrower, caving in, until Jason had the brilliant idea to ask the kid, Goose Jr., for money. That rookie got a two-million-dollar signing bonus and didn't know his ass from his elbow. Jason knew where to find him—they were always criss-crossing paths in the casino—it was just a question of sidling up at the right moment, in the right way. And he did, doling out the beer and the conversation, the "come with me" camaraderie. Then, so late it was early, the ask: Might he spot him some cash?

He could see Goslin doing the calculation in his head; what it would mean to be linked to Goodyear, what his mother would do when she found out his money was gone. What made him feel more powerful. "Sure, Goody, no problem." Good kid, right call. The whole thing took ten minutes on a laptop.

The teller looked some sort of spooked when Jason asked her to put half a million in cash in the L.A. Lions duffel bag—but she did it. Then he had to go to the drop-off, the back lot of some shopping center in North Scottsdale. He had parked and was looking for his transfer when he saw Tami tottering toward him on platform sandals, each hand holding a heavy grocery bag. Then he spotted her creaking Cavalier, parked a few spots over, looking dustier than ever. How had he missed that? Herb had told him under the strictest terms: no contact. But here she was, and when she saw him she yipped, almost, rushed up and gave him a sideways hug, her paper sack thumping him on the back. They talked awkwardly, her trying to apologize for that night a dozen different ways. As she did, he noticed new details of her tan and freckled face, the skin around her eyes looking older than he remembered. Then the handle on one of her bags ripped and grapefruits went rolling in every direction. He scrambled with her, grabbing up an armload of the fruits. He started reaching for a few that had rolled under a truck, when Tami put a hand on his shoulder. "For god's sake, Jason, leave them be."

It was when he stood back up that he saw the man, his shark's awful muscle, watching from the shade of the loading dock, arms crossed and glaring. *Muscle* wasn't the right word—Jason was bigger and stronger than this guy, but there was something in his eyes, an intensity and unpredictability, that made him frightening.

Tami saw him staring, noted the guy in the shadows and

the overstuffed bag on Jason's shoulder. "You got a meeting or something?"

"Something like that." The guy started striding over, scowling.

"Have a good day, Tami." She set two fingers on his shoulder, the lightest sort of touch, and walked away.

The exchange was quick, as easy as giving away half a million dollars can be. Easy enough when it's someone else's money. "Where's the interest?" the guy wanted to know, and when Jason explained he didn't have it, the guy nodded at the Jeep.

"My Jeep?" Jason had had it since he was sixteen. The car was something between a lucky charm and a constant companion. He knew that on the resale market it couldn't have been worth more than five grand, but maybe it'd pull in more, coming from him. Celebrity affiliation or some bullshit like that. "Right now?"

The guy nodded.

"Fuck, fine." He handed over the keys.

"We do need to know where to find you. For the rest."

Jason flipped through the options. Not the stadium. Never at the stadium again. What if it had been someone other than Sara who had seen their exchange? Not the house here—Liana didn't deserve that, and it would be a violation of his own rules. Not the house in L.A.—the new owners were moving in this week. Not his mother's house, not any of his teammates'. Trey could've helped him, but Trey was already unpacking on the other side of the country and pissed about it.

He's memorized Herb's L.A. address, and recited it now. Marlene'd be some sort of freaked to have this guy on her doorstep, but better that greeting than this guy on the doorstep of Stephen Smith. And who knew where Herb would be in a few weeks' time. He talked about heading to L.A. with the team next week, acted like this season was the same as any other. But they both knew that wasn't true.

And so the man drove away in Jason's Jeep, down the aisle and out onto the thoroughfare. Only then did Jason tap his pocket and remember his phone, his wallet—everything was in the car. "Fuck."

Looking at his watch, looking at the sky, looking at the casino tower shimmering on the horizon, he knew he was going to be late for first pitch. Dorsey would blow a gasket.

◇

The sun is fierce, and he's drenched in sweat after a mile, heaving for breath after two. There are three days left in spring training, but this feels like Southern California at high summer. He slows but keeps running.

The lot is full when he gets back to the complex, the mumble of the announcer sounding like it's the middle of the third. As he weaves through the left-field lot, he is thinking about what he'll tell Dorsey, trying to come up with an excuse, wondering about whether the clubhouse attendant has washed his sanis and cleaned his cleats and set out his uniform. It's a special treatment he usually resents, because he is one of the guys, he can handle his own gear—but today he is hoping someone has done him the favor. He is thinking about who they put in left and what Dorsey will say and—

And then he sees him. Jason is passing between parked cars in the players' lot and spots a little kid curled up on the back seat of a faded blue Toyota, slick as a seal pup, cheeks glowing red. His shaggy head is tucked into his knees, his back showing Jason's name and number. Baseballs are scattered all around him.

Maybe Jason should've worried about glass shards, about what would happen if he cut up his hand. Maybe he should've thought about the sound it'd make and considered if that might scare the kid. But all he can think of at that moment is how damn hot it must be in there, it feeling like a furnace outside, and so he picks up a stone from the stadium's nearest rock garden, fits it like a spear tip between his knuckles, and brings down his fist upon the glass, as hard as he can.

The glass shatters. Jason reaches in, opens the door, pulls out the kid. He is so small—young, but skinny, too—limp like a rag doll, and hot to the touch. Jason starts yelling for help, and someone from the grounds crew—the guy he paid off at the start of the season, the short one who gave him keys for the shed—is there in three seconds flat, cold water in hand. He pours it over Jason and the boy like champagne after a pennant win. He passes another bottle to Jason, who tips it to the boy's lips.

$$\diamond$$

That's when I come over, too, having been trailing Jason at an inconspicuous distance all morning—the shed with Goslin, the bank visit, the parking lot handoff, back to the stadium. I could have offered him a ride, I suppose, but Jason's been so jumpy, so suspicious of everyone, it's not likely he'd have accepted anyway. A fan must've seen us gathering and called the cops, or an ambulance, I'm not sure which—but Jason and I both hear the wail of sirens at the same time, how it slips in between the notes of Lester's organ. My reaction is relief, relief that help is coming. And, if I'm being honest, there's a sliver of selfishness there, knowing I won't have to watch someone die today.

And what about Jason? What does he think? When he hears the wail he leans over the limp boy and squeezes him tighter. "Hang on, little man," he whispers into the boy's tiny ear. He caresses the boy's damp cheek, leaving streaks of blood. He's cut up his hand pretty bad, smashing that window. That'll be stitches, a week out of the lineup—if not more. I take off my shirt and hand it to him. He wraps it around his mitt.

"Hang on," he says again. Jason Goodyear means it as some sort of hope for that wilted, red-faced kid in his arms, but goddamn it if his words couldn't have been meant for himself, if they couldn't have been meant for us all.

## ACKNOWLEDGMENTS

To everyone at FSG, especially Emily Bell, Jackson Howard, Brian Gittis, Alex Merto, Hannah Goodwin, Abby Kagan, Mitzi Angel, and Jonathan Galassi—thank you for believing in this book, and giving my made-up baseball team a beautiful home field. Jessica Friedman and Jin Auh, thanks for the early support and the unwavering belief in this book. Harry Stecopoulos was a wonderful early reader—thank you for seeing the book's promise and making it better. I offer the same thanks to Adrianne Harun. Steve Kettman and Dan Hoyt, thank you for being my ideal readers, and Sandy Alderson, thank you for your careful review from the field. I worked on this book at the Hermitage Artist Retreat, the Betsy's Writers Room, and the Sewanee Writers' Conference—thank you to everyone at these organizations for the support. Thank you as well to everyone at *The Paris Review*, particularly Terry McDonell, for encouraging me through the book's proverbial ninth while I was just starting off at *TPR*.

This project began in Baton Rouge, with the encouragement of the Louisiana State University English Department. Thank you to everyone there, particularly Jennifer S. Davis, James P. Wilcox, William Demastes, and Phil Maciak for steering me through early drafts, discussing the intersection of sports and culture, and getting me into the football press box. I am grateful for the wonderful friends and creative community I found in Baton Rouge, especially Alyson Pomerantz and Sandra Wolle, Atom Atkinson, Katie Boland, Kevin Casper, Vincent Cellucci, Matt Dischinger, Emily Frank, Leslie Friedman, Lara Glenum, Zack Godshall and Jillian Hall, Robbie Howell, Jill and Mike Kantrow, James Long, Brad Pope, Hannah Reed, Will and Liz Torrey, Josh Wheeler, Dylan White and Annie Bauman, Jason and Ali Wolfe, and all the Zemels. Thanks to everyone at *The Southern Review* and LSU Press—contributors and colleagues—for your encouragement in person and through bighearted correspondence. And thank you especially to the Gehebers—Leah, Philip, Laurin, Aaron, plus Hayes Brian and Laura Bergeron—for welcoming me into the family.

Writer and editor friends, thank you for checking in on the book as well as its author over these past nine years. I'm particularly indebted to the friendships of Olivia Clare, Jenny Croft, Alan Grostephan, Christian Kiefer, Nick Mainieri, and James Scott, and I've been overwhelmed by the open arms and kind words of my New York colleagues since returning to the city. Thank you for breaking bread and for your encouragement. Anna Berman, Karisa Butler-Wall, Elana Fishman, Gwen Fuertes, Diana Greenwold, Lily Guenther, Jordana Heller, Katie Lorah, Donna Meredith, Rose Nestler, Gale Orcutt, Faye Reiff-Pasarew, Talia Shalev, and Charise Castro Smith: what good fortune, to have girlfriends like y'all—I find you inspiring every single day.

And thanks to my family, from my earliest baseball games in Omaha with Grandpa Rich to the many, many seasons of Mariners games, in Seattle and Phoenix, with my dad, David. We probably should have paid more attention to the game, but we were having too much fun. Jessi, thank you for being the best sister a gal could hope for. Brian, Dan, and Karen: thank you for making our family better, and for cheering me through the process of writing this book. Mom, thank you for the endless encouragement, the bottomless love, and the good reading recommendations. Keel, thank you for being my partner in reading, dog walks, and everything else—I may have started this book before we met, but I couldn't have finished it without you and Willow.

## A Note About the Author

Emily Nemens is the editor of *The Paris Review*. She was previously the coeditor of *The Southern Review*. Her work has been published in *Esquire*, *n+1*, *The Gettysburg Review*, *Hobart*, and other outlets.